A Cold Harbour

Glasgow-born Lynne McEwan is a former newspaper photographer turned crime author. She's covered stories including the Fall of the Berlin Wall and the first Gulf War in addition to many high profile murder cases. She currently lives in Lincoln and is an alumna of MA Crime Fiction at the University of East Anglia.

Also by Lynne McEwan

Detective Shona Oliver

In Dark Water
Dead Man Deep
The Girls in the Glen
The Gathering Storm
A Troubled Tide
The Winter Dead
A Cold Harbour

A Cold Harbour

LYNNE McEWAN

canelo
CRIME

First published in the United Kingdom in 2026 by

Canelo Crime, an imprint of
Canelo Digital Publishing Limited,
20 Vauxhall Bridge Road,
London SW1V 2SA
United Kingdom

A Penguin Random House Company
The authorised representative in the EEA is Dorling Kindersley Verlag GmbH.
Arnulfstr. 124, 80636 Munich, Germany

A CIP catalogue record for this book is available from the British Library.

ISBN 978 1 83598 070 5

Cover design by Blacksheep

Cover images © Despositphotos and Shutterstock.com

Printed and bound in Great Britain by Clays Ltd, Elcograf S.p.A.

Look for more great books at
www.canelo.co | www.dk.com

1

MIX
Paper
FSC™ C018179

For Joyce and Ian Cochrane, tireless champions of books, readers and writers

Chapter 1

That was another meeting that should've been an email, Shona Oliver thought as she followed her Galloway counterpart, DI Kenneth Dalrymple, from the grey conference room at Newton Stewart Police Office. Immediately, she rebuked herself. By introducing the *community stake holders* – business owners, councillors, landowners' agents – the key players in the networks that made this largely rural area tick, Dalrymple was giving her the best shot at being him for the coming weeks. He'd spent his whole career here and was obviously well liked. Shona was under no illusion. On that level she faced a daunting task.

The location wasn't helping her mood. Her own office in Dumfries Police Headquarters was hardly state of the art, but here the building had an air of abandonment – blinds pulled down, curled posters on the noticeboard by the front door, rusted guttering. It felt like the dejection was already seeping into her bones. A few more hours of this and her priority would be finding where they kept the confiscated drugs.

'Why don't you head back to my… our office.' Dalrymple smiled. 'I'll get us some coffee and talk you through the active cases.'

When she'd first met him a couple of years ago he'd reminded her of a country vet from a 1950s drama. Today, the tweed suit was a lightweight summer one, but with his neatly trimmed sandy hair and authoritative manner he still exuded an air of quiet confidence. Any animal, or indeed investigation, placed in his care would receive his utmost attention.

Shona's priority was making the temporary transition as smooth as possible, but her heart sank at the prospect of yet another meeting. Secondment to southern Scotland's wild west hadn't been her idea. Since Dalrymple would be on compassionate leave caring for his terminally ill wife, Isobel, Shona would lay money on it not being his preferred option either. Sneaking a look at her watch she saw it was after four p.m.

'Honestly, Kenny, your briefing document was comprehensive.'

Dog attacks on livestock, damage to ancient monuments, minor fire-raising, puppy farms, road rage against tractors and horse riders.

He must've seen something in her expression for he offered a look of commiseration. 'I'm afraid you'll find it very quiet here.'

Shona smiled, anxious that he didn't get the idea she was looking down on his operation. She tucked a strand of her straightened brown bob behind her ear.

'Quiet is good.' She meant it. Time to attend to family matters, time to think, time to just breathe was something she'd been short of lately. 'And any lessons I can take back to Dumfries, particularly on rural community engagement, will be useful.'

He nodded, mollified. Checking his own watch, he clapped his hands together like an attentive host suddenly remembering his manners. 'Well, perhaps it'd be best to get you settled into the cottage.'

'That'd be great,' Shona said, hoisting her handbag over her shoulder and trying not to sound too relieved. The place he'd arranged for her – a holiday let called Coldharbour Cottage – was forty minutes away on the coast at Portpatrick, owned by a friend of Dalrymple's and close to his own home.

'When is your daughter arriving?'

'Monday,' she replied. 'I'll drive up to Glasgow in the evening and get her.'

He nodded again, apparently satisfied by the plan but made no move towards the carpark. She could see he had something on his mind. Most likely, he'd picked up on the frostiness earlier in the CID room as the Galloway team had surveyed Shona and was about to offer advice on getting the best out of them.

'I know your officers have a great deal of local experience,' she began. 'I'm convinced we'll quickly arrive at a productive working relationship. If there's the odd teething problem, you needn't concern yourself.' Which was code for – *don't listen if they come running to you behind my back*.

But he waved away her concern. 'I have every faith, Shona. Your CID operation at Dumfries is a credit to you, and I should know.'

It wasn't so long ago that their roles had been reversed. Dalrymple had stepped into Shona's shoes when Hollywood had hit the Solway to shoot a Robert Burns biopic. She'd been seconded to liaise with the film company, reconnecting with an old friend in the process. She hadn't been half as gracious as Dalrymple was being at handing over the reins and she winced inwardly at the memory.

He fished the cottage key from his pocket and handed it to her. 'I'll need to get back to Isobel. Will you find it all right?'

'No problem. I have your directions.'

'There is something else you might do for me,' he began. 'I've the file in my desk.'

Jeezo, Shona thought, the place was shaping up to be Hotel California. She was never getting out of here.

But instead, she smiled once more. 'Fine. I'm at your disposal.'

-

Ten minutes later she was sitting opposite Dalrymple in his bunker of an office. High, barred windows ran along one side which, combined with the faded décor, instilled the room with a soupy light, even on this bright summer's day. He took a brown folder from a drawer and slid it across to her.

Shona noted the hand-written name and date on the front. *Ailsa Scott, July 1986.*

'A cold case?'

Dalrymple nodded.

Shona flipped open the cover and found herself face-to-face with a smiling young woman of about her own daughter's age. Ailsa stood on a clifftop, an artist's paint-brush in her hand, long brown hair whipping behind her in the wind.

'Ailsa Scott, seventeen years old,' Dalrymple said. 'It's the only unsolved murder on our books.'

'And you'd like me to look at it?' Shona felt a familiar curl of curiosity while recognising the desire to immerse herself in a forty-year-old case might be down to a wish to escape her current personal and professional challenges.

'I want you to look at the original investigation, see if they missed something. The conclusion at the time was that Ailsa was the victim of a random encounter, likely someone from Glasgow, the central belt or further afield, cruising around for a victim.'

'And you're wondering if this ties in with any other past cases?'

They needn't necessarily be murders. Most serial offenders had a past history of other crimes – robbery, house breaking, assaults, sexual or otherwise, abduction, possession of weapons.

The A4 file was as thick as Shona's thumb. Dalrymple had done a thorough job. She flicked through a few pages. In addition to the typed sheets, she glimpsed copious notes in his neat hand.

He leaned forward, resting his elbows on the desk. 'If there's new evidence or lines of enquiry I can have it referred to the cold case unit in Glasgow.'

Shona thought that was a bit of a long shot. Budgets were being slashed. They were having enough problems funding current investigations, never mind old ones. The state of the building they were sitting in was proof of that. But she also saw the determination in Dalrymple's face. He must be at least fifteen years her senior. Perhaps he'd be retiring soon. Doing that with a clean slate, getting the last unsolved murder off their books, would be his swan song.

'Was Ailsa's murder sexually motivated?' Shona said, turning the page to the case abstract.

'No evidence of an assault but the location on the coastal path was a public one.'

The crime scene was listed as close to Black Point Lighthouse.

'You're thinking the attacker was disturbed?' Shona said.

Dalrymple spread his hands, indicating he considered it possible. 'It may have been a random killing. But there is another, more disturbing possibility…'

'…That the murderer is still living among you,' Shona finished. Policing your own community was something she knew all about. It was never easy but the thought that a killer was going about their day, witnessing not only the family's grief, but the pain of not knowing why their loved one had been killed, and who was responsible, was like twisting a knife. 'Suspects?'

'Next page.'

Shona ran down the list. Five names, each tripping a recent connection in her mind. Suddenly, she understood that Dalrymple had had an ulterior motive in introducing her to the men at the earlier meetings. When she saw the last name she felt a jolt of shock and looked up at Dalrymple.

'Roddy Rutherford?' She raised her eyebrows in disbelief. Roderick Rutherford, respected local solicitor, lifeboat volunteer coxswain at Portpatrick, father of her daughter Becca's boyfriend, Jack. 'Kenny, I should declare an interest here.'

She told him of her past acquaintance with Roddy via neighbouring lifeboat operations and how that had led to their offspring becoming flatmates while attending Glasgow University.

'I was aware of your connection. I have one of my own.' He sighed. 'Ailsa Scott was my wife Isobel's older sister.' He paused, flexing his hands into fists as the flicker of some strong emotion passed like a cloud quickly over his face. 'You're aware Isobel has a terminal diagnosis. It won't be long. She's the last of her family. Her parents died never understanding what happened to Ailsa. I know it's on Isobel's mind. I'd like to give her what peace I can. I suppose you could call it my last gift to her.' He smiled sadly. 'Will you help me?'

Shona bit her lip, then nodded.

'Since no charges were brought, everyone on this list must've been cleared, right?'

'Maybe. Or there was just insufficient evidence, at the time.'

Dalrymple's face was now an unreadable mask. Had he really spent years in meetings with businessmen, councillors and charity leaders that he suspected had murdered his wife's sister in cold blood? Suddenly she glimpsed another, steely side to the affable country detective, one who knew he had quite possibly shaken hands with a killer and watched them walk away.

But could that person really have gone undetected in the heart of such a close-knit community? From her own experience she knew it was possible. Some secrets were buried deep. And whoever was responsible would want to keep them that way.

Detective Inspector Kenny Dalrymple's mind must've been working along the same lines.

'I appreciate your help on this. But one other thing – Shona, take care.'

Chapter 2

Shona pushed open the door to the carpark of Newton Stewart Police Office and the sun hit her like she'd swum up from the ocean depths. After a day of talk she craved silence. Turning off the radio as she took the A75 west, she drove through woods dense with summer. Once onto minor roads, the silver expanse of Luce Bay opened up on her left, and the tension in her shoulders began to ease. Here, the sky expanded to a great blue dome above the vivid green of open fields, their smooth surface broken only by a few wind-sculpted hawthorns hunkered in the hollows by the roadside.

It wasn't just the day's endless meetings she was keen to get a break from. Dalrymple wasn't a man to bear grudges, but his team in Galloway CID – a detective sergeant, one detective constable and two civilian support officers – had made it clear they regarded Shona with deep suspicion. The irony of it was she understood why – she'd previously sent one of their number to prison. That it was for corruption and the murder of a serving officer didn't seem to matter. She simultaneously loathed and recognised the twisted logic of their feelings. In a job that potentially put your life on the line, loyalty to your fellow officers trumped everything. Publicly, they condemned their perfidious ex-colleague. But earlier, as she'd stopped outside the CID room door to check her phone messages, her shadow already falling on the frosted glass, she'd heard it as clear as day – *Look out, lads. Here comes the spy in the camp.*

She'd weighed up whether to confront or ignore the jibe. With her own team back in Dumfries, she wouldn't have hesitated to give them all a rocket. *Wee Shona* would invite them to consider their thinking, their life choices and their future on her team. But in Galloway, she was on unfamiliar ground.

Shona was still contemplating what to do when her phone rang and a name flashed up – Inspector Simon Wallace of the Ministry of Defence Police. A bubble of joy rose in her chest. Over the last six months they'd been taking things slowly, but she'd already begun to wonder if their relationship was leading somewhere more serious.

'Hey, you,' she grinned, switching to the hands-free. 'How's your *conference*?'

This was code for the military police training exercise Simon was currently running in Berlin.

'Hey, yourself. It's going fine.' His voice was warm, his accent a mix of middle-class Edinburgh and soft southern England, a souvenir of well-educated beginnings and a life spent constantly on the move, first in the army and then with the MOD Police. 'How was your first day in the wild west?'

'Interesting.'

'That good, eh?'

'I'll knock them into shape.' She wouldn't mention McCulloch's surliness, Kyle's lack of confidence, and Erin's state of panic every time Shona addressed her. It would feel like a lack of leadership on her part and, as a fellow cop, she didn't want him to think she couldn't handle it.

‘And no more phone calls from our London friends?’

It boosted her spirits to hear him use *our*, as if they were in it together. She’d told Simon that the National Crime Agency had interviewed her about historic corruption allegations surrounding her former boss DCI Harry Delfont and seemed intent on pinning his double dealing on her. She’d also revealed how the man had filmed himself drugging and sexually assaulting her, and others, in an attempt to blackmail them into not reporting his crimes.

What she hadn’t mentioned was witnessing her friend and fellow victim Thalia Brookes dispensing her own justice and tipping Delfont’s lifeless body into a Cumbrian lake, and how Shona had helped her flee the scene. It was for Simon’s protection, she told herself. But the truth was she couldn’t bear to see his disappointment, his revulsion. The woman he thought he knew and loved – DI Shona Oliver – accessory to murder.

‘No. Nothing from the NCA,’ she replied, calmly.

‘What about your Super?’

Detective Superintendent Mark Davies, sensing an NCA scandal, if not the details, made it clear her secondment to Galloway wasn’t optional. Just a necessary, temporary, move out of the limelight, he’d said.

‘Well, I’ve made it through the first day without him checking up on me.’

‘Gold star for you then. When’s Becca joining you?’

‘I’m picking her up Monday.’ At the thought, Shona’s spirits lifted again. It was her student daughter Becca’s agreement to the temporary move that had convinced Shona to embrace it. ‘I doubt I’m the principal attraction though.’

Simon laughed. 'How's Jack doing? Is he still back home in Portpatrick then?'

'He's doing well. Becca's determined to get him fit enough to return to uni in the autumn.'

'God, he was so lucky.'

Simon's tone was heartfelt and Shona realised he must also be thinking about his own son, Gabriel, now a post-graduate student at Glasgow University. The near-fatal mugging of Jack Rutherford was every parent's worst nightmare.

'Having you around to help Jack and Becca meant we were all lucky,' Shona said, her reply equally sincere. 'And hopefully you'll get a chance to see for yourself soon?'

Thinking of Becca and Jack Rutherford inevitably recalled his father, Roddy, and his inclusion among the suspects for Ailsa Scott's murder. Adolescence was a notoriously difficult period of immense physical and psychological upheaval. Might Ailsa's death have stemmed from something as simple as a falling out between peers, or some petty jealousy? Or had she become swept up in something criminal? But the most important question of all was – did Roddy pose any threat to Becca? She was on the brink of asking Simon what he thought when she realised how ridiculous it'd sound. As a cop and lifeboat volunteer she was best placed to make that judgement, and there'd never been a sniff of impropriety around the Portpatrick coxswain. But running other ideas about the cold case past Simon was something she could do when he visited.

'So, Inspector Wallace, when can Europe safely spare you without descending into chaos and anarchy?' she teased.

'I'll be making a strong case that the free world can cope without me as soon as possible. Maybe next weekend?'

Shona felt a twinge of disappointment that it wouldn't be sooner, followed by a spasm of guilt that she was asking him once more to juggle his work plans and make the trek to where she was.

'I miss you,' Shona said, as the call came to an end.

'And I miss you too,' he replied with such warmth that Shona drank it in, hoping it would sustain her through the rest of his absence.

On the outskirts of Portpatrick, the road descended into a narrow gorge and she could sense the sea long before she saw it. There was something in the altered quality of the light that fell on the colour-washed cottages, guest houses and hotels and she immediately understood why the picturesque village was so popular with artists and holidaymakers. The place had once been the main ferry port to Ireland for livestock, passengers and mail, before the transfer to Stranraer in the mid-eighteen-hundreds, after which herring fishing gave it a second life. The outer harbour followed the curve of the bay, extending its outstretched arms of stone ready to gather in grateful vessels, which these days consisted of a small local fishing fleet, pleasure craft and Portpatrick's all-weather lifeboat, which was moored in the inner harbour. The waterfront pavements were busy with families and elderly couples, all enjoying the sunshine.

Shona checked the directions Dalrymple had given her and, realising she'd missed a turning, doubled back and headed up the hill once more. She took a side road, passing his home, a two-storey stone 1930s villa with its swathe of green lawn and view over the village. When the tarmac ran out, the Audi grunted and grumbled over gravel, climbing higher. Just as Shona thought she must have mistaken her way again, a low white cottage with a grey slate roof appeared at the end of the track.

Coldharbour Cottage was hunkered down in a shallow dip, its gable towards the prevailing southwesterlies, but it still commanded a spectacular view. When she'd told Becca where they'd be staying, and speculated that it might've belonged to the coastguard, her daughter had laughed. Not that kind of harbour. It's nothing to do with ships, she'd said. More in the sense of *harbouring a criminal.* Coldharbour was an old term meaning a temporary place of refuge or shelter, often found on pilgrim ways, and near Neolithic sites, she'd added. A temporary place of refuge just about summed it up, Shona thought.

She got out and shivered as the fresh breeze lifted her hair from her neck. To her left, beyond Portpatrick, the coastline marched away towards Scotland's southernmost point, the Mull of Galloway. To her right was an expanse of golf course, then a stretch of cliffs and bays leading to the white nub of the old Black Point Lighthouse. Shona imagined that on a clear night, she might see the lights of Carrickfergus across the North Channel. In summer this was an idyllic spot, which she was sure Becca would love. In winter, when it was blowing a hoolie, it might be a very different experience.

Inside was a sitting room with a woodstove, two bedrooms and, at the back, the bathroom and a kitchen big enough to eat in. She dropped Dalrymple's file on the table and filled the kettle. On the worktop were storage jars of tea and coffee, plus bread, scones and a bag of oatmeal for porridge. She checked the fridge freezer and found a stack of quality frozen meals, along with milk, a local cheese and some salad items. While the tea brewed, she brought her bag in from the car and left it in the hallway.

A few minutes later she carried her mug outside and sat down on the bench by the front door. An ominous line of black clouds sat on the horizon to the north, but elsewhere the sky was still a perfect blue. It'd be light until ten p.m.; plenty of time for a walk down to the village, or along the coastal path. Shona's gaze fell once more on Black Point Lighthouse. If Dalrymple wanted to draw Shona's attention to the site of Ailsa Scott's murder, he couldn't have picked a better spot. She drained her mug and set it down, then collected her boots and RNLI fleece from the car. Picking up the buff file Dalrymple had given her, she stuffed it inside her jacket, along with her notebook, and set off for the cliff path.

Chapter 3

Long grass brushed against Shona's legs as she crossed the field to the cliff edge. A marker post stamped with a stylised thistle and a crossbar bearing *Southern Upland Way* told her she was, quite literally, on the right track. In the hiatus between serious walkers and evening strollers the path was empty, and Shona welcomed the lack of potential cheery greetings and curious questions about what she might be doing there armed with the file. Ahead, the cliffs of grey rock were blackened by sea and weather; the lighthouse stuck out of the headland like a bleached bone. Shona pulled up her collar against the breeze and began to walk.

Dalrymple wanted answers for his dying wife, but Shona had a reason of her own for solving this forty-year-old mystery. With the NCA closing in she might only have a short time left as a police officer. If this was to be the end of her career, she wanted to feel she was still on the side of the good. She wanted to get justice for Ailsa Scott. If she could give one more family peace of mind, then maybe that would be some consolation.

The path followed the indentations of the coast, flowing in around a cove, jutting out around a promontory so what she'd estimated was a five-minute walk took three times longer. Turning her back to the wind, she eased the folder out of her jacket and checked the map.

The crime scene was in a sheltered dip just off the path itself, where the clifftop drifts of purple and white wildflowers seemed most dense. Below, on the shoreline, lay the broken and rusted wrecks that were a testament to the lighthouse's necessity.

Now Shona was here, the locus was more private than she'd anticipated. Perhaps the original investigation, and Dalrymple, had dismissed too quickly the possibility that sexual assault had been the initial motive. She studied a crime-scene photograph. Ailsa had been posed as if she'd just slipped and fallen on the clifftop rocks, paintbrush still in her hand. Shona returned the picture to the file.

She could see why the young woman had chosen to paint here. With its everchanging light and weather, dramatic shipwrecks and striking cliffs, it was a place both beautiful and menacing. Shona couldn't resist imagining all the other ways in which folk could get themselves into trouble on this coastline. Inflatables blown out to sea. Misjudging the tide and getting trapped in the bay. Dogs chasing gulls off cliffs and their owner going into the sea after them. Twisted ankles on rocks. Bread and butter for the lifeboats.

Ahead was the cluster of buildings around the base of the lighthouse. The lamp itself had been decommissioned and the coastguard accommodation was now holiday cottages. Four SUVs were lined up in the adjoining carpark. The shouts of children playing and the smell of barbeque swept over her, carried on the wind. A man, one of the children's fathers probably, stood next to the vehicles and, just for a moment, she had the uncomfortable feeling he was watching her. After a minute, he turned away and disappeared into a cottage. He'd been taking a well-earned breather, she told herself. But even on this sunny evening she couldn't shake the unsettling atmosphere that seemed to hang about the place. Perhaps it was because she was thinking about Ailsa's murder. Or perhaps it was just her RNLI experience telling her they didn't put lighthouses in tranquil waters.

Shona sat down on the hollow's sun-warmed grass out of the wind and opened the file once more. It was always difficult not to judge a cold case by modern standards, but perhaps it didn't matter if she did. What Dalrymple wanted was an assessment that referenced not just the possibilities of newer forensic techniques, but innovative ways of thinking and a greater understanding of offender psychology than was available to their predecessors.

Ailsa Scott was a promising young artist whose death was initially deemed accidental – she'd slipped on rock and fallen. But the postmortem revealed a fracture to her temple bones which was inconsistent with the crime scene. It was likely that she'd been struck from behind, and that her body had been moved after death. The Scott family had lived in the area for generations. Both parents were from farming backgrounds. Her father repaired, then sold, farm machinery. Ailsa's mother had taught at the local primary school.

The investigation team, led by a Detective Chief Inspector Dalziel, had quickly discounted family and close neighbours, and identified the five potential suspects but couldn't find sufficient evidence to charge any of them.

The Southern Upland Way long-distance footpath had opened just two years previously, and in addition to Roddy Rutherford, who'd been a fourteen-year-old volunteer at the lighthouse, there'd been a walker reportedly seen in the area at the time of the murder. Despite a photofit created from witness statements and a wide-spread public appeal, he'd never come forward, nor been identified. Perhaps it wasn't surprising since the two photofit images – one face and one full length – fell firmly in the *could be anyone* pile: tallish, youngish, slim-ish, khaki waterproof jacket, jeans, walking boots and navy woollen hat.

In the hollow, the shadows began to lengthen as the sun slipped lower. Shona's stomach growled – she'd eaten nothing since a sandwich at lunch – but she was too absorbed in the file to set off back to the cottage just yet. Dalrymple had included separate sections containing their personal details, family and employment background and whether they were previously known to the police. She took out her notebook, checking off the suspects' names against her notes from today. Ailsa's boyfriend was Graham McLean. At the time of her death, he was a seventeen-year-old working on a local caravan site, which he now owned, along with a string of other businesses. His best friend, Bruce Campbell, had a summer job there too. He was now the head of a plumbing firm with key local contracts. Both were at the meeting this morning to discuss crime prevention and workplace security.

The final suspect, Ailsa's art teacher, Jeremy Young, had been a little older at twenty-four, which put him now in his mid-sixties. He was rumoured to have been besotted with his pupil and had left the area soon after Ailsa's death. Shona checked her notebook. At this afternoon's meeting to discuss youth crime, Jeremy – *call me Jem* – had told her he'd recently retired from teaching but had come back to the area so that his wife, Alison, could be close to her elderly parents, but also so he could head up a charity community arts initiative. He'd struck her as earnest but rather bland.

Shona closed the file. The wind had gone round and was reaching into her sanctuary. In the time she'd sat there, absorbed in the case notes, the warm grass had become cold ground. There was a wad of witness statements, forensic reports and interviews with the suspects to read through, not to mention detailed photographic evidence. Becca wasn't arriving until Monday. Shona had the weekend to get through the file and begin fitting the pieces of the puzzle together.

Her phone rang. As she fished it from her pocket, she saw the Kirkness lifeboat skipper, Tommy McCall's name flash up.

'Tommy. How's things?' she said as she got stiffly to her feet. Out over the North Channel, the dark clouds had raced in, faster than Shona had thought possible.

'No' so bad. Where are you?'

'I'm in Portpatrick. Just saw the all-weather lifeboat moored up in the harbour.'

'You defecting tae Galloway then?'

'Temporary secondment to Newton Stewart for a few weeks. I told you.' She felt the first spots of rain on her cheek and stuffed the file and notebook inside her jacket.

'I mind you did. So, I cannae count on you this weekend if we get a shout?'

Shona frowned. It wasn't like Tommy to phone after she'd notified him. She carried her RNLI pager most weekends when she was in Kirkness. Her Dumfries CID officers operated an on-call rota, only contacting her in the rare instances of murder, rape, armed attacks or other threat-to-life situations.

'You short of folk?' Shona said.

Tommy hesitated, then he said, 'Aye. We're a bit tight.'

Rain was drawing in like a curtain across the sea, stippling the surface of the now grey water. Shona remembered her packed bag in the hallway. She wasn't due back in the office at Newton Stewart until Monday. She checked her watch. The roads would be quiet.

'I can be back in a couple of hours,' she said. 'Half pint of shandy in the Royal Arms?'

'You drive a hard bargain, Mistress Oliver, but I think we can run to that.'

With a last glance at the unlit beacon of the lighthouse, Shona set off back along the path, her shoulder angled to the wind, protecting the file from the now driving rain.

Chapter 4

The next morning, Shona came downstairs at High Pines to find Tommy's partner, Freya, already in the kitchen. She'd come to do the changeovers of the two self-catering units, located on the lowest floor of the four-storey building wedged into the hillside above Kirkness estuary. Freya stepped in to do the odd bit of cooking too, when she wasn't behind the bar at the Royal Arms, and Shona knew she'd never manage without her and appreciated the older woman's steady friendship.

'I'll give you a hand if you like,' Shona said, putting her RNLI pager on the kitchen countertop and reaching for a mug.

'No, you're braw, thanks,' Freya replied in her Orcadian lilt. She was smartly turned out as usual in cropped jeans and a crisply ironed floral top, styled, short blonde hair and light make-up. 'I've just seen one load o' guests leaving, so I'll make a start.' She flapped her hand at Shona. 'Sit doon and eat your breakfast.'

'You saying you'll be quicker without me?' Shona put on a mock look of outrage.

'Don't take this the wrong way but you're pretty slap-dash when it comes tae mirrors.'

'My police driving instructor said the same,' she grinned.

'Well, he wasnae wrong. And Tommy wouldnae be best pleased if you fell off a ladder dusting and broke an arm.'

'Is he really having problems with crew numbers?'

Freya pressed her lips together. 'It's the time of year. Folk away on their holidays. We've no' had as many young uns back fae university this summer. Wi' money tight, they're staying where they are an' getting jobs.'

'That's true,' Shona said. 'Becca's away all next month working on a dig.' It was unpaid, but it counted towards her archaeology degree.

'But she's joining you in Galloway for a bit?'

'Picking her up from the flat on Monday night.'

'An' what about that nice friend of yours, Simon?' Freya gave her a conspiratorial look. 'He's very charming. Very good-looking. And I suppose him being a polis as well helps the two o' you get along.'

All those things were true, but mostly it was the steadiness, the lack of drama that Shona was enjoying. They could go to the movies, have dinner, make love, stay over at each other's places without the experience descending into farce or tragedy, which Shona had come to believe were too often the defining features of her relationships.

'So will we be seeing him this weekend?' Freya pressed.

'Unfortunately, Simon is away at a conference in Berlin.'

Having spent a good chunk of last night and this morning texting, Shona resisted her irrational desire to turn her phone screen face down on the countertop.

'Och, that's a pity,' Freya smirked, then her expression turned more serious. 'You any further forward wi' thon other business wi' yer mother?'

Shona sighed. Since her estranged mother, Angie MacDonald, had got in touch, Shona's initial conviction that she could put aside the difficult memories of her childhood had proved premature. Months later, they still hadn't met, although there'd been video calls and phone chats. Mostly, Shona wished she could list Angie's reappearance under a case number, and file it away until she was ready to deal with it. Becca, who'd already been in contact with her counsellor grandmother, albeit in a professional setting, was urging her mother to take that next step.

'I don't know what's holding me back,' Shona admitted.

Freya folded her arms and leaned against the kitchen door frame. 'Could be you feel meeting in person is like handing her a free pass tae forgiveness. And if you meet once, then change your mind, it's like you're leavin' her – the exact thing you cannae forgive.'

Shona blinked at Freya. 'Yes, that's it exactly. You should do this for a living.'

'Aye well, you dinnae spend thirty years working behind a bar and no' get tae hear folks' problems.'

'You think I should meet her?'

Freya pushed off from the door frame and shrugged. 'Up tae you. But you could ask yourself how long you're prepared tae be stuck in limbo?'

Shona nodded, thoughtfully. 'Thanks, Freya.'

'My pleasure. Anyways, cleaning waits for nae woman.' She opened the connecting door down to the lower level. 'And eat yer breakfast,' Freya called over her shoulder as she left.

Shona did as she was told. There wasn't a lot in since she'd planned to be away for a few weeks, but there was coffee, muesli and bread in the freezer for toast. She took her breakfast up to the lounge where the semi-circle of floor-to-ceiling windows gave a view over the sparkling firth. The rain that had followed her from Portpatrick last night had gone although the strong wind remained. She eyed her RNLI pager, now sitting on the table next to the buff folder Dalrymple had given her. Below, she saw a few yachts and dinghies taking to the water. Families were beginning to arrive at the narrow cockleshell beach. There was plenty of time for folk to get into difficulties or be caught out by the tide.

Shona closed her eyes, as if that might shut out Freya's words, which had been running on a loop in her head. She had to make a decision. Eventually, she texted Becca and asked if she thought it was a good idea to meet up with Angie when she came to pick her up on Monday. Their return journey to Galloway would give Shona a valid excuse to end the meeting quickly if she felt it wasn't working. Becca's thumbs-up emoji came straight away, along with a suggestion for a bar in Ashton Lane with a roof terrace.

Before she could change her mind, Shona texted Angie suggesting the meet, then slid the phone into the pocket of her jeans. Swallowing the last of her coffee, she pulled Ailsa Scott's case notes towards her.

Everything, from Dalrymple's comprehensive file to his choice of accommodation for Shona, seemed intended to help her solve the mystery of Ailsa's death, and now she wondered if it had been his suggestion to their Super, Mark Davies, that Shona fill in for him, rather than drafting someone down from Divisional HQ in Kilmarnock. She sighed, feeling the weight of his faith resting upon her shoulders. After forty years, and Dalrymple's own extensive enquiries, would apprehending the murderer even be possible? Memories faded. Perceptions of events shifted, overlaid by others' opinions. Everything conspired against Dalrymple's desired outcome, his final gift to his dying wife.

Only one of the three men, whose notes she'd begun to read through the previous night, was known to police. Shona turned to the section on Ailsa's boyfriend's best mate, the plumbing magnate Bruce Campbell. He had a police youth record that made Shona's cop-senses tingle – petty theft, fire-setting, possession of drugs. Dalrymple had also thought it worth adding a handwritten note detailing reports of crimes that hadn't been pursued – animal cruelty and a complaint of voyeurism at the caravan site. It all pointed to an escalating pattern of offending. But his adult record was clean, setting aside speeding tickets and a Sheriff's warning for breach of the peace at a 40th birthday party. Having gotten away with murder, would Bruce Campbell suddenly become a near-model citizen?

Shona's first impression of Bruce the plumbing boss had been that he was a wee bit under the thumb of his loud and opinionated best friend, Graham McLean. Now she wondered if that had always been the case, and if the dynamics of this friendship had any bearing on Ailsa's murder. Would they lie for each other? She thought it likely. She placed them top of her action list for further investigation. Both their statements and any alibis would need careful cross-checking.

The art teacher was also high on Shona's list if only for his maturity over the other suspects. Ailsa's death had almost been written off as an accident. The murderer must've kept a cool enough head to arrange the scene to fit that narrative, before making his escape, unnoticed, from a public place. Jeremy 'Jem' Young had struck her as unassuming and bland yesterday. Shona consulted her notebook. Jem's arts project aimed at – *engaging at-risk young people helping foster positive relationships with mentors and authority figures like youth workers and police officers.* Viewed in a sympathetic light it spoke of a person wedded to public service. In a less charitable light, this individual might enjoy exercising power over, and manipulating, others, particularly those younger than themselves. How might he react if challenged?

Shona turned to a fresh page in her notebook and jotted down a number of actions including checking which witnesses were still alive and reinterviewing them, establishing if all potential witnesses had been interviewed at the time, and exploring whether further forensic tests on any stored evidence were viable.

Shona tapped her pen against her teeth. Ailsa's murder took place on 30 July, 1986. What else was happening then? Shona, a toddler at the time, was in her own life-or-death struggle with fate and her junkie parents. She googled the date. Thatcher was in Downing Street and Reagan in the White House. By July, there'd already been the *Challenger* Space Shuttle and Chernobyl disasters. The football World Cup and Maradona's Hand of God. South Africa was still under apartheid, and *Top Gun* was the big summer film. Fashion revolved around Sloane Rangers in Barbour jackets, acid-wash denim, neon colours, shoulder pads and big hair. It was a Wednesday in prime holiday season. The Commonwealth Games in Edinburgh had opened a week earlier, but without the blanket TV coverage that would keep people indoors glued to their set. Shona thought again about the unidentified walker. The Southern Upland Way was the UK's first officially recognised coast-to-coast long-distance route and had attracted plenty of serious ramblers – two and a half thousand in the first year. Most walked west to east, their backs to the prevailing weather, and would have left Portpatrick in the early morning, passing close to the lighthouse soon afterwards. It seemed to Shona that when Ailsa's murder took place, in the late afternoon, only those walking shorter distances, like the elderly couple who'd found her, would likely be around. But the original investigation hadn't discounted their statement of the man on the path, and neither could she.

From this first pass of the case file, it looked like the investigation had a number of viable suspects but had just run out of steam. These days, case reviews by outside officers could kick in as early as a fortnight after the event if sufficient progress wasn't being made. Back then, they were allowed to stagger on long after any meaningful momentum had evaporated. There comes a point in every investigation when you realise no more witnesses, forensics, or breaks are coming. If you haven't found the culprit, the chances of doing so recede like a coin dropped down a well. You keep listening for the splash, but it never comes. It's easy to convince yourself it's still falling, all the while knowing it sank long ago. Four murder suspects with alibis of similar strength. All equally innocent or guilty.

In her jeans pocket, Shona felt her phone vibrate. Her heart skipped and she was irritated with herself for allowing her anxiety to overcome her. Gingerly, she took out the phone. The alert had indeed heralded the arrival of her mother Angie's message – she'd love to meet on Monday evening.

It was done. There was no going back.

Chapter 5

The sun had just set, the sky a bright, glowing ember above the purple-tinted banks of the estuary, when Shona's pager went off.

Phone. Shoes. Car keys.

She was out of High Pines and into the Audi in under a minute.

At the lifeboat station, the boat hall doors lay open, spilling light and the sound of the tow tractor, onto the concrete apron. The lean figure of the helm, Tommy McCall, appeared, already kitted up and carrying his white helmet.

'Mayday from a yacht aground,' he said, following her in.

Shona pulled on her immersion suit over leggings and T-shirt, shoving her phone and car keys into a locker.

'Vessel out of Maryport, Cumbria, taking on water,' he went on. 'Two crew members on board.'

Mayday – *life in grave and imminent danger.* It meant immediate launch. But they needed a minimum of three to make a rescue with the D-class *Margaret Wilson* viable. With high tide an hour away, the stranded yacht was in the gravest danger.

'Workington are sending their big boat in support,' Tommy added, but shook his head. 'They'll no' get anywhere close enough.'

Their inshore lifeboat's inflatable hull and shallow draught made it invaluable among the constantly shifting and treacherous sandbanks of the Solway Firth – if they could get out there.

Seconds later, Shona heard running footsteps and felt a wave of relief. The tension lines on Tommy's weathered face eased too as Callum, the village postman, appeared in the crew changing room, his blonde hair damp with sweat.

'Had to sprint home,' he said. 'Was out with the dog.'

Seven minutes after the initial call came in, the lifeboat cradle was backed into the choppy water by the tractor, and the *Margaret Wilson*, with Tommy at the helm and its navigation lights blinking, set off into the gloaming. The yacht *Samphire*'s last reported position was three miles out in the Solway.

Beyond the shelter of the estuary, the reflections of the vivid sky lay like a fiery oil slick on the tumultuous surface of the firth, as an unseasonal north-east wind had picked up to a steady thirty miles per hour. Combined with the heavy swell of the incoming tide, it made for an uncomfortable ride. Shona and Callum gripped tightly to the inflatable's handholds as they thumped through the waves. She was already running a worst-case scenario – people in the water – and knew Tommy and the big postman would be doing the same, preparing to act instantly if they needed to.

Approaching the co-ordinates given by the yacht skipper, they spotted the grey bulk of the 35-foot *Samphire* thrashing on the edge of the sandbank like a stranded whale, her navigation lights extinguished, all power gone. Her mast was swinging from upright to almost horizontal, like some maritime metronome, as the vessel was pummelled by the waves.

Callum radioed the coastguard that they were now on scene, but as he turned back to Shona and Tommy his face was grim. 'The skipper reported *Samphire*'s fibreglass hull is cracked. Can't raise them on the radio.'

There was no sign of the two men aboard.

Shona knelt in the bows, shone her torch towards the yacht and hailed it.

'*Samphire*! This is Kirkness lifeboat. Is there anyone aboard?' She felt a creeping dread that the casualties had already been washed away, and this had just become a search for their bodies. But as she was about to call a final time, a man appeared above the swaying hatchway blinking in the torch beam. A second figure followed. Both were wearing waterproofs and lifejackets.

'Stay where you are,' Shona called, motioning the flat of her palm towards them. When the lifeboat arrived, there was always the chance that panicked casualties would throw themselves towards it and end up in the sea.

'In twenty minutes, thon tide'll be o'er the boat,' Tommy shouted above the wind. 'We'll need tae transfer the casualties one at a time. Port side o' the lifeboat tae starboard side o' the casualty vessel.'

Shona motioned once more for the men, who were clinging to the rigging and each other, to stay where they were. In the shallow water, with the waves breaking over the yacht, it'd take all Tommy's skills to get close enough.

They did a practice run, assessing every wave to find the rhythm of the tide's approach, and the wash back from the sandbank. Shona looked ahead and Callum behind, calling out to Tommy as the surf rolled in and he battled to steady the lifeboat. Hitting each breaker already felt like being rammed into a brick wall. It had become a race against time. The longer they were out there, the worse the sea would get as high tide neared.

As they approached the *Samphire* again Shona pointed to the man nearest the starboard side.

'You first,' she yelled.

Both she and Callum were on their knees on the port side of the lifeboat as Tommy swept them in. The first casualty was gripping the rigging, but as a wave pawed at his feet he slipped and found only empty air. Callum shot out an arm and grabbed him by the lifejacket hauling him into a space occupied a second later by the lifeboat.

Shona helped the casualty sit upright and began checking for injuries.

'Okay?' She gave him a thumbs-up. He looked pale, but after a moment he nodded and responded with a thumbs-up himself. Shona patted his cheek, encouraging him to make eye contact as a way of assessing his alertness and whether he was going into shock.

'What's your name? Are you hurt at all?'

'David. David Gallagher.' Then he shook his head to indicate he wasn't injured.

'Who's that with you?'

'My brother, Alec.'

Despite the strength of the wind and the flying spray, Shona thought she was getting a strong whiff of alcohol off him.

Before she could ask him how much he'd had to drink, they'd circled round for the second crewman and Shona saw in the twilight that the port side of the yacht was now under water. Only minutes remained before the vessel would be completely submerged.

'Stay sitting there,' Shona ordered Gallagher, as she wrapped an emergency blanket around him. He didn't look like he had the strength to do anything more than blink.

The last casualty clung petrified to a stanchion of the yacht's broken safety rail, reluctant to leave the perilous safety of the *Samphire.* He was facing backwards to the lifeboat, couldn't see their hand signals and didn't seem to hear their shouts.

'Alec!' Shona yelled.

'Turn around!' Callum roared, but their instructions and shouts were carried away by the wind.

A second later, he half-turned to look over his shoulder at a wave approaching like a freight train.

'Go, go, go,' Shona yelled.

Callum half-stood and grabbed Alec Gallagher as the wave washed over them both and the casualty toppled into the upswing of the lifeboat.

In an instant, Tommy pivoted the *Margaret Wilson* around and they headed away from the churning breakers around the sandbank and into deeper water. He immediately set a course for the rendezvous with the Workington lifeboat to transfer the two casualties. Even if both were uninjured, hypothermia was a real danger and they could be warmed up more quickly inside the cabin of the larger Shannon-class vessel.

Shona turned back to David Gallagher as Callum began running through the initial casualty checks with the other brother, propped up opposite. In the minutes after being rescued, most people were numb, disorientated. Some apologised profusely for the lifeboat being called out, some cried and confided they were sure they were about to die. What happened next took Shona utterly by surprise.

As she leaned closer to Tommy to catch what he was saying above the roar of the wind and the outboard engine, and Callum was on the radio updating the coastguard, David Gallagher struggled up from his seated position onto his knees and threw himself at his brother, grabbing the front of his lifejacket.

'You did this, you fucking useless bastard,' David shouted. 'You sunk us.'

Before Shona could stop him, he landed a punch on Alec, who swung back.

'It was all your fault,' Alec yelled.

Tommy immediately cut their speed. In the cramped confines of the lifeboat, in choppy conditions, there was a real danger one or more of them might go overboard.

'Oi, you two,' Shona grabbed David's raised arm. 'You need to calm yourselves.'

She gripped his wrist, but as the lifeboat bucked in the swell, his elbow came back and caught her a blow on the nose. Pain exploded in her face as she immediately tasted the blood on her top lip.

As the *Margaret Wilson* tipped again, Shona, her eyes stinging, used the casualty's weight to wrestle the flailing man to the floor, pinning him face down. Callum had wedged the other brother, who admittedly looked like he had little fight left in him, against the instrument console in the bow.

Her free hand went reflexively to her belt, where her cuffs would've been during numerous London night patrols. When they weren't there, she felt a surge of frustration at just how much danger David Gallagher was putting them all in.

'I'm a police officer,' she yelled close to his ear. 'Do you want me to arrest you? Do you? Cos just try me, pal.'

He continued to struggle; she tightened her grip until he cried out in pain.

'We're not in Scotland. You can't arrest me.'

'Tommy? Have we crossed the midpoint of the Solway yet?'

'No. We havenae.'

'So, we're still in Scotland, Mr Gallagher. Not your lucky day, is it?'

'Here,' said Tommy, holding out an orange strap normally used to stabilise fractured limbs. 'He's endangering ma vessel. You'll need tae restrain him for his own safety.'

With a hand still on the tiller, Tommy shuffled forward and gripped one of David Gallagher's wrists and Shona slipped the line around and made it secure.

'David Gallagher, I am arresting you for breach of the peace, assaulting a police officer, and obstructing and endangering a rescue operation under the Emergency Workers Scotland Act 2005.'

When she'd completed the caution, Shona shouted, 'Callum. Tell the coastguard to get Cumbria police to meet Workington lifeboat when they come ashore.'

'Can we no' just throw them back?' Callum said through gritted teeth as he lifted the radio handset. Alec Gallagher at least had the sense to look alarmed.

She leaned close so Gallagher could hear her. 'I'm letting the Cumbrian cops have you for the night, but I can always come down there and rearrest you for whatever marine contraventions the coastguard can add.'

After ten minutes face down with the cold spray washing over him, David Gallagher finally calmed down.

Given the motion of the sea and the amount of alcohol he'd likely had, Shona and Callum kept a close watch on him in case he vomited and choked. *Less for your preservation and more to avoid the paperwork*, she muttered to herself, wiping the blood from her nose with the back of her hand.

When the *Margaret Wilson* met up with the Workington boat, Alec was taken across first and the forewarned crew kept the brothers apart. Many of the volunteers on the larger all-weather lifeboat had day jobs working the trawlers. Shona didn't fancy David Gallagher's chances with them if he kicked off again.

'Did you ever see the like?' Callum exclaimed as they turned for home.

'Oh, aye,' Shona exclaimed. 'But not in the middle of the Solway.'

As the Kirkness crew headed back in the last of the fading summer twilight, they passed what was left of the yacht – only the topmost section of the mast was sticking above the white frill of the waves. It must've sunk within minutes of recovering the brothers. It was a rule that the RNLI never judged those who needed their help, but Shona was having a hard time not attributing the loss of the *Samphire* to the Gallaghers' own recklessness. She was just grateful they hadn't taken a lifeboat and its crew down as well.

It was after midnight by the time they got back to the station. The floodlights on the front of the building illuminated a wedge of activity at odds with the darkness that lay on the rest of the village. The shore volunteers began washing down and refuelling the *Margaret Wilson*, ready for her next shout.

In the crew changing room, Shona felt a sudden tiredness overwhelm her as she slotted her white helmet back in its cubbyhole above the line of hanging immersion suits.

Tommy took her by the shoulders, his grey eyes studying the damage to her still bloody nose.

'D'you need patching up, lass?'

Shona shook her head.

'Had worse,' she said, and dabbed a tissue to her face. She knew from long experience that if Gallagher had caught her nose slightly higher up, she'd be sporting two black eyes tomorrow. In that sense, she'd come off lightly.

He patted her shoulder and let his hands fall. 'Aye, I suppose you have. It'll go in the report. I'll leave it up tae you if you want tae get thon fella charged, but you know Callum and me will back you. Come up for a cuppa. We'll get the de-brief o'er quick an' you can away tae yer bed.'

'Ever had an incident like that before?'

Tommy tipped his head to one side. 'Drunken sailors? Aye. But whatever was between them two, it wasnae just about the yacht, was it?'

'Suppose not,' Shona agreed, though she couldn't imagine what past grievance would prompt such a near-suicidal loss of control.

-

By the time they'd done the paperwork, it was after one in the morning. It was only as Shona walked to her car parked near the lifeboat station that she checked her phone. The rest of the world would be asleep and she expected to find it blank, but there were a string of missed calls. She frowned and opened a voicemail message from an unknown number.

'DI Oliver, it's DS George McCulloch from Galloway. There's been a suspicious death. I've called a few times. Since you're not picking up I expect you're asleep. But don't worry, I've rung DI Dalrymple and he's on his way.'

'Shit,' Shona said. 'Shit, shit, shit.'

DS McCulloch's tone dripped with sarcasm. She looked at the time stamp on the message. When he'd called, she'd been wrestling a fratricide-fixated drunk in the middle of the Solway. There was nothing she could have done, but still she felt her Galloway secondment had just got off to the worst possible start.

Chapter 6

When Shona got through to Dalrymple's mobile, he assured her it was fine; they hadn't explicitly arranged for her to be on call this weekend. The incident had taken place on a farm close to Portpatrick. One man was dead in suspicious circumstances. She should get some sleep and come over in the morning. They'd know more by then.

So, at six a.m. on Sunday morning, she set off on the hour-long journey and arrived at the Newton Stewart Police Office with little more than the knowledge that she'd likely be leading a murder case, and the sense she was already playing catch-up.

The CID office was compact, barely room for six desks of which only four were ever occupied – one sergeant, one constable and two civilian staff, who all looked up as she came in. She let her gaze rest on each in turn, unsure who had previously spoken the *spy in the camp* jibe. It made little difference since her arrival had been greeted with universal hostility.

Detective Sergeant George McCulloch was in his fifties, cruising to retirement. He was tall and broad with a ruddy farmer's face and bottlebrush moustache. His suit said he modelled himself on his inspector, but he lacked Dalrymple's charm and restraint. Shona doubted DS McCulloch would ever find himself mistaken for local gentry.

The detective constable, Kyle Wilson, was a couple of years into the job and had been parachuted in from Ayr after his predecessor's hasty departure for the jail. On Friday it had taken Shona less than ten minutes in their company to notice the way Kyle kept his eyes on DS McCulloch, as if interrogating every comment, and even his body language, for clues which he himself might follow. He was completely in the older man's thrall. Mentorship by experienced hands was something Shona generally approved of. Her own sergeant, Murdo O'Halloran, was the type of compassionate and experienced officer every cop could learn from, but Shona wondered if in this case Kyle was merely picking up bad habits.

'Boss is in his office,' McCulloch offered, not getting up.

She was a senior officer. He should be on his feet.

At that point the inner door opened and Dalrymple put his head out.

'Ah, Shona. Thank you for getting here so quickly after your busy night.' His gaze fell on George McCulloch, who immediately half-rose behind his desk. 'DI Oliver was involved in the rescue of two men from the Solway,' Dalrymple informed the room. 'And undoubtedly saved their lives. Kyle, can you get us some coffee.'

Dalrymple turned on his heel. The CID team exchanged glances Shona couldn't yet fully interpret – close to a sneer from McCulloch to wary curiosity from the others.

The rest of the squad was comprised of two civilian staff. Erin Brown, the twenty-eight-year-old digital analyst was the sole woman and only technical support member. She sat at the back of the room behind a barrier comprising of two outsize monitors and gave Shona a cautious half-smile.

The final member of the team, Ian Smith, was a whippet-thin retired detective, a 'rejoiner' in his early sixties who'd taken up a civilian investigator job last year. Recently, this had become a popular option for filling Police Scotland's rural and island posts. Shona judged him the canniest of the bunch. But beneath his apparently neutral expression, even he seemed to be taking in her high-end brand navy suit and white silk blouse and scorning her city ways.

But so what; she was a city girl at heart – Glasgow-born, ex-City of London police. Her return visits to either place always felt like a homecoming, despite the mixed memories they inevitably conjured up. And five years in Dumfries hadn't blunted her appreciation of culture, or decent coffee, she thought, gingerly accepting the proffered mug of grey liquid from Kyle Wilson, and following Dalrymple through to his office.

'You said last night you were treating the farmer's death as suspicious?' she said as Dalrymple took his customary seat, then stood up again and offered it to Shona, seemingly remembering it would be her case now. 'It's fine,' she said, motioning him to stay where he was and drawing up a chair opposite.

'It's murder. No doubt about it I'm afraid,' he replied gravely. 'I've got uniform guarding the scene at Eastcraig Farm until forensics get here, but I doubt they'll find it was anything other than deliberate. The thieves targeted quad bikes and tractor GPS units on a farm. Seems the farmer, Muir Maxwell, tried to stop the van they'd loaded the bikes into. Drove straight over him. Then, they reversed, to make sure.'

Shona's eyes widened. In more than twenty years as a police officer, in Dumfries and in the City of London, she thought she'd seen it all. But this was a whole other level of cold, deliberate malice.

'I know.' Dalrymple shook his head as if to reorder his own thoughts of shock and disbelief. 'We've security camera footage and a witness. The dead man's mother, Margaret Maxwell, lives at the farm with the family, and saw it happen.'

Shona winced. 'That's terrible. How is she?'

'Shocked, upset. But she's given us a brief statement. You'll need to talk to her again, of course.'

'Is this related to Operation Raven, d'you think?'

The previous autumn there'd been a joint investigation between the Galloway and Dumfries offices after a spate of agricultural thefts across the region, carried out by a Manchester-based organised crime group.

Dalrymple nodded. 'That was my first thought too. That the thieves are back so quick is disturbing, but insurance money means new kit.'

'A return visit is a favourite tactic of housebreakers, so maybe it's to be expected,' Shona said. 'Won't be the same OCG, of course. It's always been the way. As fast as we dismantle one, any folk on the fringes regroup. They spring up like mushrooms.'

'The Maxwell farm wasn't hit the last time, but it doesn't mean it wasn't on their list of targets. If they'd already done the planning it makes sense to just update their intel and start there. It gives us a place to begin too.'

'You can leave that to me,' Shona said firmly draining her mug. 'I'm really very sorry I was unavailable last night. How is Isobel?'

Dalrymple sighed. 'Putting a brave face on it. But every day that passes, it's like a little bit more of her is gone, as if she's fading before my very eyes. And if I look away, for just a minute…' He stopped.

'It must be hard,' Shona said, gently. There was a time when she imagined she and her own husband Rob would be together for the rest of their lives, that one of them might be faced with the prospect of watching the other suffer an end like Isobel's. But now Rob was divorcing her from his jail cell, and who knew what lay ahead for either of them.

'In a way, it's a privilege not everyone gets,' he smiled sadly. 'We both have time to say what we want to each other.'

'I read the cold case file you gave me,' Shona began. 'There are some areas I'd like to look into more closely. Would it be okay to speak to Isobel at some point?' It had occurred to Shona that Ailsa's sister, and only remaining family, might have her own theories on who the killer was. 'D'you think she'd be okay with that?'

Dalrymple nodded. 'I'm sure she'd want to help.' He pressed his hands to his knees and stood up. 'But I really must get back to her and let you get on. This is your investigation now but do call on me if I can help.'

Shona smiled, gratefully. 'I will. Thank you, Kenny.'

-

With such a small team there was no need for a conference room so she called them into Dalrymple's office. Perhaps if they saw her behind his desk it'd send a clear message that she was now in charge – whether they liked it or not.

She stood while they all found chairs and drew them up.

'Thank you all for coming in this early on a Sunday. I'm sure you're as eager as I am to catch whoever is responsible for this shocking crime,' she said, then sat down. 'Do we have an update on when forensics will arrive at Eastcraig?' Shona glanced down at the briefing sheet Dalrymple had left her. 'Kyle, I believe you're liaising on that.'

Kyle Wilson looked horrified at being the first one singled out and his reflex glance towards George McCulloch for guidance confirmed Shona's earlier inkling of the power dynamic between the two detectives.

'A ballpark time is okay,' she reassured him with a smile.

'Er, later this morning, ma'am,' he stuttered.

'Thank you, Kyle. And you don't need to call me ma'am. Boss is fine.'

In the tail of her eye, she saw George McCulloch bristle at that.

She ignored him and continued. 'We have first accounts from the family, but I'd like you to begin house-to-house this morning and establish initial lines of enquiry.'

'The boss has already put that in place,' McCulloch said, his expression just short of a smirk.

'That's good,' Shona said smoothly. 'Any update on when Mrs Maxwell will be fit to interview?' The local doctor who'd attended the scene and pronounced Muir Maxwell dead had also checked over his elderly mother as a precaution and administered a sedative.

'Should be okay this afternoon,' Ian Smith replied.

'Thank you, Ian. And where are we with alerting neighbouring forces and ports?'

'All done,' McCulloch cut in. 'The boss already asked for any intel on farm thefts involving quad bikes and GPS units to be forwarded directly to us. Cairnryan port police will check any suspicious vehicle.'

Shona stared at him for a beat, her face expressionless. 'Good. Let me know as soon as anything comes in. And talking of the vehicle,' she turned her attention to the young data analyst, 'Erin, how are we doing with the CCTV from Eastcraig?'

The young woman nervously wound a strand of her long red hair around her finger.

'I've sent it up to digital forensics at Gartcosh for further enhancement. The van was a white Ford Transit Connect, but they've taped over the number plate.' Her blue eyes were wide in her round face as she waited for Shona's reaction.

'It shows there was planning involved. But it's useful to know the vehicle type when it comes to cross-checking with other nearby incidents.' It was one of the most common makes and models on the road, but she didn't want to discourage her only in-house tech-support. 'What about from traffic cams?'

'I'm gathering the digital files,' Erin replied.

'Okay. Let me know if you find anything.'

It was a simple enough request but the young woman still looked unsure. Shona needed to get down to the crime scene; she didn't have time to spell it out for her.

She'd prefer to take Ian Smith with her. He was competent if supercilious, but he was a civilian investigator, here to provide office-based support. And it would put both detectives' noses needlessly out of joint. Her twin weapons would be rewarding good work and instilling the fear of God into them, the proportion each would receive dependent on how they performed today. She settled on the young constable.

'Kyle, you'll be coming with me to Eastcraig. DS McCulloch, I'd like you to co-ordinate with uniform this morning on the house-to-house.'

All through the briefing, George McCulloch had been shifting impatiently in his seat, now he looked fit to explode. Shona guessed he'd been counting on shadowing her for the day and reporting back how useless she was.

Before he could say anything, she added, 'I'm sure you're already aware there's a potential link to Operation Raven. DI Dalrymple and I were just discussing it and he thought this was something you could look at.' It wasn't strictly true, but close enough.

She'd landed him with two largely administrative jobs and given Kyle the preferred spot of wingman to the boss, but he could hardly complain if DI Dalrymple had rubber stamped it. And after her battering on the Solway last night the last thing she needed was DS McCulloch for company on what promised to be a long morning at the crime scene.

The sergeant was eyeing her like he knew she'd boxed him in. 'Okay. I can look at Operation Raven for you.'

He made it sound like he was doing her a favour.

Shona took a deep breath. 'I'm aware you may not deal with many murders here.' Until last night, Ailsa Scott was the single unsolved case in the last forty years. 'But I have every faith that you have the skills and determination to bring whoever murdered Muir Maxwell to justice.'

The whole team were staring at her. If they expected her to react to McCulloch's lack of deference they'd be disappointed. She'd met plenty of George McCullochs. The police had always attracted its share of bullies, because it was a job that came with a lot of power. With a warrant card, you could take people's liberty away.

For a moment she thought the pep talk had been ineffective and they'd succumbed to a shocked collective muteness at the senseless horror of the crime, and the task they now faced.

Then, Ian Smith said, 'Boss?' He touched a finger to his nose.

Shona's hand went to her own face and she looked down just in time to see a large gobbet of blood fall on her white silk blouse. 'Fucksake.' She pulled a tissue from her bag. 'Thank you everyone.' She dismissed them. 'Kyle, give me ten minutes then we'll go.'

When the office emptied, to her dismay, she suddenly realised that the nosebleed might look like a sign of nerves to officers that didn't know her. She could've told them how it happened, a jokey tale of wrestling with a drunk that might resonate with their own past experiences. But this wasn't the time or the place. Too early for confidences that were better suited to the pub. And she didn't want them to think here was the new girl beg-friending them.

Considering her companions for the next few weeks, Shona was suddenly overcome by so deep a longing for her Dumfries team, a team she'd so carefully built and nurtured, that she felt a physical pain in her chest that was nothing to do with her ruined silk blouse. She wanted a team that would bring her knowledge, experience, insight and key critical-thinking skills. That seemed a tall order for a CID operation that would fit comfortably in a single squad car.

Chapter 7

Eastcraig Farm consisted of a modern farmhouse that sat at ninety degrees to a run of byres, stables and animal sheds. A line of police exclusion tape across the main entrance vibrated like a violin string in the brisk wind. A uniform officer checked Shona and Kyle's IDs and directed them to a makeshift parking area off to the left.

'Where are the family?' Shona asked Kyle as they got out of the car.

'Old Mrs Maxwell, and Muir's wife, Anna, and the two kids are at the brother's farm. It's about a mile and a half further up the road.' He pointed to a line of woodland on the low hill behind them. 'We've a uniform crew with them, just in case they need anything, and to give them some privacy.'

Shona had raided her suitcase in the boot and swapped her suit jacket and stained blouse for a red RNLI T-shirt and black Police Scotland fleece. She zipped this up now against the strong breeze that was blowing in off the Irish Sea just visible a couple of miles away to the west. In the distance, Shona thought she could just see the white exclamation mark of Black Point Lighthouse.

'What d'you know about the farm?' she said.

Smooth green fields, edged with golden gorse, spread outwards in every direction marked only by sheep scattered across them like grains of rice. In the nearest paddock, a flock of hens scratched at the grass, shepherded by a cockerel with spectacular tail feathers, all under the eye of a large grey farm cat. Beneath the sunshine and the lambs' tail tufts of white cloud, it looked the picture of a rural idyll, if only you could ignore the blue forensic tent in the trackway and the hi-vis of police officers and vehicles.

'Eastcraig is about a hundred acres,' Kyle said. 'They do good business producing free range, grass-fed meats and eggs to restaurants and local shops. Lamb, and beef.' He pointed to a field of black cattle with a distinctive white band around their middle which Becca insisted on calling 'Oreo cows' but which Shona knew, thanks to Murdo, were the native Belted Galloways.

Kyle stood on tiptoes and indicated an enclosed area near the farmhouse.

'Turkeys for Christmas.'

Shona, somewhat shorter, could only glimpse smuts of grey feathers through the hedge.

'And they do honey in the summer,' he said. 'The old farmhouse is a holiday cottage.'

Shona's eyes lighted on a gable end, all that was standing of some ancient home.

'The other building, by the road,' Kyle grinned. 'They have open days and guided tours of the standing stones.' He pointed out a pair of upright rocks which Shona had taken to be old gateposts. 'They breed Border Collies and do shows,' he continued. 'The sheepdogs are pretty valuable. Lucky they didn't take them.'

Puppies too. The place was a dream. Until it turned into a nightmare for Muir Maxwell and his family.

Kyle indicated a metal outbuilding. 'That's a storage barn, but it's empty at the minute.' He continued around to a squared-off unit like a shipping container. 'That's the butchery operation. All done on the farm.'

Perhaps death wasn't such a stranger here, at least if you were a sheep or a cow.

Shona couldn't help noticing how relaxed Kyle had become since they were out of the office.

'Are you from a farming background yourself?'

'Yes, Boss, Ayrshire. But arable – barley and potatoes – not beasts.'

'You'd have a lot in common with one of my DCs at Dumfries,' Shona said.

'D'you mean Jess Johnstone?'

Shona looked at him surprised.

'She always calls in to Stranraer Police Office for a cuppa on her way to the ferry home to Northern Ireland. Just for a chat.'

When Shona thought about it, perhaps it wasn't so surprising. Jess grew up on the family farm in Antrim, run by her father who'd also served as an RUC officer during The Troubles. Jess herself had transferred to Dumfries from Police Scotland's Highland Division, to be nearer her parents as they got older. She was an officer who knew personally the power of community links when it came to rural policing.

Just at that moment a van pulled up beside them and Shona spied the familiar figure of Senior Forensic Scene Examiner Colin Boyd. He stepped out and extended his hand.

'Shona. Didn't expect to see you here. You're a bit off your manor,' he said as they shook.

'Keeping you on your toes, Colin. Never like to be predictable.' Shona smiled, then introduced the two men to each other and explained her secondment.

'What've you got for me?' Colin said, sliding open the side door of his vehicle.

'Farmer. Muir Maxwell,' Shona began. 'Forty years of age. Hit by a vehicle last night. Thieves were attempting to make off with farm equipment. He was trying to stop them. His mother witnessed it.' She nodded to Kyle. 'Show Colin the CCTV footage.'

He hesitated, then pulled out his Pronto, the mobile-phone-sized digital notebook linked to the case-management system.

'The CCTV is positioned about thirty metres away from the incident.' Shona pointed to the main animal shed, which was straight in front of them at the bottom of a shallow incline, which included a duckpond. 'Camera is on the byre to cover the animals since they're the most valuable thing on the farm.'

When Colin raised his eyebrows in question, Kyle added, 'It's not just the cost of replacing the animal itself, it's the loss of breeding lines. Four to six generations of refining desired traits. The farm equipment, tractors and quad bikes are more easily replaceable. They're stored in the furthest shed.'

He pointed out a newer, pale green corrugated building beyond which the blue forensics tent was visible, then handed Colin his Pronto.

'It's not an easy watch,' Shona warned.

Despite the distance and darkness, the image was good quality. A compact white panel van sat with its open rear doors towards the camera. Two figures were pushing a quad bike up a ramp into the back. One was tall and broad, the other shorter and of a lighter build. Both wore dark hoodies, balaclavas and dimmed headtorches. They'd just got the quad bike inside, and were pulling away the ramp, when there was a shout. Both turned towards the camera, then slammed the rear doors and bolted behind the vehicle. Muir Maxwell came running into shot, making to follow the men. But out of sight they must've climbed in the passenger door, for a moment later there was the sound of the engine.

Maxwell changed tack and headed towards the open gate of a track that ran across the fields at the back of the farm. It looked like he intended to close the exit and trap the thieves in the yard. Muir Maxwell was a tall, fit man. Perhaps he planned to confront them himself or just slow down their escape enough to gather more information on who the culprits were, so they'd be caught quickly and his kit returned. Whatever he intended, it had all gone wrong. Maxwell was nearly at the open gate when the van caught up with him. The actual point of impact was mercifully hidden from the camera by the van itself, but the momentum propelled Maxwell in the same direction as the vehicle for a few sickening seconds until he fell sideways from a height and crumpled onto the track. There was a flash of brake lights as the van came to a halt. Then the vehicle sped backwards, hitting Muir again, before driving over him a third time and speeding off into the darkness.

Shona suppressed a grimace. She'd watched it a dozen times now. Each time the vehicle stopped there was a suspended moment where a different outcome seemed possible. The van stalled. The thieves repented. An ambulance was called. Muir's injuries were not as bad as it looked. But then the sickening realisation hit. For Muir Maxwell there were no second chances.

'Dear God.' Colin shook his head, running a hand over his close-cropped dark hair as he gave the device back to

Kyle. He sat down in the vehicle and began pulling on his Tyvek suit. He was in his fifties, a career forensic officer, but even he seemed shocked by the casual brutality of the crime.

'Muir Maxwell was declared dead at the scene,' Shona said. 'His body's been taken to Glasgow for the post-mortem. We had a spate of farm machinery thefts last year. They were carefully planned raids by a Manchester-based OCG. The thieves did their homework, used satellite maps and drones to find where kit was stored. In some cases, they pushed quad bikes and the farm's all-terrain vehicles quite a way before starting them up.'

'You think this is some of the same crew?' Colin said.

'Could be. As well as the quad bike in the van, they'd already loaded another onto one of the farm's trailers in the shed, intending to tow it away. They'd also nabbed three GPS devices. Easy targets as they're so portable. Basically, a seven-inch tablet in the cab that runs on Android-based software with a sunlight readable touch-screen display, and a small, dome-shaped, roof-mounted receiver, attached with a magnetic pad. We're looking for anything that gives us a link to the individuals or their vehicle. The tent preserves the point where the victim was found.'

'I'll start by recording the whole scene, interiors and exteriors,' Colin said, stepping into his wellies. 'A collision at that speed, the van will be damaged. Looks like the ground is fairly soft. Tyre tracks might help ID the vehicle.'

'Will you be able to tell us how fast the driver was going and whether he braked before he first struck Maxwell?'

Colin raised his eyebrows. 'That would be the natural reaction if someone stepped in front of you.'

'It might also be the difference between a murder charge and one of culpable homicide. I don't want any mitigating circumstance presented by the defence to reduce a jail term. I want to nail these bastards.'

'Looks like it's rained recently,' Colin said.

Remembering the storm clouds on Friday night as she'd left Portpatrick, she nodded.

'A rolling tyre would produce straight, crisp tracks on this soft ground,' Colin continued. 'If the driver braked, or took avoiding action, you'd expect smears. Any evidence like that, I'll find it.'

'Thank you,' Shona said, quietly.

With uniform officers helping with the door-to-door and Colin single-crewed, Shona told Kyle to suit up and give the SOCO a hand searching the barn. She thought the young DC might push back against such a mucky job, but to her surprise he seemed keen. Perhaps he missed the hands-on aspect of farming, even when there were *beasts* involved.

They already had first accounts from the family but she'd need to interview them this afternoon. Sometimes, sleep and a little distance shook loose a memory, a recent encounter or some out of the ordinary occurrence that had a bearing in the case, but which had been buried by the initial shock. Despite how useful it might prove, she wasn't looking forward to it.

Shona had a word with both constables on sentry duty, emphasising that no one – two-legged or four-legged – was allowed through until Colin had finished. Then she pocketed her Airwave radio and a couple of forensic bags and set off down the track the thieves had taken when they'd made their escape. It was a search for any evidence, but she'd taken it on partly because she just needed time to think. She had an odd, aching itch between her shoulder blades, which she knew was probably a physical manifestation of being mentally off kilter. New office, new patch, new team, new case – two new cases if you counted Ailsa Scott – was probably all it was.

Once clear of the farmyard itself, she stopped and surveyed the size of her task. The twin buff lines of the vehicle track ran across the grass, then disappeared into a fold in the undulating terrain, beyond which Shona knew was another field and then a single-track road which doubled back towards the nearest village and the main road. She took a sip from her water bottle and slid it back into the pocket of her fleece. Fishing out a band, she secured her hair, which the wind seemed intent on blowing into her tired eyes. She replaced her sunglasses and dabbed at her nose, satisfied that if the bleeding started again at least it'd be camouflaged by her red T-shirt.

The expanse of the landscape suddenly felt like a metaphor for the size of her task. The men who had killed Muir Maxwell could be miles away by now. Back in Manchester or, having evaded the port police or abandoned their vehicle, they could have walked aboard a ferry and be in Belfast, or even Dublin by now. The bigger the crime, the bigger the network needed to facilitate it, and successful OCGs were well resourced. Her main hope was that the brutal killing of a farmer had panicked the perpetrators into making mistakes. All she had to do now was spot anything they might have dropped in their haste. If she was right about the OCG, they needed every bit of forensic evidence they could get.

Chapter 8

An hour later, Shona was back at the farmyard with a clearer idea of the property's layout, and three evidence bags containing a pair of Red Bull cans and an unpaired glove. They were probably all from Muir Maxwell or his workers, but they'd still need to be tested. At the final field exit onto the single-track road there were more tyre marks and numerous scrapes of paint on the gatepost. Whether those belonged to the killers' vehicle or were the commonly acquired patina of agricultural equipment coming into contact with farm structures, would be up to Colin to sort out.

As she'd retraced her steps along the track, the press office had called to confirm they'd released the name of the victim, along with some photographs supplied by the family, and an appeal for any information about the vehicle. It would be the cue for the phones to light up. It would mean another ordeal for Muir Maxwell's family as media interest peaked, but it could also bring them a witness and an important break for the investigation.

Shona waved to Colin, who was leaning against the forensics van, clutching a mug of something hot. He raised his other hand in acknowledgement, then tapped Kyle on the arm to alert him to Shona's return. He was still wearing his Tyvek suit, the top half-off, arms tied around his waist, and also holding a mug. At the sight of his boss, he hurriedly downed the contents and began shedding his forensic suit in earnest.

'It's fine,' Shona reassured Kyle when she arrived at the van. 'I wasn't about to tell you off for slacking. In fact, if there's anything left in that flask…' She nodded to the bumper-sized metal Thermos by his feet. The breeze was keeping the heat bearable, but she was still parched and in desperate need of caffeine.

Colin reached over his shoulder into the van and produced a clean tin mug.

'Made sure we kept plenty for the boss,' he said.

Shona smiled. 'That's why you're my favourite SOCO. Here, I'll trade you.' She held out the three evidence bags. 'Not much I'm afraid.' Then, she updated him on the possible paint scrapes on the gatepost. 'I'll show you on the map. You can drive around by the main road to get to it.' She'd taken a welcome sip of the sweet black coffee. Her expression became grave. 'So, is it what we thought?'

Colin put down his empty cup, folded his arms and nodded grimly. 'The tyre tracks back up the CCTV. There's no sign that the driver braked.'

Shona sighed. 'Too much to hope one of them dropped photo ID, then?'

'Afraid so,' Colin replied. 'I've taken prints and DNA swabs from the trailer hook-up and the tractor cab where they took out the GPS. You never know. Both fiddly jobs in the dark so they might have got sloppy and taken off a glove. I'm gonna need elimination swabs and prints from the family and anyone who works here.'

'I'm seeing the family this afternoon. I'll get them sent over.'

'I can pick up a fingerprint scanner,' Kyle offered. The Pronto had a range of attachments which linked directly into the biometrics database. It sped up ID searches at traffic stops but it also meant the families like the Maxwells wouldn't need to make a trip to police offices at the worst moments of their lives, something Shona was profoundly grateful for.

She nodded her thanks to Kyle, then turned back to Colin. 'Are you happy there's nothing else to be gained forensically from the site?'

The SOCO rubbed his chin. 'I'll do the gatepost on my way out and give you a buzz later today when I've logged everything at Gartcosh. Then you should be good to go. Probably don't want to let the family back until we've cleaned up.' He nodded towards the forensic tent which covered the bloodstained soil.

'Let's say they can come back tomorrow,' Shona replied. 'Kyle, can you let uniform up at the farm know. The Maxwells have probably been asking.' It had occurred to her that she hadn't appointed a family liaison officer, but she couldn't spare anyone from her team for that specific role. She'd have to talk to her Super about borrowing one from somewhere. 'Here.' She took the Airwave radio from her pocket. After a brief pause she also handed him her water bottle. 'Stick this in the car for me, would you?'

When the young DC was out of earshot, Shona said, 'Colin, can I pick your brains on something else?'

It wasn't that she mistrusted Kyle, or the rest of Galloway CID, but this was a small community and she'd rather the local rumour mill didn't start grinding out fanciful theories that would hinder her from finding the truth. And then there was Dalrymple's warning that the perpetrator could still be around. She hadn't taken that lightly.

'Aye, go on then,' Colin replied.

'There's a cold case I'm looking at. What's the likely forensic viability of evidence for testing?'

'How far back are we talking?'

'Mid-1980s.'

Colin began loading the Thermos and mugs back into his van and blew out a long breath.

'Forensic investigation now is a technology heavy and highly protocol-driven affair, but forty years ago they had very few tools at their disposal – mainly fingerprints, ballistics, toxicology – so evidence was gathered on that basis. They'd test for the presence of semen and saliva. Do handwriting and shoe marks comparison. Blood analysis was limited to blood group typing. And a lot of what was collected was largely down to individuals' powers of observation.'

'What about DNA?' The forensic archive boxes containing Ailsa's clothes and some of the painting equipment had been moved to the stores at Kilmarnock more than fifteen years ago.

'DNA profiling's first use was in 1986, but it didn't become widespread here until the Scottish DNA Database was established in 1996. Whether any material from your cold case is viable for testing depends on how well it was handled and archived. But I have to warn you, Shona, I've spoken to plenty of forensic scientists who won't even touch a case if the evidence has come out of police stores because they can't guarantee its integrity.'

'Okay, Colin. Thanks.' Shona tried hard to keep the note of frustration out of her voice. 'I'll let you get off now. And thanks for today. Text me when we can release the scene.'

She'd half-expected his response but still felt a plunge of disappointment that her options were already narrowing before she'd even properly begun to reinvestigate Ailsa Scott's murder. Yesterday's quick search through phone numbers and addresses attached to the case had shown that while the suspects were all still living, most witnesses – Ailsa's parents, a few locals who'd seen her that afternoon, and the couple on the coastal path included – were long dead.

Shona returned to her own vehicle, mulling over Colin's words. Kyle was standing by the driver's door, tapping his phone against his hand as he watched her approach. She opened the passenger side, but Kyle made no move to get in.

'What is it?' Shona eyed him.

'It's just…' he began awkwardly. 'I've just had a chat with Erin.'

'Has she found something?'

'Not yet. That's the problem really.'

Shona raised her eyebrows, inviting him to go on.

'I'm not sure how to say this…'

'If this is an operational matter, I'm happy to hear it,' she said, stifling her irritation.

'Oh. Okay. She needs help.'

Shona glanced at her phone. 'I've had no calls or messages from her. What kind of help?'

'That's just it. She's a bit nervous of asking you…'

'Why?' Shona asked, genuinely puzzled.

'Erin is worried you'll think she can't do her job and she'll end up getting transferred and…'

'Oh, for goodness' sake. I'm not a monster!' Her data analyst's shyness and lack of confidence was obvious. Shona thought she'd adjusted her manner appropriately. Obviously not. The CCTV load was considerable. Her team in Dumfries was such a well-oiled machine that they supported each other's taskings without involving her, but perhaps she was wrong to assume the same happened here. 'I'm open to discussing issues anyone is having.' Kyle still looked uncertain. Keen to show she practised what she preached Shona said, 'What d'you suggest?'

'Well, it might take a couple of days to bring someone in from division and get them up to speed. I could give Erin a hand. I mean, I know the crime scene and the local area. With both of us on it we should get through it quickly.'

'Okay. I think that would be sensible. Thank you, Kyle.'

Her detective constable gave her a relieved smile.

It was something Dalrymple would have known. She'd missed it. But Shona congratulated herself that the speedy resolution of the issue was another step towards team confidence and cohesion, all the while knowing she'd landed herself with the mucky end of the stick. If Kyle was helping Erin with the CCTV load, that left only one option to accompany her for the interview of Muir Maxwell's family – DS McCulloch. And she couldn't honestly say she was looking forward to that.

Chapter 9

As Colin left, and Kyle headed back to Newton Stewart in a squad car, the two remaining uniformed officers parted the crime tape for a battered pickup, nodded at its occupant, and admitted it into the parking area.

Shona looked enquiringly at the man in overalls who got out. At first, she'd thought he was a contractor brought in to look after the animals, or a concerned neighbour, but it only took a moment longer to see the resemblance to the dead man. He was a stockier, younger version of Muir, though he still stood over six feet tall, and had the same round face and receding hairline. The deep blue of his eyes was enhanced by the ruddiness of his fair complexion beneath the day or two of growth on his chin. He looked like he hadn't slept in a month.

'You must be John Maxwell. I'm DI Shona Oliver, senior investigating officer on your brother's case. I'm very sorry for your loss.'

He took her hand like a bird in his calloused paw and shook it gently. As he did so, he pressed his lips together, as if he didn't trust himself to speak.

Shona took a step away from the uniform officers. With a tilt of her head, she invited John Maxwell to follow. They walked in silence the short distance to the fence beyond which the Belted Galloway cattle grazed.

'How are you all coping?' Shona began.

John Maxwell plunged his hands into his overall pockets and shrugged. 'Gey shocked. No' properly sunk in yet.'

'I guess this'll mean extra work for you.'

'Dinnae mind that. And Billy will come in tae help oot if he's needed.' He pointed to a scrubby hedge line where an older man was walking among cows and checking their water trough. Billy saw them looking, held up a hand to Shona and John in acknowledgement, and began walking down the hill towards them.

'This time o' year,' John continued, 'the yowes and kye are oot tae grass. Just need an eye kept on them wi' the heat, but we've plenty o' shade.'

All around, lambs and calves followed their mothers or lay soaking up the early sunshine.

'How will you manage the farm shop?' Shona said.

'Anna always keeps the freezers full o' stuff. And we'll no' start the slaughter tae September.'

Shona supposed if you lived always with this cycle of birth and death you became accustomed to the turning points of the year. She ate meat herself, though not in front of Becca, and knew it was hypocrisy to separate the product from the animal. But still she found herself wondering if these mothers in the fields before her, by the colouring of the leaves or the shortening of the light, were counting down the last days of their offsprings' lives.

Shaking the thought off as city-girl sentimentality, she turned back to John Maxwell.

'I know you've given an initial statement to my officers, but is there anything that's come to mind since? Did your brother Muir ever mention being worried about farm security, or that he'd seen folk hanging around?'

John leaned his elbow on the top of a fence post, cupping his chin in his hand. He was silent for a moment, then shook his head. 'I cannae mind anythin'.'

'No nighttime visitors?' Shona prompted.

'We get folk askin' tae camp. The Southern Upland Way is just over by.' He indicated the stand of trees on the hill. 'We dinnae encourage them. Cannae guarantee they'll no' fricht the yowes, or mak' a fire. Or leave a midden. And there's a bothy a couple o' miles further on.'

'Did that ever result in a confrontation?' Shona frowned. An orchestrated hit by an OCG wasn't the only possibility. Those rarely resulted in a confrontation, never mind the killing of a farmer. Their MO was to get in and out quickly and unseen. Move their haul of agricultural equipment on fast, preferably into a shipping container and out of the country, sometimes before the theft was even noticed. If the job went wrong, it was abandoned and the gang regrouped to hit another target elsewhere. It wasn't like there was a shortage of farms with tantalising equipment. She remembered Dalrymple's list of current investigations – dog attacks on livestock, damage to ancient monuments, minor fire-raising, puppy farms, road rage against tractors and horse riders. All those crimes could potentially impact a place like Eastcraig Farm. This in turn might easily have led to an encounter that escalated beyond angry words. She was in no way blaming Muir Maxwell for what happened, but there was no denying clashes between locals and visitors were a potential tinderbox.

'Cannae mind Muir talkin' aboot a confrontation,' John replied after a moment's thought. 'But I suppose there coulda been. This time o' year there's plenty a' folk wi' awe the fancy gear. But you get bunches o' lads, just eejits fae Glasgow. They see stuff on YouTube an' TikTok an' think they're Bear Grylls or in the SAS. It's no' so much fun when yer in the dark, ringin' wet and freezin' cauld. Cannae just call an Uber oot here. Happens a couple o' times every summer.'

Shona nodded. It was a possible motive. Muir Maxwell had sent a bunch of lads packing. They'd come back to teach him a lesson and get themselves a wee holiday bonus in the shape of a couple of quad bikes and GPS units. They might've indulged in a bit of pilfering elsewhere – fill and drive-off at a petrol station, or shoplifting – before everything went wrong here at the farm.

'Okay, thank you. We'll look at that.'

When Billy arrived, he pulled off his cap as they shook hands. 'Billy Fraser, inspector.'

Shona smiled, surprised and touched by the arcane and respectful gesture. Close up, he was older than Shona had first thought, late sixties perhaps, but still fit. He'd probably been quite the charmer in his youth. His thick hair was steel grey and his blue eyes shone out in his weathered face, though above one eye was a bruise, at the centre of which was a small nick that'd been closed by a strip of surgical tape. John saw Shona looking.

'Tell her how you got that, Bill,' he smirked.

'A kye got the better of me.'

'We cry her The Princess. Barged him intae the gate.' He nodded up the hill.

As if she recognised her name, one of the larger cows stopped chewing and stared at them.

'She's a thrawn beast,' Billy said, shaking his head good-naturedly. 'I dinnae mind, lass. I still got ma guid looks.'

Shona smiled. Agriculture, forestry and fishing constituted the most dangerous occupation in the UK and

Shona had plenty of experience of accidents, and sometimes fatalities, on her home patch. But it was good to see the warmth of John and Billy's relationship, and Shona was glad that Muir's younger brother would have support at this terrible time.

'I'm sorry, I was just asking if Mr Maxwell, Muir, had had any trouble recently?'

Billy bowed his head. 'Terrible business, it is. Terrible.'

'You're not aware of anyone coming onto the farm, or making threats?'

He looked from John to Shona, then shook his head.

'There's something else I need to ask you both.' Shona pulled out a plastic bag from her pocket. 'Are you happy to provide DNA, for elimination?' When John frowned and looked uncertain, she added, 'We're asking everyone who's regularly on the farm – family, anyone who works here. We'll need yours too, Billy.'

'Will it tell ye I'm a quarter Norwegian? Or the true king o' Scotland?' He winked, but Shona could tell his heart wasn't in this enforced jollity, that it was for John's benefit. She'd seen it many times before. A shield to keep the horror of what had happened at bay.

'I'm afraid not,' she smiled. 'And your DNA sample won't be retained after the case.' She took the plastic tube containing the swab from a bag. 'You just run it up and down inside your cheek.' She motioned what they should do. 'We'll compare it against the samples our forensics officer took. It'll help us not waste time chasing false leads. It'll help find Muir's killers.'

John nodded his agreement. 'Aye. Of course. Anythin' we can do. Anythin''.

'And we'll need both your fingerprints as well,' Shona added, as she deposited the swabs in the forensics bag.

McCulloch was bringing the Pronto scanner with him to Moine Farm. 'I'm just heading up to see Mrs Maxwell and Anna. We can do it then. Will you be back home soon?' she said to John, aware she sounded like she was hurrying him. 'I mean, have you much more work to do here?'

'I've no' much more noo,' Billy said. 'Need tae move the kye, but I'll wait tae the gloaming, when it's nae so roastin'. I'll just finish up, if that's all, inspector?' He indicated the cows. 'I'll be up tae Moine in a bit.'

'That's fine, thank you,' Shona said. He raised a hand in farewell and set off back across the field.

'I'll no' be long. Just the dogs tae feed.' John indicated the kennels behind her.

Shona turned to see six adult Border Collies penned behind the wire, silent but focused, their laser-like concentration fixed on John Maxwell's every move. Two of the sheepdogs had a chorus line of leaping pups in with them, who were doing their best to drive each other into a yipping frenzy of excitement, despite the occasional chastisement of their mothers.

'They look quite a handful. Do they need much exercise?'

'I'll tak' the lads oot later an' work them a bit. The bitches are fine fur noo.'

'And you'll both remember to come by Moine Farm for fingerprints?'

'Aye, sure.'

'And you'll get in touch if you remember anything about threats made to Muir?'

John nodded, his jaw set hard, then wiped the back of his hand across his eyes.

'I'm sorry,' Shona said, softly. 'This must be very hard.'

From the background DC Kyle Wilson had supplied, Shona knew that John wasn't married, and there were no other siblings. John and Muir's father had died more than twenty years before. Officially it had been an accident. But the shotgun blast that'd killed him came in the wake of the Foot and Mouth outbreak and had left the unanswerable possibility that it was self-inflicted. On top of the trauma of Muir's murder, John would be expected to step up for his mother, sister-in-law and his two nieces, just as he was grieving himself.

John Maxwell looked up and Shona noted the blue of his eyes exactly matched the sky. But there was something else there too, a steely determination.

'Folks here will help us oot. We'd do the same for them. Are you off up tae Uncle Pat's now?'

'I'm sorry?' Shona said, not understanding.

'Moine, I mean.' He gave her a small smile. 'It was ma uncle's before it wis mine. Cannae shake the habit.'

'Oh, I see,' Shona said, returning the smile. 'Yes. I will try to make things as straightforward as possible for you all and keep you up to date with any developments.'

'Aye. Appreciate that.'

Billy had disappeared through a gate at the top of the field. The cows had wandered down towards John Maxwell until they formed a loose semi-circle on the other side of the fence. Absently, his eyes on the ground, John put out his hand and scratched the nearest animal beneath her jaw. The others pressed closer and as Shona turned to leave, she had the oddest sensation both man and beasts were united in the same grief.

Chapter 10

The road rose before Shona, the fields of beasts giving way to fields of tiny trees, row upon row of them, their plastic guards lighting up like cats' eyes in the afternoon sunshine.

Moine Farm was only a mile or so up from Eastcraig, but it was like stepping back a century, and several rungs down the economic ladder. Laid out in the old steading style, buildings ran along three sides of an open courtyard, the central one being the farmhouse itself. The barns, pigsty and byres were mostly roofless. Some held rusting farm machinery covered by old tarpaulins. The only anomalies were the two, brand-new-looking agricultural buildings further up, on the opposite side of the track.

The uniform patrol that had been assigned to the family was nowhere to be seen. DS George McCulloch's car was in the yard, but he wasn't with it. In the farmhouse, shapes moved behind a deep window set in a repurposed doorway. Shona scrutinised the glass until she was sure. McCulloch's fat white calf peeped from below his trouser cuff; a teacup balanced on his knee. To her irritation he hadn't waited, or called her, but had gone straight inside and, apparently, made himself at home.

The door was answered not by the detective but by a slight, blonde woman in her thirties with dark circles under her eyes – Anna Maxwell, the victim's wife. She looked so frail that Shona immediately stepped forward and put a hand under her elbow.

'Perhaps you should sit down, Mrs Maxwell. I'm Shona.' She had her police lanyard and ID around her neck. Further introductions could wait.

The front door opened straight into a sparse kitchen with a stone-flagged floor, a sink, a couple of freestanding cupboards and an ancient electric cooker. It had the kind of stripped-back aesthetic that might land it in a home interiors magazine, if only it wasn't so authentic. In the middle stood a bare wooden table and a single chair. Mrs Maxwell stepped backwards and sank into it.

'Sorry,' she said. 'I must've got up too quick. Call me Anna.' She gave Shona a weak smile. 'Too many Mrs Maxwells gets confusing otherwise.'

Shona took a glass from the draining board and filled it from the tap.

The elder Mrs Maxwell bustled through from the adjoining room, McCulloch in her wake. Shona had imagined a woman more elderly and frailer. It was evident both her sons had inherited at least some of their heft from her. She looked fit and strong despite her deeply lined face and cropped white hair.

'You shouldn't have got up at all,' Shona said to Anna, handing her the glass and shooting a disapproving look at McCulloch, who merely stared blankly back at her.

Shona turned to Maggie Maxwell and repeated her name and rank. 'I'm the SIO on your son's case. I just came to introduce myself, and to ask if you had any questions.'

'Where's thon fella we met afore?' the elder Mrs Maxwell said, indignantly, folding her arms.

From the tail of her eye, Shona caught George McCulloch's smirk.

'DI Dalrymple is attending to a family matter. He's fully briefed me. I am the detective inspector based at Dumfries CID and I worked alongside DI Dalrymple on the agricultural thefts last year.'

'Cannae huv done yer job that well if they're back,' Maggie Maxwell retorted.

Shona felt the barb but kept her expression sympathetic. 'I'm so sorry you and your family have suffered such a terrible loss. I will do everything I can to catch the people who did this.' She held the woman's gaze until she saw her anger dim and the realisation of why they were all standing in this bleak kitchen hit her anew. Maggie Maxwell looked down at the crumpled tissue in her hand and bit her lip.

'Shall we go through?' Shona ushered the two women into the room next door. It was barely more furnished than the kitchen. Even in the height of summer the place had a chilly air. Shona dreaded to think what it would be like here in winter. On a sofa by the empty fireplace, Muir Maxwell's daughters in jeans and sweatshirts sat colouring. Neither six-year-old Olivia, nor her five-year-old sister, Ava, looked up at Shona's arrival.

'You,' Shona hissed, stepping back into the kitchen and pointing a finger at McCulloch, 'should have answered the door. And where are the uniform officers? If I'd been a journalist, that poor lassie could've been all over the news by this afternoon.'

'The boys have gone for a sandwich. And I saw it was you when you pulled up.'

'Even more reason to answer the door then, Sergeant.' Shona glared at him. 'Now, make yourself useful.' She nodded towards the kettle. 'Black, no sugar for me. I'm sure you already know what Anna and Maggie take.' She made to step through the doorway, into the living room, but paused, then came back for the sole kitchen chair with a look that said – *you're done parking your arse for the day, McCulloch.*

Maggie Maxwell had taken the armchair and regained both her composure and her fiery expression. Shona didn't take it personally. She thought the current prosperity of Eastcraig was likely the result of a long and hard-won battle fought by this woman and her departed husband, and her prickly and determined manner had become her default as a result.

Maggie gave a long sigh when Shona asked her to go over what had happened the previous night once more. McCulloch handed round the teas and withdrew to stand behind Shona, out of her eyeline.

'I dinnae sleep well,' Maggie began. 'Dogs were makin a racket. I went doon and Muir was at the table but had his...' She pointed repeatedly at her ears.

'Headphones in?' Shona supplied.

'Aye. I tellt him aboot the dogs. Mibbaes a fox. He went ower tae the byre. I went oot tae. Rain had stopped. He shouted an' it wis then I saw the van.'

On the sofa beside the girls, Anna stiffened and began chewing her thumbnail.

Maggie jutted her chin towards her grandchildren. 'I'll no' say any more. It's a' written doon fur ye.'

'Of course,' Shona said. 'Again, I'm really sorry to have to ask you this, but is there anything else you've remembered, or would like to add?'

Maggie shook her head, her jaw clenched shut with a line of hard muscle.

Shona could see the shutters coming down. 'Tell me about Muir. What was he like?'

'Kind,' Anna said, her eyes shining with unshed tears. 'He loved his family. Spent all his free time with the girls, though there's never enough of that running a farm. He would help anybody. All the neighbours have been saying how kind he…'

Shona handed Anna a tissue from her bag and gave her a smile of encouragement. 'And what about the people who worked on the farm? No one he had trouble with?'

'No.' Anna's eyes were wide with shock as she dabbed them. 'He's known most of them all his life. Billy was born on this farm, grew up when his father worked here. And John always makes the time to help if we need him, though he's work of his own.'

'John mentioned you'd previously had incidents with wild campers.'

'Aye,' Maggie said, her look shrewd. 'D'ye think that's wha did this?'

'It's a line of enquiry.' Shona could see the cogs turning behind the woman's expression. 'Did Muir have any recent confrontations?'

Maggie frowned, gave Anna a quick look. 'None that I mind.'

To give Maggie and Anna time to think, to sift their memories, she said, 'Have you lived at Eastcraig a long time?'

'Aye, ma husband's folk. Fower hunnert year. Give or tak.'

Four hundred years. Shona's eyes widened in genuine surprise. She had no idea what her ancestors were doing back then. Probably fighting someone. Or in prison. Or both.

Maggie Maxwell looked suitably gratified by Shona's reaction.

'And what about this farm? *Uncle Pat's*, John called it.'

'My husband's brother left it tae John.' Maggie made a face. 'It's aw bog and moor. Naethin tae be done wi' it.' She shook her head. 'I dinnae know what'll happen tae us all wi' oot Muir.'

It looked like Maggie didn't consider the work now being done by Muir's younger brother would be sufficient to keep both farms going. But the blow was still raw, the freshness of the shock she was suffering had a habit of driving out rational thought.

'I saw all the wee trees…' Shona began, but Maggie's look of disgust deepened.

She opened her mouth to speak, but Anna cut in.

'John sold the land to a habitat restoration project.' Her voice was light – Edinburgh, Shona thought. 'He used the money to invest in the new byres. He takes cattle from other farms for overwintering, and in the summer works as a contractor.' She looked fondly at her two children. 'I like to think my girls' grandchildren will see the trees. It'll be called Maxwell's Wood, after Muir's father.'

At that, Maggie's hard expression relented a fraction. It seemed to Shona that to the elder Mrs Maxwell, family was the most important thing in the world. She'd suffered a life-changing blow with the death of her eldest son, so could be forgiven for wanting to fight the world.

They all sat in silence for a moment, then Shona said, 'So, is there anything else you'd like to add to your statements?' Both Anna and Maggie shook their heads.

Shona took a card from her pocket and laid it on the low table. 'If you remember anything, please give me a call.' She looked for McCulloch, half-expecting that he'd slid off somewhere, but he was still leaning on the wall behind her chair, no doubt sending daggers at the back of her head. 'If it's okay, DS McCulloch will be taking your fingerprints and a DNA swab for elimination. I spoke to John and Billy at the farm and they'll be here soon. And if you can tell DS McCulloch who else is regularly at the farm, that would be helpful. We just need to establish where they were at the time of the murder and eliminate them from the forensics.'

When both women agreed, she made her goodbyes.

She indicated McCulloch should follow her into the kitchen.

'Wild campers. What d'you think?'

McCulloch seemed momentarily taken aback that she was asking for his opinion. Then he gave her a sour look.

'Cannae see it. It'll be an OCG. I went through the files like the boss suggested and there's several promising leads.'

By *the boss*, it was clear he meant Dalrymple, not her.

'Are there any other reported thefts with a similar MO within a reasonable timeframe?'

'Enquiries are at an early stage.'

Shona gave him a quizzical look. That was the sort of reply you fed to journalists. Who did he think he was talking to?

'Have any other divisions reported a white van with two suspects targeting farms?' She reckoned if they had, her phone would be ringing by now. The murder would've hit the Scottish national case-management system, though it was always worth having her team calling their contacts, including forces south of the border.

McCulloch shook his head dismissively. 'It's an OCG. And some farm always has tae be first.'

'Well, I'd like the campers line pursued as a priority. Some elements of this theft feel chaotic, poorly planned – going in while the lights were on in the farmhouse, the clumsy exit. Why not park the van further away and just push the quad bikes silently while carrying the GPS units? It's possible this was an opportunistic theft by disgruntled city lads. It's possible they reversed over Muir because they knew he'd recognised them from the previous confrontation about camping or lighting a fire. Go back through any low-level criminality for the last two weeks and see if we can place the vehicle or the individuals there. Put Kyle on it.' He was helping with the CCTV, but he could start the ball rolling with calls to uniform.

McCulloch scowled. 'Is that no' a job for Ian or the lassie?' He pulled back his shoulders, using his height to look down on her in every sense of the phrase.

Shona held his gaze and didn't budge.

'It's a job for whoever I say it is,' she retorted, trying to keep her voice from travelling to the two women next door. 'And I shouldn't have to remind you that this investigation is about getting justice for Muir Maxwell's family, which means that no stone is left unturned, no line of enquiry discarded, particularly at this stage of the investigation. Have I made myself clear.'

They stared at each other.

'Well? Have I, Sergeant?'

She doubted if Dalrymple ever had this much bother with the man. It was true every team needed an attack dog. Someone you could send in to rattle cages. Shona was lucky that Murdo, Ravi and Jess all had that capability in differing forms. But McCulloch was mistaken if he thought she'd tolerate him as pack leader.

'Yes,' he said through gritted teeth.

'Yes, what?'

'Yes… boss.'

'Good. I'll see you shortly at the office,' Shona said, closing the farmhouse door firmly behind her to emphasise this wasn't a request.

She was still fizzing with irritation when she braked hard to avoid a dawdling pheasant in the narrow lane down from Moine. She took a big breath and let it out evenly. Now slow down, she told herself, or DS McCulloch will be the death of you. Let's not give him the satisfaction.

Chapter 11

Shona sent the CID team home that evening as soon as the initial actions were complete so they'd be rested for tomorrow. The second full day was generally when the adrenaline prompted by the crime began to dissipate, and the real work started. They had an accurate chronology of the incident from the farm CCTV, and a motive – theft – but no suspects. All the local news channels, and many of the nationals, had led with the story of Muir Maxwell's murder, but none of the responding slew of calls had provided any convincing information or fresh lines of enquiry yet. Come Monday morning, it'd be the time to get grafting.

As she took the road up to Coldharbour Cottage, she came to the Dalrymples' neat villa and on impulse pulled into the drive.

Kenny Dalrymple was casual in dark cotton trousers and a pale linen shirt open at the neck when he answered Shona's knock. She'd never seen him quite so informally dressed. It felt a little awkward, like she was intruding on somewhere private, which in a sense she was. The feeling only lasted a second or two until Dalrymple smiled.

'Come away in, Shona. Lovely to see you.'

'I thought I'd just give you a quick update on today, since I was passing.'

'That's very kind of you.'

He showed her into a wood-panelled study on the ground floor. The walls were decorated with family photographs and mementos of his policing career. There were also several landscape paintings, modern in style – cliffs, fields and sea made up of bold blocks of blues, oranges and greens. They lifted the otherwise stern atmosphere of the room, filling it with life and colour.

From deeper within the house, Shona could hear women's voices.

'The nurse is with Isobel,' Dalrymple explained.

'I hope this isn't a bad time?'

'Och, no.' He stretched out a hand inviting her to sit in one of the two brown leather armchairs that stood opposite his desk. She wondered if what constituted *good* or *bad* altered drastically when time was running out for someone you loved. 'Would you like to pop up and say hello in a bit?'

'I would,' Shona replied. 'How is she today?'

'You know.' Dalrymple shrugged, giving her a sombre look, followed by a perfunctory smile. Shona realised that she didn't know, and probably never would unless she experienced the agonising slow loss of someone she loved for herself.

'Anyway, so how are you getting on?'

'We've two lines of enquiry so far. The OCG we discussed earlier and a potential clash with wild campers on the Southern Uplands Way that runs near the farm.'

'Both credible?'

'I'd say so. The family have had consistent trouble, and have chased a few off, mostly young lads. Perhaps Muir recognised them. We think this could be a bit of tit-for-tat gone badly wrong.'

'That makes sense.' He nodded, then lapsed into silence.

Shona looked around at the half-dozen or so colourful landscape oils.

'Those are Ailsa's paintings,' Dalrymple said, eventually. 'Striking, aren't they?'

'Yes,' Shona agreed. 'The death of any young person is tragic. But to lose such potential, the pleasure her work would've given people, and how much pride her family would've felt makes it worse somehow.'

Dalrymple nodded, then clasped his hands together signalling a change of topic. 'Let's see how Isobel is doing.'

-

Dalrymple led the way upstairs, carrying a tray of coffee and biscuits. He called out to his wife as he pushed the door open with his elbow. Shona steeled herself for the inevitable change in Isobel from the lively sophisticated woman she'd seen in the photographs on the study wall. She'd expected to find her in a bed moved downstairs, but when Shona came into the room, she saw why Isobel had chosen to remain here: the window, which gave a panoramic view of Portpatrick and the beautiful coast beyond. Evening sun flooded in, illuminating sanded floorboards and rugs, the tasteful pale green wallpaper of chrysanthemums and lilies.

More of Ailsa's landscape paintings shone from every wall, but there were also smaller, darker scenes, nightmare images of twisted faces in reds and black. Opposite the window, in the centre of the bed, Isobel lay propped up on pillows. The long blonde hair was gone, replaced by snowy stubble. She wore eye make-up, deep red lipstick, and a pair of chunky silver earrings which highlighted her blue eyes. There was no hiding the pallor of her skin or the hollow cheeks, but the effect was one of defiance. A beautiful woman who was beautiful still. By the bed was a photograph of Ailsa and Isobel, both in T-shirts and jeans, their arms around each other's shoulders. Ailsa's dark hair flying in the wind. Isobel's blonde locks escaping from a beanie hat. They were like mirror images of each other. Shona recognised it from the case file. It must've been taken the summer Ailsa died.

Dalrymple was soon dismissed. 'Women's talk,' Isobel said, shooing him out of the room.

'Interesting pictures,' Shona said, sipping her coffee. 'Do you paint?'

'Oh no. They're all my sister's work. Books are my thing. Literature. History.'

'My daughter's at university doing archaeology. She's visiting with me now. Well, it's really her boyfriend she's here to see.'

'Kenny told me. Jack Rutherford.' Isobel smiled. 'He was one of mine. I taught him in primary school. Lovely boy. It was terrible what happened to him. Is he better?'

'He is. Becca has made it her mission to get him out and about.'

'She's very welcome to borrow any of my books. I've a lot of local history. Kenny will show her where they are.'

Isobel took two great breaths. Talking seemed to have tired her out. Shona started to rise but Isobel reached out and laid a hand on her arm. 'I know you're looking at what happened to Ailsa. Kenny believes I need closure before I die, and maybe I do. But mostly I let him think that because he so desperately wants to solve the case and has done for years. So, ask me anything you like.'

'Are you sure you're not too tired?'

'We didn't always get on, you know,' Isobel said, ignoring Shona's question. 'Do you have sisters or brothers?'

A perfectly ordinary question which, until recently, Shona would've had no trouble answering. It was equally possible she did and she didn't. Like Schrödinger's cat? Probably not, but pretty close.

'Err, no.'

'People forget that your relationship with your parents doesn't go on for all your life. You expect them to die before you. But your sister, or brothers, are the ones with whom you have a whole life. That's the bit I regret because no matter how bad it can seem at times, there's always the possibility of change. I wonder if Ailsa will be waiting for me?'

Shona was at a loss for an answer.

'Oh, don't mistake me. I'm not religious.' Isobel hauled herself a little more upright against her pillows, waving away Shona's help. Peering at the view, she said, 'The harbour down there was made by St Patrick himself, as he leapt across the North Channel, his footprint carving out the hollow in the rocks. A little way from here St Ninian came ashore in 397AD to bring enlightenment to the Picts and Scots, founding the country's first church. Who wouldn't be a believer, even just a little, here in this land of saints?'

Shona smiled. 'I think what you believe is true is more important than what others tell you is true.'

'So do I,' Isobel declared. She gave Shona a smile of such warmth that it eclipsed even the sun that streamed through the window and Shona saw why Kenny

Dalrymple would do anything he could to give this woman peace. And so would she.

-

Back at Coldharbour Cottage, as Shona washed the bloodstains from her silk blouse in the bathroom sink, she considered phoning Murdo and getting him to rearrest the drunken sailor who'd given her the bloody nose in the first place. It was doubtful she could claim the cost of replacing the blouse off David Gallagher. And it wasn't just her wardrobe and her life he'd endangered; the whole lifeboat crew had been in peril. But pursuing him would mean she'd need to give a statement to an impartial investigating officer. There'd be phone calls back and forward with them and with divisional HQ at Kilmarnock, and probably a medical examination to confirm she was operationally fit. The RNLI would need to be involved, and that would mean more paperwork. With two killers on the loose, and possibly a major OCG operating in Galloway, she'd need all her focus on that. She didn't want to risk a repeat of last night, no wait, technically early this morning, with Dalrymple being dragged from his dying wife's bedside to cover for her.

And then there was Becca and the meeting with her own estranged mother. She'd considered scrapping the whole trip to Glasgow and asking her daughter to get the train to Stranraer. But the postmortem on Muir Maxwell was taking place tomorrow afternoon at the mortuary suite in the Queen Elizabeth University Hospital, so she'd be in the city anyway. It would be hard to sell the excuse of being too busy to spare half an hour to Becca, if she was less than a fifteen-minute drive away. In that sense, fate seemed to be conspiring against her wish to put Angie MacDonald off for as long as possible.

Shona hung the blouse on a coat hanger over the bath to let it dry and went through to the darkened front room without turning on a lamp. Portpatrick twinkled faintly below, but thick cloud obscured the Northern Irish coast. She texted Simon but he didn't reply. Berlin was only one hour ahead of BST, but he could be already asleep or on a night exercise, and she didn't attribute anything to his silence. In truth, she often relished these rare moments when she was completely alone and she didn't have to be in command, or in control, or show-up for the many friends and colleagues she was lucky to have in her life. When she could look inside for her younger self, that wee lassie off a housing scheme, and tell her that no matter how tough life was, she was doing fine. Everything was going to be okay.

She climbed onto the broad ledge and pressed her face to the window. Whichever way she looked the lighthouse, with all its attendant secrets, seemed to be there at the edge of her vision. The murder of Muir Maxwell, and the possibility that his killers were still in the area and might strike again, necessarily put a forty-year-old cold case on the back burner operationally, but Shona was finding it hard to make the same mental shift. Meeting Isobel had shown her that the bond between the sisters had endured beyond the grave and the loss of Ailsa still felt as fresh as it had done forty years ago. For Isobel, it was still very much a current case, with a murderer still out there.

The glass felt cool against Shona's cheek. After a night prising two sailors from the Solway's grasp, and the scouring hours of wind and sun at the farm, she felt she could fall into a doze right here. There'd be more long days to come before she would see Simon or be back in her own bed in High Pines. She tried to picture a positive outcome for both cases – Muir's and Ailsa's – the perpetrators caught; the families offered a firm resolution on which to build their futures. A relaxed lunch with Simon in one of Glasgow's trendy cafes would follow. And just as the coffee arrived, she'd glance up and see Becca and Angie approaching. Shona would smile and the familiar knot of anxiety twisting in her stomach would be gone. She'd forgive her mother for a lifetime's hurt that she barely acknowledged even to herself. Her blood family would stretch beyond Becca once more, closing a circle that had been broken since Shona was a small child. It would be a bulwark against the future. Someone in her life who always had her back. Blood ties give you that.

In a brief sliver of time, the shoreline between wakefulness and sleep, all seemed both possible and just out of reach.

She roused herself with a start and felt the stiffness in her limbs, the glass, which had taken on the warmth of her cheek, suddenly chill once more. Blinking, she looked down again at Portpatrick, but a sea mist had rolled in. The faint lights were gone and everywhere, it seemed, was only darkness.

Chapter 12

Next morning at Newton Stewart Police Office, Shona went through the updated actions, with one eye on the clock. It was a two-hour drive to Glasgow and she needed to be there for the postmortem this afternoon. The briefing went ahead without McCulloch, who texted that he was tracking down farm workers for biodata elimination. She couldn't really blast him for that, however much she was itching to.

Half an hour later, as Shona left the office and pointed the Audi north towards Glasgow, she anxiously replayed what they had. Erin and Kyle had collated the house-to-house, or in this case, farm-to-farm, statements, and made a sizeable dent in the CCTV from the traffic cams. However, neither action had so far yielded a new lead. When she asked Kyle if McCulloch had messaged him about the wild camping line of enquiry he looked blank, so she briefed him herself.

Ian had confirmed that the port police at Cairnryan hadn't detained their suspects, so if they'd left the area it hadn't been in their van via ferry to Northern Ireland. He'd also reviewed the current intel on farm thefts. Eastcraig was the only place to have been hit recently. Harvest was in full swing; machinery was in use. If it had been the depths of winter, a break-in at an isolated barn might not have been immediately noticed. She reluctantly had to admit that McCulloch might be right about Eastcraig being the first target, possibly of a newly formed and inexperienced OCG team who'd panicked. She knew what was driving her anxiety. Twenty-four hours in, unless McCulloch came good with his *promising leads* from the old Operation Raven intel, what they had amounted to nothing.

Her normal route to Glasgow from Dumfries was mostly motorway, but this far west it was all A-roads and she had to resist the urge to put her foot down. The day was bathed in sunshine and the drive lush and green, but Shona's frustration wasn't all the result of the inevitable queues behind tractors. She couldn't look at the rolling farmland without thinking about the lurking threat from the perpetrators of Muir Maxwell's murder. They'd got away with a single quad bike, brutally murdered a farmer and drawn a tidal wave of publicity. Would there be a boss somewhere – Manchester, Liverpool or Glasgow – threatening dire retribution for their failure? Perhaps they'd dole out their own justice and she'd have two more bodies on her hands? Would they hit another farm, try to make up for their poor haul from Eastcraig? Desperate folk were unpredictable. The only way to neutralise the threat was to catch them.

Finally, Shona hit the coast road. Galloway became Ayrshire, and the Irish Sea was transforming itself into the Firth of Clyde. Her mind skipped over the postmortem to what waited for her afterwards – the meeting with her mother. Searching her heart, she found no spark of warmth for the woman who'd given birth to her. In the cold light of day there was only anger, and, if she was honest, a kind of disgust. If Shona found a child in the conditions her mother had left her in, it'd lead to a prosecution for wilful neglect, if not outright cruelty. She'd regularly been left alone, tied to her cot for hours in a filthy, freezing flat. When her gran had eventually tracked her down, three-year-old Shona was so hungry and dehydrated, that she couldn't even cry. That Angie was a hopeless addict and a target of violence herself somehow didn't elevate her enough in the hierarchy of victimhood to win Shona's pity. She knew it went against everything she'd learned in her police career about the insidious and overwhelming nature of what folk like her mother had to deal with. But it was trumped by one unalterable fact. Angie was her mother. She should have protected her.

By the time Shona had arrived at the Queen Elizabeth University Hospital in Glasgow's southside she'd made up her mind to call off the meeting with Angie. She was busy, preoccupied by both a cold case, and a hot one. And with the NCA in her rearview mirror and closing fast, she was desperate to get results. Once she'd parked in the multi-storey, she took out her phone but couldn't think how to phrase her message without prompting a discussion about rearranging it. She could truthfully claim work was the issue, but how would Becca react? She'd see straight through her mother and there'd be a right rammy. Not the best start to their weeks together in Galloway.

The day had turned oppressively hot and humid. The postmortem was fixed for two p.m. She had less than ten minutes to get a coffee first. Dabbing her still aching nose with a tissue, it came away disappointingly damp and pink. She tossed her phone into her bag and set off for the main entrance. The Angie problem could wait.

Shona had changed into scrubs and was attempting to force down her still-too-hot coffee in the cool of the mortuary corridor when she saw a tall, muscular and familiar figure approaching.

'It's good to see a friendly face,' Shona said. It came out more heartfelt than she'd intended.

Professor Sue Kitchen smiled and pointed to Shona's drink. 'Take your time with that. Don't want my post-mortem rescheduled cos you're in A&E with self-induced burns.'

'Oh, you're all heart,' Shona replied, returning the smile.

Sue's grey eyes peered at her from behind gold-rimmed glasses. 'Talking of friendly faces, what have you done to yours?'

Shona put her hand self-consciously to her nose. She'd seen the dark line of a bruise this morning, but thought it faint enough to be covered with make-up. 'Is it that obvious?'

'Only to folk with medical training. Or eyes.'

With a sigh, Shona recounted the Solway rescue and the fight in the lifeboat.

Sue stood listening, one hand propped against the corridor wall, until she bent double giving Shona a flash of concern. But when Sue stood upright again, wiping tears from her eyes, it was clear she found the whole thing hilarious.

'It could only happen to you,' she snorted. 'Wrestling with a drunk in the middle of the Solway. Do you not get enough excitement in the day job?'

'Well, I'm glad you find it amusing,' Shona replied, smiling despite herself. With a little distance, she was beginning to see the funny side too. It did sound like a farce. And it felt good to laugh.

'I mean the *Gallagher brothers* should've been warning enough not to get between them.'

'I didn't know their names when… Oh, I see,' Shona said, catching on. 'Never had you down for an Oasis fan.' She lobbed her empty cup in a nearby bin.

'Good to know I can still surprise you.'

'I'm hoping there won't be any more of those this afternoon. Come on. I suppose we better get going.'

The examination room was a few degrees cooler again, goosepimples rising on Shona's arms. It took her a moment to recognise Sue's regular assistant, Ciara, whose vivid hair colours, make-up and piercings were usually a source of fascination. Today, however, the purple hair had been superseded by two blonde pigtails held back by daisy clips, and a pink Cupid's bow of lips and rosy cheeks on her normally goth-pale face.

'It's *cottagecore*,' Sue confided, knowledgably. 'Takes a bit of getting used to, doesn't it?'

'No, it's interesting. It's nice,' she said, and was rewarded by a smile from Ciara as she left the room. Shona tried, and failed, to picture Becca in such a romanticised getup. Her daughter had never shown much of an interest in changing her appearance dramatically, though Shona herself had given her gran a few near heart attacks as a teenager, progressing through a full rainbow of hair colours.

A moment later, Ciara returned with the cadaver trolley.

'Right,' said Sue, her face growing serious, her tone functional, professional. There'd be no jokes in the presence of Muir Maxwell's body. 'Let's get started.'

The violence of his death was clear. There were extensive injuries to Muir's face and head. The lower part of his left leg lay at an atypical angle, and there were abrasions on every part of his body. Such was the visible damage that the X-ray images that Ciara had taken previously and now displayed on the wall screen were almost superfluous.

Equally clear was that even with speedy medical attention Muir Maxwell wouldn't have survived. The driver had done this deliberately and taken off without a second thought. It only reinforced the urgency of catching him.

The postmortem proceeded with the typical speed that had earned the pathologist and former fencing champion the nickname *Slasher Sue.* Within a short space of time, the external assessment was complete and Sue had opened the torso and removed the internal organs.

Shona noted those things that Sue brought her attention to – the heavy muscling on the shoulders and chest, indicating a level of physical fitness, the health of Muir's heart and lungs – but she knew better than to interrupt or ask for any conclusions before Sue was finished. The professor taught at Glasgow University, where she also coached the rowing and fencing teams, and Shona often thought the urge to lecture had become a reflex, one that was probably appreciated by some police officers more than others.

Finally, Sue stood away from the dissection table. She leaned against the worktop that ran down one side of the room and folded her arms. Shona recognised the invitation to pose her questions.

'Cause of death?'

'The catastrophic head trauma alone would've been fatal. All your victim's injuries are typical of a collision of this kind.'

'Can you tell if the initial blow to the head was the fatal one?'

'Difficult to determine in RTAs, particularly with head trauma, which can result from either contact with the vehicle, or the ground, or both within a very short time frame.' Sue studied her. 'But you believe it's important. Why?'

Shona replayed the farm CCTV in her mind. The first impact, the body falling like a rag doll. The van reversing, a second horrifying jolt as the wheels went over Muir Maxwell, then the third as the killers made their escape.

'I suppose I want to tell his family that death was instantaneous, and I don't want to lie.'

The pathologist reached for a stoppered plastic tube that Shona had seen her filling earlier with traces extracted with tweezers from a forehead wound. 'Small fragments of glass. The primary impact was with the vehicle's windscreen. The victim was facing it at the time. If he suffered no other injuries, this alone would be enough to kill him. The damage to the frontal lobe was unsurvivable. Is that sufficient to answer your question?'

The language was bare, scientific, but the expression in Sue's grey eyes was sympathetic. She'd given Shona a form of words that would bring a crumb of comfort to Muir's family. Sometimes that was the best you could do.

'We'll do the standard toxicology screens for alcohol, prescription and non-prescription drugs, but there's one other thing,' Sue said, beckoning Shona back to the table where Ciara was closing the Y-shaped incision on Muir Maxwell's torso. Sue lifted the man's right hand. 'Have a look at this.'

Shona studied the knuckles, which were scraped and swollen with visible bruising.

'These are antemortem?'

'By about a day, maximum. The question is, did he get these injuries farming, or was he in a fight that is pertinent to his death?'

Shona nodded, thoughtfully. 'It ties in with a line of enquiry. Trouble with unauthorised camping. The victim's brother mentioned *lads from Glasgow who think they're in the SAS*.' There was something else. She'd caught the look that'd passed between Maggie Maxwell and Muir's wife, Anna, when she'd asked them about the wild campers – somewhere between fear and a warning. Did they think they'd be in trouble for making it clear the campers weren't welcome? Or was Muir's anger directed towards his womenfolk. Injuries from domestic violence weren't always visible and she could understand shame making them cover it up, even with him dead. 'I don't have a clear enough picture of the victim yet to understand how he might react in that situation,' Shona said, thoughtfully. 'The Maxwell farm seems to be operating well, with multiple income threads, and he's not known to us. But running a business like that can put a lot of pressure on relationships.'

Sue patted Shona's shoulder. 'Something for you to think on. I can only tell you what the body tells me. It's up to you to build the who, the when and the why.'

As Ciara drew a sheet over Muir Maxwell's body, obscuring the bruised and torn flesh with a consoling blankness, Shona felt the corresponding weight of Sue's statement settle on her like an enveloping shroud. The answers were there, but only if she could find them.

Chapter 13

Shona arrived back at the hospital's multi-storey carpark. The afternoon sun cast alternating bands of light and shadow on the concrete bays. As she walked, her mind seemed to change in time with the illumination. Should she go through with meeting her mother? No. Yes. No.

A short drive away was Simon Wallace's flat, high in a sandstone terrace overlooking Kelvingrove Park. She pictured him at the window raising a hand in welcome, his cropped fair hair and white shirt bright against the darkness of the interior. But there was no point in seeking refuge there. Simon was still in Berlin. He wasn't due back until the end of the week.

She threw her handbag onto the passenger seat of the Audi and cranked up the air-conditioning. On impulse, she pressed Simon's number. He'd sent a text that morning, as he did most mornings and evenings. He was likely to be busy most of the day but would call her later. Perhaps the calmness of his voicemail message might tip her into thinking straight.

'Hi Shona.'

'Simon.' She sat upright in her seat. 'I thought you'd be busy.'

'Happily, you caught me on a break. Everything okay?' he said, alerted by something in her tone.

'Yeah, fine. It's just… this meeting with my mother this evening. I think I'll cancel.'

'Why?'

'I'm just feeling a bit overwhelmed at the moment.'

'That would be understandable.'

'And, maybe, I've only just realised how angry I am at her.'

'That shows admirable self-knowledge. But, you've been considering this for six months, right?'

'Which is why I think it might not be a good idea. I mean, I thought she was dead. Her turning up after nearly forty years. What could I possibly have to say to her now? The whole thing just seems… ludicrous.'

'Daft question, but you're absolutely sure she is who she says she is?'

'I've checked her birth certificate, criminal record, driving licence, electoral roll, employment history and social media. It's her, Angie MacDonald.' The woman's name was like a blade in her chest. 'Problem is, Becca really wants it to happen.'

'If this was a case, what would you do?'

Shona sighed, knowing Simon had skilfully exposed the ridiculousness of her indecision. 'I'd gather more data to expand my hypothesis. You think I should talk to her?'

'Don't go to talk. Go to listen.'

'Okay. You're right.' She sighed. 'Isn't it annoying to always be right?'

'I've gotten used to it. How is Becca?'

'She's good. Coming straight from work to the meeting. Then we're heading to Galloway. Any chance you could come down on Saturday?'

'I'll be back in the UK by then but I promised I'd go to Gabe's hockey match in Perth.'

'Oh.' He had mentioned his son's game, but it'd slipped her mind.

Simon must've heard her disappointment because he quickly added, 'How about Sunday lunch? You can show me Portpatrick.'

Shona brightened. 'Yeah, that'd be great. I miss you.'

'I miss you too.' He paused. 'I know this isn't the right time to say this, but there's an obvious solution to missing me.'

'And what's that?' She smiled, ready for some saucy suggestion or bad joke.

'I guess what I'm asking is, do you want to spend the rest of your career in Dumfries and Galloway? Would you consider moving to Glasgow? You know I'd like to see more of you.'

'Oh.' Shona was momentarily lost for words.

It was true the reasons she'd come to Dumfries and Galloway in the first place had mostly gone – her soon-to-be ex-husband Rob's dreams of running a boutique B&B back on his home turf. A different way for Becca to grow up, with fewer bad influences. Did Shona really want to stay here forever now that so much had changed? It was as if she spent so much of her time processing the demands placed on her – the Super, her CID team, the victims, Becca, the guests, the lifeboat – the list was endless, that when asked what she wanted for herself, she struggled to come up with an answer.

'Just think about it,' Simon said. 'And Shona, it'll be okay, you know with your mother, whatever happens.'

He paused, leaving space for her to agree, but still she felt a kernel of lingering doubt about the reunion.

'I'm sure you're right,' she said eventually. And could she really leave behind the Solway and the life she'd built, return to her home city? Becca was here, so was Simon. On one level it made perfect sense, on another, she just wasn't sure.

They ended the call with Shona promising to update Simon later with news of how the meeting had gone. Then she sat for a moment, her hand poised on the keys in the ignition, considering her interview strategy. Honestly, she was a right eejit not to have thought of this before. Her breaths became deeper, her heart rate slowed. Here was yet another reason why Simon was good for her.

Primary aim of the interview – obtain accurate and reliable information to further the investigation by building a non-confrontational relationship with the interviewee to encourage co-operation. Clarify and challenge their account, then evaluate the information given.

She switched on the ignition and fastened her seat belt.

Simple. She could do this standing on her head.

–

The bar's roof terrace was quiet, the perfect late afternoon spot to unwind. But relaxing with a chilled glass of wine was the last thing on Shona's mind. The space ran the length of the building, bordered by overflowing purples and reds of summer planting, and covered by an orange awning, tinting the scene with the hyperpigmentation of a dream, or possibly a nightmare.

At a corner table, an older woman with cropped, wavy white hair, a geometric top and Doc Martens, sat chatting with a younger woman in jeans, her long brown, equally wavy hair loosely tied up in a scrunchie. Between them, an empty chair. She studied the pair – her mother, her daughter. There wasn't a huge resemblance between them, but even in these few moments there was something in the tilt of a head, the gesture of a hand, enough to extinguish hope that this was all, somehow, a big misunderstanding they could laugh about later. The realisation solidified in her arms and legs like clay, holding her there. Shona looked again at the empty chair between them, and the impossibility she could ever fit in it overwhelmed her. For a fraction of a second, she almost turned and fled. The thumping of her heart sent tremors through her. Water splashed from the glass she was holding onto the hot tiles.

'Mum!' Her daughter got up and hurried towards her. 'Can I carry your drink?'

'It's fine, darlin' honestly.' Shona had armed herself against hugs or even a handshake from her mother, with drink, handbag and phone. There would be no Insta-ready tearful reunion.

As they approached, the woman half-rose from her seat. Shona gave her a polite smile. 'Hello, Angie.'

Angie's reply was a nervous smile. 'Hiya.'

The emails had been hesitant at first. But gradually they'd fallen into a pattern. Not every week, but every other. The small details that made up a life. She knew her mother lived alone and loved her job with a restorative justice charity, having fought for years to get, and stay, clean. She'd never married and had no more kids after Shona. She went to occasional country and western gigs with friends from work, often as the designated driver since she didn't drink. Standard practice for ex-addicts, thought Shona, who couldn't help checking out both glasses on the table – orange juice. She'd found it easier to picture Angie as a distant family member who'd got in touch, rather than the estranged mother who she'd assumed was dead. It had only struck her recently that she could have used her police position at any time to verify this, but she hadn't. Bury the woman, bury the hurt with her. Now, that was no longer an option.

Angie's hungry gaze was travelling over her, taking in her face, hair, clothes, handbag, shoes, as if making judgements. Even as Shona turned to kiss at Becca's cheek, she saw the evaluation continue in her peripheral vision.

'Is it okay if I call you Angie?' Shona began. The woman had folded her hands in her lap, so Shona did the same, subtly mirroring her posture.

'Aye. Of course.'

'I'm gonna keep calling you Angie too,' Becca declared. 'I've never had a gran growing up, and it'd be a bit weird since I know you already.'

Shona was still suspicious that Angie had somehow engineered their chance encounter through the restorative justice counselling programme Becca had attended after Jack's stabbing.

'Angie, can I ask you why you got in touch now?' Shona said, her tone calm and reassuring. Her own Glasgow accent had been filed down by years in London, a necessary move to be understood by folk who'd never travelled further north than Barnet, but she let it slip back – a better match to her mother's own.

Angie shifted in her chair, considering. 'I've been thinking about it for years, on and off. Seen you in the papers once or twice with the police and the lifeboat.' She gave her a rueful smile tinged with what Shona recognised uneasily as pride. 'And I just had my sixtieth birthday. When Becca turned up in my waiting room, I took it as a sign. None of us know how much time we've got left.' She smiled fondly at her granddaughter, who grinned back. 'She's a wee doll, isn't she? Image of you.'

Shona had a clear, professional strategy, a pathway of questions leading to a key objective – what did Angie want? But in a single hot rush of fury, it all slid away. The day suddenly darkened, a cloud across the sun.

'How do you know what I looked like at Becca's age? Or at twelve, or at five, or at any time when I was a kid?'

'Mum.' There was warning in Becca's tone.

Angie's eyes widened. The heel of her DMs dug into the paving slabs as she edged back from Shona's furious gaze and folded her arms protectively against herself.

'Mum, it's okay.' Becca's hand was on Shona's arm.

Shona began to throw it off but then grabbed it instead. 'We need to go.' She made to stand up but Becca pulled away, landing her back in her seat.

'Mum, you've only been here five minutes. You need to give Angie a chance to explain.'

But an image flashed through Shona's mind – four generations of women around the table – Becca, herself, the ghost of her grandmother and Angie – all caught in the fallout of one person's selfish recklessness.

Shona opened her mouth to tell them both the interview was at an end, but Angie got in first, her voice like a crack of summer thunder in the drowsy atmosphere of the roof terrace.

'Oh, you're right to be angry. I destroyed lives, my own most of all. I'm not making excuses. But I'm sorry you had to suffer too.'

Shona shook her head, her face filled with scorn at the insufficiency, the weakness, of the apology. 'I suppose it was all other people's fault, like my father,' she hit back, 'if you can remember who he was.'

'Oh, I mind him right enough. He did his bit to keep me hooked. He's dead, by the way. OD-ed just after you started school. You'll both be thankful I cannae see anything of him is youse two.'

Becca had shoved her chair back against the low wall of the terrace. She sat white-faced, out of her mother's reach. At the other tables, where drinkers were reading or murmuring to each other about their day, heads turned and a sticky silence fell.

Angie was breathing hard. She pointed a finger at Shona. 'But you're wrong if you think I didnae know what you looked like as a kid. I watched you in the playground. I came to my mother's house for years, but no way was she letting me see you.'

'Convenient to blame someone who's dead,' Shona shot back, regaining some of her composure.

'She got custody of you. Went to court to stop me. Threatened me with the jail.'

Shona shook her head in disbelief.

'Wasnae the same back then,' Angie went on. 'Now, social workers keep the contact going. If I'd gone back inside, that'd be it. I'd never've seen any of youse again. Took me fifteen years to get clean and into education. I came back just after your eighteenth birthday, but there were other folk in the house. Told me my mother had died and they didnae know anything about you. Few years ago, I saw you were in Dumfries. Different name. Married name. But I knew it was you.'

Part of the story might be true. Her grandmother had died soon after Shona joined the City of London police, but that didn't mean the rest of it was.

'I'm sorry for what I did,' Angie said, her voice dropping to barely a whisper. 'But you weren't the only one who lost their family.'

Shona stared at her. 'You asking me for sympathy?'

'No. I'm not.'

'So, what do you want?'

This meeting had been a mistake. She didn't blame Simon for encouraging her to go ahead with it, but she'd satisfied her curiosity about her mother from the emails. She couldn't ban Becca from seeing Angie, and it'd probably be counterproductive to try, but she'd discourage contact. Chances were, Becca, who had her own refined sense of natural justice, would move on soon enough anyway when she'd processed how much damage Angie had done to her mother.

'I've been asking myself what I really want for years,' Angie replied. 'I don't expect you to help me get it. But mibbaes it's a thing you've a right to know too about the rest of your family.'

Shona leaned forwards, her elbows resting on the table, recomposed. 'I had all the family information I need from my grandmother, thank you. I have seen enough in my professional life, as you must've yourself, to understand there needn't be a fairytale ending for people to make peace with their past and move on.'

It wasn't strictly true. The desire for a happy outcome clung on in folks' hearts long after their brains had told them it was a total bin fire and they should walk, no run, as fast as they could in the opposite direction. But Shona was determined not to be one of them. If she needed to talk about her mother, she had Simon. She had her work family, Freya and her lifeboat family, she had Becca, and she didn't ultimately discount the possibility of professional counselling. There was nothing this woman could give her.

Becca, who'd edged closer to the table again, said, 'Angie, what d'you mean, *the rest of your family*? You said before, prison meant you wouldn't've seen *any of youse* again.'

Shona pressed her lips together to avoid snapping at her daughter. Becca was an only child. Her father's only brother, Sandy, and his wife had no children, so there were no cousins either. From an early age Becca had been obsessed with large families. Jack Rutherford had a huge number of Galloway kin, and Shona had wondered if this was part of his appeal.

'Becca, we need to get going,' Shona said evenly, then turned to face Angie. 'I'm sorry this hasn't worked out.'

'I said I didn't have any more kids after you. But you never asked about before.' Angie shrugged. 'I was nineteen when you were born, so I suppose that's natural.'

Shona felt a cold dread overtake her. 'So, I've a half sibling. Still alive?' Mostly she just wanted this to be over. Becca's hopes of cousins, an auntie or uncle, would be soaring.

Angie shrugged again. 'Don't know for sure. Davey and Helen.'

'Two of them?' Shona gasped, unable to hide her shock.

Angie nodded. 'Went into care and were adopted. Same father, so, not half. You've a brother and sister out there. I want to find them. I can't do anything about the past, but maybe I can give you back your family in the future. Up to youse what you do with that. But at least you'll know the truth and that you weren't alone.'

An avalanche seemed to hit Shona. She'd achieved her aim, discovered what her mother wanted, but now she wished she hadn't. Shona stood up, unsure if her legs would carry her. When Becca did the same, she strode across the roof terrace without a backward glance.

Chapter 14

The next morning, at Coldharbour Cottage, as Shona was setting the table for breakfast, she was surprised to see Becca outside on the bench, coffee in hand, and already dressed. It had been too late to visit Jack Rutherford when they'd arrived last night, and this was most likely her daughter's motivation for an early start. They'd spoken little on the journey south, each processing the dramatic turn of events at the bar, and had been careful to give each other space since they'd arrived. Shona made herself a coffee and went to join her.

The weather was bright and fresh – blue sky and high summer clouds above the metallic sheen of an Irish Sea stippled with tiny white wave crests. But Shona couldn't muster the optimism the day seemed to promise.

'Looking forward to seeing Jack?' Shona said with a forced smile as she sat down. 'His father emailed me last week singing your praises.' Her recollection of Roddy Rutherford as a suspect in Ailsa Scott's cold case, and Becca's potential reaction should she ever find out, made Shona's stomach turn over.

'That's nice of him, but I'm only doing what anyone would.' Becca smiled. 'Yeah, I'll have some muesli and walk over.'

The Rutherford house was on the other side of the village, a little up the hill from the harbour.

'I can take you.' Shona meant it as a peace offering.

'Don't you have work?' Becca replied, eyeing her mother.

'It's on my way.' And a reconciliation with Becca would at least alleviate some of the pressure she was feeling. All night, when she wasn't replaying Angie's revelation, she was going over the implications of Slasher Sue's findings at the PM and what that meant for Muir Maxwell's family.

And maybe seeing Roddy counted as work. Shona was anxious to get that first meeting since she'd read Ailsa's case file, over with. He'd been panicky and evasive in the original interview, but then he was only a teenager at the time. She had to balance that with what she'd always believed him to be – honest, hard-working, community focused. Coxswain of the Portpatrick lifeboat, single dad to Jack after his wife's premature death. Was it really possible he was the murderer of Ailsa Scott, and he'd hidden in plain sight in this close-knit community for decades? That'd take some nerve. But then you didn't head out in the treacherous Irish Sea in a storm to rescue strangers without plenty of that. He must've saved dozens of lives. Is that how he'd justified not confessing? His service at sea the penance for an early transgression? In Shona's experience, people who murdered couldn't rationalise their actions forever. Sooner or later, the façade they'd built broke down and then other lives were at risk.

Becca nudged her. 'Thinking about yesterday?'

'A bit,' Shona replied, truthfully. She stood up. 'C'mon. Breakfast.'

Becca remained on the bench. Shona could see from her daughter's determined expression that she wasn't about to let her mother wriggle off the hook.

'It's good that you're reconnecting with Angie, Mum. It might give you some resolution. Heal old wounds,' Becca said, with the resolute certainty of youth.

Shona had been a little economical with the truth when she'd called Simon last night. There'd been some shocks, she'd said, but she knew it all now, hopefully, so that was a relief. From his short silences before each reply, she recognised he wasn't convinced he was getting the whole story. But he was prudent enough not to enquire further at this stage, unlike her daughter. Shona's ears had begun to buzz, a pressure building in her head. Every detail of her mother's expression was etched in her memory, how the revelations had tumbled from her, despite Shona's obvious discomfort.

'You must be curious to know about your brother and sister,' Becca pressed. 'I might have cousins. You'd be their auntie. And we don't have much family.'

'You're my family.' Sudden tears were pricking at Shona's throat. 'You're the only family I need.' And she might not have had many relatives, but she was blessed in her colleagues and friends.

'Oh Mum, it's not that I need anyone else. It's just… it might be nice to have a few relatives that aren't in jail,' she added in a weak attempt to lighten the mood.

Shona couldn't help but think of the NCA investigation circling her. They were intent on proving she'd shared in her husband's corrupt ways, which wasn't true. She'd arrived at a place where the border between what was true and what was right had blurred beyond understanding. It was as if she'd walked casually out into the Solway at low tide, heedless of the peril, only to find herself surrounded by quicksand. Every turn was fraught with disaster. Becca couldn't know how prophetic her words might be. At the thought of what lay ahead, Shona shuddered.

'Cold?' Becca got up and hugged her.

'A bit,' Shona lied, glad of the diversion.

'How did you find this place again?' Becca turned and shaded her eyes, taking in the view of the village, then the coast running north to the lighthouse.

Shona interrogated her daughter's tone for approval or disapproval but couldn't make out which it was.

'It belongs to a friend of Detective Inspector Dalrymple.'

'It's nice. There's lots of interesting archaeology in the area, and lots of sites that haven't been properly recorded yet. I'm gonna take Jack out on walks to look at them, if he feels okay.'

'That's good.' Shona watched a shaft of sun illuminating Black Point Lighthouse, transforming it into a chalky column of pure white against the blues of the sea and sky. The whole landscape felt steeped in stories it was reluctant to give up. She thought of the briefing she was due to give this morning. At least they knew what had happened to Muir Maxwell. With hard graft and a bit of luck, they'd find the perpetrators. But there'd been no CCTV cameras forty years ago for Ailsa. Only the lighthouse had witnessed it all and it was keeping its secrets.

She became aware Becca was studying her.

'Are you all right, Mum?'

'I am, darlin'. Just got a lot on my mind.'

'I know. You can always talk to me.'

'Yeah, of course.' Shona smiled, then scrubbed a hand through her hair, letting the wind catch it in an attempt, both physical and metaphorical, to blow the dark thoughts from her head.

Becca's phone buzzed and she checked the message. 'It's Jack. He's not at home.'

It looked like Shona's opportunity to sound Roddy out had slipped away. 'Everything okay?'

'Yeah. He's at the lifeboat station helping his dad.'

'Even better,' Shona replied, as Becca gave her a puzzled look. 'It's closer. You'll see Jack quicker,' she teased. It was also a neutral location for Shona to quiz Roddy. 'Right, let's have some breakfast and get you down there.'

-

They arrived at Portpatrick Lifeboat Station just before eight a.m. The big, all-weather Shannon-class lifeboat rode the gentle swell in the inner harbour as gulls followed a returning creel boat to its nearby mooring. Roddy had discarded his suit jacket and was by the raised tailgate of his car, unloading first aid supplies, the sleeves of his white office shirt rolled to the elbow.

'Sorry to drop in on you so early,' Shona said as they shook hands.

'No bother, Shona. And here she is,' he beamed at Becca.

Shona felt a twinge of discomfort as her daughter came forward and hugged him.

He was tall and broad shouldered, his close-cropped hair and beard was more salt than pepper now, but Shona reckoned he'd have another ten years as the all-weather lifeboat coxswain, if his health held out, before compulsory retirement at sixty-five.

'Jack's onboard. Run and surprise him,' he said to Becca.

'Bye, Mum,' Becca called over her shoulder as she headed down the gangway.

Jack must've heard them draw up. He climbed stiffly from the lifeboat, then did a self-conscious little dance for Becca, as if proving his recovery was more complete than it looked. He was the image of his father, with thirty-five years wiped from the clock – tall, slim, dark-haired and with a ready grin that quickly put people at their ease. Becca braked into a cartoon, slow-motion run, gingerly putting her arms around him as if he was made of glass that might shatter at any moment, before they both dissolved into laughter.

Shona and Roddy both smiled at their antics and she was just wondering how to bring up the subject of her presence in Portpatrick when he spoke.

'Is that right you're filling in for Kenny Dalrymple?'

'Yeah, I am,' Shona said, casually.

'Things not so good with Isobel then?'

She shook her head. 'D'you know the family?'

'Aye, of course. Everybody kens everybody here. And I've been there myself,' he added, quietly.

It was only then that Shona realised Roddy had probably also nursed his own wife through terminal breast cancer. Any replies he might give would inevitably be tinged with that painful remembrance.

'I might pop in and see them. D'you think that'll be all right?' he said.

'I'd give them a ring. I think Isobel has good days and bad days.'

Roddy stuck out his bottom lip and nodded.

She wanted to ask if his offering Dalrymple support meant he had no hard feelings with the police but knew that was too blunt an approach.

Instead, she said, 'D'you remember her sister, Ailsa?'

'I mind her well. Whole place was shocked at what happened. Terrible. Black Point always had a reputation as a dangerous place, but it was Ailsa Scott's death that made folk avoid it.'

'What d'you mean *it had a reputation*? Were there other deaths?'

'Other murders? Aye, during smuggling times.' He shrugged. 'Shipwrecked sailors struggling ashore and being dispatched by locals after the cargo. Their ghosts are supposed to haunt the place. You'll not find many locals walking their dogs up there. The police did a thorough job with Ailsa, though. Interviewed everyone, but they never got the culprit.' He smiled. 'They even fancied me for it at one point. No need to look so shocked, Shona. I was still at school but I was big for my age and was volunteering up at the lighthouse when it happened, so I suppose they had to. Mind you, these days, they'd never get away with interviewing a fourteen-year-old without a solicitor. And if that was a client of mine, I'd make damn sure I lodged a formal complaint.'

The evidence against Rory was purely circumstantial. Ailsa's body had been found by walkers – an elderly couple – who were the primary witnesses to the unidentified rambler and had helped create the photofit image. Roddy Rutherford had been second on the scene when the shocked and distraught pair had come to the lighthouse for help. But he'd also presented so badly at interview – jittery and evasive – that he remained under suspicion.

'That must've been very distressing. D'you think it influenced your decision to study law and train as a solicitor?'

He made a show of considering the question. 'Aye, you might be right there. Hadn't really thought about it.'

Shona swallowed. 'Did you ever have any suspicions yourself who was responsible?'

He shook his head. 'Feeling was it couldn't be anyone who lived local. Had to be the fella walking the coastal path they never found. Got clean away with it. But really who knows.' He closed the boot of his car, a signal their conversation was coming to an end. 'Anyway, don't want to hold you up. If you're filling in for Kenny, you'll be dealing with thon farmer who was killed.'

'Yes, I'm just on my way now.'

'Terrible business. Someone from outside, surely. I mean it makes no sense to rob a farm on your own doorstep. How would you get rid of the proceeds without someone twigging?'

Shona nodded, though the obsession with outsiders being responsible for nefarious deeds was something she'd heard many times before, often just before the real and very much local culprit was unmasked. 'Becca has a key to the cottage so she can go home any time if Jack needs to rest.'

The pair were sitting on the end of the dock with their backs to their parents, Jack pointing out local landmarks.

'Oh, I've no worries on that score.' Roddy smiled, opening the driver's door. 'Becca's been that good for Jack. She'll know he needs a rest before he does. See you later, Shona.'

She watched him navigate the dockside with practised ease, tooting his farewell to Becca and Jack who raised their hands in acknowledgement. Was it just her imagination or was his exit a little too hasty? Their encounter had left her feeling oddly uneasy, though she couldn't put her finger on exactly what was troubling her. Then she saw it; the first aid box Roddy had unloaded was still sat on the tarmac. He'd failed to deliver it to the lifeboat and see it safely stowed. Perhaps he was just distracted, late for work, but it was a potentially costly mistake and a significant oversight for someone of his experience. Either way, she'd text Dalrymple and warn him that Roddy might be in touch. She wouldn't need to spell it out. He'd understand if Roddy's visit included being on a fishing trip about a potential new investigation into Ailsa's murder. Because however much Shona didn't want it to be true, it'd be a sign they needed to look much more closely at their local lifeboat coxswain.

Chapter 15

When she got to Newton Stewart Police Office carpark, her phone buzzed with an incoming call. She thought it might be Roddy attempting to rectify his forgetfulness with the first aid box, which she'd already given to Becca and Jack. But checking the screen she saw it was Colin Boyd, the senior forensic scene examiner.

'Hi Colin. What can I do for you?'

'As always, it's what I can do for you, Detective Inspector.'

'I'm listening.' Her heartbeat skipped up a notch at Colin's tone.

'Got a match on the fingerprints.'

'You have? Brilliant. Hang on a second.' She grabbed her handbag, got out of the Audi, locking it with a flick of her keys over her shoulder. 'Okay Colin, what've you got?' she said, as she hurried to the back door. It was already hot, her back clammy from the car seat.

'Michael Elliot, known as Midge.'

'Address?' Shona keyed in the code and yanked open the security door.

'Right on your doorstep. String of previous convictions.'

'He's local?' This was even better than she'd hoped. 'Text me the details, Colin, and thank you.'

As she swept into the CID room, the team all looked up from their desks. Shona crooked her finger at Sergeant George McCulluch. He got up with less urgency than she'd have liked and followed her into her office.

'So, Michael "Midge" Elliot, what d'you know about him?' Shona looped her handbag and suit jacket over the coat stand in the corner behind the desk and sat down.

McCulloch sank into the chair opposite and sighed as if he had better things to do with his time than answer random questions. She'd have preferred him to wait for an invitation to sit, but this early in the day she let it pass.

McCulloch shrugged. 'Midge Elliot? Petty thief fae Stranraer. Small-time dealer who's got a habit himself. Multiple drug rehab orders. Thinks he can run with the big boys but is just feckless enough tae no get himself into proper bother.'

Shona wasn't sure who counted as big boys in Galloway, but she got the gist of it.

'What if I told you we've a match for his prints at Eastcraig Farm?'

McCulloch raised his eyebrows and looked genuinely surprised.

'Was he on your list of farm workers for fingerprints and DNA elimination?'

McCulloch shook his head.

'Anyone mention him?'

'I double-checked wi' the farm payroll and Maggie Maxwell. She didnae say anyone was missing from it.'

'But he could've been a contractor, or casual labourer?'

'His name has never come up.'

It was like pulling teeth. God, how she missed Murdo, currently sitting at his desk back in Dumfries. He'd have been all over this. 'Well check again. His prints are on the quad bike and the trailer hook-up, and they didn't get there by magic. Don't go to Maggie. Ask Muir's wife, Anna. She does the books. Bury Midge Elliot's name in a list of others we're interested in talking to. Say they're tip-offs from the public appeal. See if she bites.' Shona thought presenting Maggie Maxwell with a single suspect at this stage would result in her rounding up a posse of farmers intent on stringing up Midge Elliot from the nearest lamppost.

McCulloch remained in his seat, shaking his head. 'Can't see Midge for this.'

As the local expert on known faces, Shona was prepared to humour him, but only so far. He was rapidly reaching the end of his allocation. 'And why is that, given the forensic evidence?'

'He's a plodder. If a quad bike wi' the engine running was left in the street he'd be off wi' it. But he hasnae the brains for anythin' else.'

'CCTV shows two men,' Shona reminded him as she sat back in her chair and folded her arms. 'Either of them could have planned the theft, and I use the word *plan* loosely, since it was all pretty chaotic at the end. By your admission that fits our suspect. What about his associates? Do you fancy any of them for this?'

He shook his head, then shuffled forward in his chair and tapped her desk for emphasis. 'Still think this is an OCG.'

She hadn't completely abandoned the idea herself. But you had to follow the evidence. McCulloch seemed to have become fixated on the idea that there were no other credible lines of enquiry.

'From the Operation Raven intel,' he went on, gathering momentum, 'I've found three fellas that fit the bill. Sean and Gary Jones and a Michael McPhee. All Manchester-based. Two released fae custody before the trial and one oot last month fae a six-month stretch for a serious assault. They were the tiddlers in our net. Prosecution thought the case against them too weak tae pursue, but they'd have the skills and the knowledge. Maybe even recced the place. I've got Manchester CID on the lookout for them, but so far, no show. No hits on ANPR for their listed vehicles. Wherever they are, it's no' on their usual turf.'

McCulloch himself sat back and folded his arms, challenging Shona to shoot his theory down.

A splinter group. She had to admit he'd been right to pursue it. 'It's a line of investigation. But where are the forensics to back it up?'

'They're professional. Wore gloves. Midge is small fry. Cannae see him killing anyone.'

It was the arrogant certainty that he was right and she was wrong, even in the face of forensic evidence, that tipped her over the edge. No officer should be this closed-minded at this stage of an investigation.

Shona planted her hands firmly on the desk and stood up. 'Noted, Sergeant McCulloch. But right now, Midge Elliot is our prime suspect. I'd like you out there, calling Anna Maxwell to exclude him as a family friend or casual employee, or any other possible reason for him being at Eastcraig. And I want chapter and verse – his current whereabouts, employment history, known associates – you know the drill.' When he didn't move, she added. 'And I want it now, Sergeant. Full briefing in thirty minutes.'

She stared him down until he got to his feet and left, in his customary leisurely manner, leaving the office door ajar.

Shona took her phone from her bag. As she made the call she walked across to the door and pushed it slowly shut aware the team would be watching and interpret any show of temper on her part as a win for McCulloch.

'Murdo,' she said warmly when the call was answered.

'Boss. Hear you've got a wee job on your hands doon there.' It was classic Murdo understatement and Shona smiled in recognition. She could see him now standing by his desk in the corner, hoiking up the waistband on his suit trousers with one hand, phone clamped to his ear with the other but eyes on what every member of the CID team was doing without seeming like he was checking up on them.

'You heard right,' she sighed, hoping it didn't sound too heartfelt.

'Anything we can do for you here? Had the standard enquiry from a guy called Ian.'

'That'd be Ian Smith. He's ex-job, now civilian investigator. I tasked him with contacting other forces.' It was reassuring to hear he was doing his tasks thoroughly, though she never doubted he would. 'You've had no farm thefts reported in Dumfriesshire?' she said.

'All quiet on that front.'

'And no reports of anyone trying to flog a cut-price quad bike?'

'Not a sniff. It'd be a risky purchase anyway. Just takes a neighbour tae visit and click yer new bike matches the description of a murdered farmer's and that's you persona non grata wi' the agricultural community for the rest of yer natural life.'

'I've just got a positive ID on prints for a Stranraer local, apparently not the brightest bulb in the box. But here's the thing that's bothering me.' There was something that didn't sit right, though she would never admit it to McCulloch. 'The driver made no attempt to brake or avoid the victim. Then he stopped, reversed and went over him again. For a robbery it just seems a bit…'

'O'er done?' Murdo supplied.

'That's it. Excessive. Muir Maxwell was a big guy. But they outnumbered the farmer two to one. They were in a vehicle. Was pretty obvious no one else was going to intervene out there in the dead of night.'

'Aye it's no typical. Might have a drug habit. Could've been hyped up on something, acting like they're in a video game. It's no' real to them. Only sinks in later whit they've done.'

'That makes sense,' Shona agreed. 'Previous history of addiction.'

'You'll soon know if he was capable when you've had a wee chat with him.'

At Murdo's easy confidence in her she felt her spirits revive, only now realising how much they'd been flagging in the wake of all she'd encountered in the last week – her mother, the teething troubles with the new squad, even the battering she'd received from the Solway and the Gallagher brothers during the rescue. What she needed was people she could rely on, more familiar faces, and less new ones, around her.

'There is something you can do for me, Murdo. Can Ravi be spared for a week or so? I'm desperately in need of a decent family liaison officer and I'm short of likely candidates.'

DC Ravi Sarwar was a fellow Glaswegian with just the right mix of sharp eyes, empathy and charm to support both the victim's family and the investigation. Shona reckoned he could bring even Maggie Maxwell onside in record time.

'I'd love tae send you Ravi but he's up at the High Court this week for thon McConnachie case, remember?'

She did, dammit.

'What about Jess?' Murdo said. 'I mean it'll leave me short-handed but there's another week tae go tae the full moon, so we should be fine.'

Jess didn't have Ravi's experience in the role, or his all-encompassing charm, but she had grown up on a farm in Northern Ireland so that more than made up for it. It was such an obvious solution she wondered why she hadn't thought of it herself. It was further evidence, if any was needed, of the toll her private life was taking on her work decisions.

'That'll be perfect, Murdo.' Remembering her chat with Kyle, she added, 'I think Jess already knows some of the officers here. One told me she often pops into Stranraer Police Office for a coffee and a chat on her way to the ferry.'

'There you go then. Sorted.'

Feeling she was on a roll, she said, 'Murdo, one more thing. Do you remember the Ailsa Scott cold case from 1986? She was murdered on the coast path. No one was ever charged. I'm reviewing it on the quiet for Kenny Dalrymple. There's a family connection.'

'I mind it. An' I can see how you'd have the time tae do that wi' a hot murder case and the perpetrators at large.' He sighed. 'Go on then.'

'Head injuries. Moved and posed after death. No sexual assault. No established link to other cases. I'm struggling for a potential motive. Can I send you the abstract?'

'Wi' lassies, statistically, the partner or a rejected suitor, would be top o' the list.'

'Boyfriend investigated and cleared at the time, but that's where I've put him and his mate.'

'Good. Send me the abstract an' I'll send you Jess. No' sure I'm getting the best o' this deal, but you're the boss so I guess I'll have tae lump it.'

'Thanks, Murdo. Everything going okay?'

'Fine. I'm just makin sure that when the cat's awa all us mice are working hard.'

'I'll ignore the inference, Detective Sergeant. Listen, talking of work I better go. Bye, Murdo. And thanks.'

Shona congratulated herself on a smart move. All it had taken was one phone call. With Jess arriving and Murdo appraising the cold case she could feel the wind shifting in her favour. Time to make the most of it.

She went to the door. 'Briefing now, folks!' She felt a smirk of satisfaction when McCulloch pouted and checked his watch.

'Right,' she said when they were all in position around her desk. 'We've a positive fingerprint hit for Midge Elliot. More on that shortly, but first, has anything else come in?' The public appeal had lit up the phones. 'Has Elliot been mentioned?' The group shook their heads. 'Any further reports of farm break-ins, attempted or otherwise?' The response was the same.

'Perhaps the murder has scared them off,' Ian said.

'Nice thought, hold onto it,' Shona replied. 'Now, yesterday's postmortem showed Muir Maxwell had bruised knuckles sustained before his death. Was this from farm work or did he have a violent encounter the day before his death? It may be connected to Midge Elliot, it may not. I want every lead followed to its conclusion so the fiscal doesn't catch us out later.' Shona pointed her pen at Kyle. 'Where are we with the idea that he confronted city-boy campers and they decided to teach Maxwell a lesson. Any reports of low-level crime from lads that might fit the profile?'

'Nothing, boss. Sorry.'

Shona took a moment to digest that. It didn't rule the scenario out entirely, but it downgraded the line of enquiry. 'Okay, in that case, we'll also need to consider domestic violence.'

The whole group looked momentarily puzzled.

'You mean Muir assaulting his womenfolk?' McCulloch ventured.

'We know it happens. No visible injuries on Maggie, Anna or the girls, but it might not be the whole story. Ian, ask uniform and check the records. Erin?' Shona peered at her digital analyst over her glasses and gave her an encouraging smile. 'The CCTV you sent for enhancement to Gartcosh?'

Erin took out an iPad and turned it towards Shona, who motioned McCulloch, Ian Smith and Kyle to come around the desk and join her. The detail had been sharpened, the sound enhanced. They heard Muir's shouts, but frustratingly, nothing said by either of the two figures.

'Well? Could one of the men be Elliot?' Shona said when they'd run the video a few times. 'Ian? Kyle? Have you met him?'

They both nodded.

'It doesn't exclude him,' said Ian, tactfully.

McCulloch kept his face expressionless, but his tense posture signalled his irritation.

'Good enough for me.' Shona sent them all back to their seats. 'Muir Maxwell and his family are who should be foremost in your minds when you're asking questions, trawling through CCTV.' She wanted to solve this case for them, but also for Dalrymple. Ailsa Scott's picture, the one of her on the clifftop, her hair blowing about her, was never far from Shona's consciousness. Leaving him with another unsolved murder would feel like a betrayal of his trust in her. 'The choices you make in reviewing evidence may make a crucial difference to whether this guy at the wheel is caught, or the Maxwell family live in limbo, possibly forever.

'Go back over everything and look for him. See if you can find Midge Elliot's vehicle leaving or arriving at his home address on the night Muir Maxwell died, and any other sighting of it in the days since. Kyle, I want you to track down Elliot and keep him under watch.' The young constable gave McCulloch a reflex glance seeking approval. But Shona headed off any objection of sending Kyle single-crewed. 'Who's your handiest uniform constable here?' Every CID member knew who was rock-solid in a tight corner. 'Tell them they've a temporary promotion to plain clothes.' She gave him an ironic smile. 'No extra pay, but guaranteed pints when we nab this guy.'

The difference in the team was marked, even McCulloch. They'd caught the scent of a suspect. If they could prick up their ears they would've.

'We spend today nailing down the evidence.' They'd have twelve hours to question him and an alibi was often difficult to check at three a.m. 'McCulloch, get me a team. First thing tomorrow, bring Midge Elliot in.'

Chapter 16

Overhead, the gulls were already up and screaming. Midge Elliot's flat in west Stranraer was at the top of a four-storey block peppered with rusting TV dishes. Even in the pearly, five a.m. light of a still summer's morning the place looked defeated. Shona stood beside a patrol car, as a uniform squad in body armour made ready to detain the suspect. Detective Sergeant McCulloch was talking with his opposite number. Next to him, Kyle bounced on the spot, doing a fair impression of shrugging off the early morning chill, but Shona recognised it for what it was – nerves. He caught her eye and gave a hesitant thumbs-up.

Yesterday afternoon, McCulloch had come back with the news that Anna Maxwell didn't know any of the names on his fabricated list, including Midge Elliot's, which was precisely what Shona had hoped. Their subject's background, however, provoked mixed emotions. Ian Smith had delivered the news that Elliot was currently on a sponsored work placement run by none other than local businessman, and Ailsa Scott's former boyfriend, Graham McLean. She remembered McLean from the stakeholder meetings on her very first day – a short, mousey-haired man in an expensive suit, whose social gravity seemed inversely proportional to his physical size. Everyone in the room had deferred to him. If he interrupted, the other person stopped talking. Would he be outraged that she'd arrested one of his pet projects for murder? Or had he employed Midge Elliot in the first place because, having himself killed Ailsa and got away with it, he recognised a kindred spirit? Her interest ignited by both the cold case and the current investigation, she needed a way in and told Ian to run a background check on all Graham McLean's current personal and business interests.

The uniform sergeant approached, pulling his black balaclava below his chin to speak. He was only distinguishable from the rest of the team by his striped epaulettes.

'We're ready, ma'am.'

Nothing in Midge Elliot's background suggested he'd access to weapons but, given the cold-blooded nature of the offence, they'd agreed that deploying two specialist officers with Tasers was sensible. That, and Elliot's history of drug use, mandated that they also had paramedics standing by, which accounted for the ambulance sitting on the other side of the carpark. They were going in without forensic backup. Shona was keeping one eye on the budget. Mitch lived alone and if they found anything they could seal the flat and bring forensics down later for their regular fee rather than double time for an early in the morning call out.

'Okay.' Shona tightened the Velcro straps on her stab vest and quick-scanned the six uniform officers, McCulloch and Kyle. Satisfied, she said, 'Let's go.'

As they moved towards the building, one or two curtains twitched, but there was no sign the neighbours might pitch in to obstruct the arrest – no sign they were being filmed or angry faces with phones clamped to their ears summoning reinforcements.

Despite the brightness outside, the lobby was gloomy, lit by a single remaining bulb flickering behind an ineffectual safety grill. Above, their route dimmed by increments, the fourth floor almost in darkness. At a signal from the sergeant, each officer switched on both their torch and their body worn cameras. Silently, they began to climb.

When they reached the top landing, they found the stairhead window had been boarded up, but Shona's eyes had begun to adjust. She wrinkled her nose at the overflowing binbags outside Elliot's door. The rank smell of rotting food filled the cramped space and made it even more claustrophobic. She strained for any sound that might indicate what was going on inside Elliott's flat, but all she could hear was her own breathing and the blood pumping in her ears. Kyle was just ahead, his attention fixed on Elliot's door. McCulloch had been with him when they'd begun to climb, but was now several steps behind Shona, though he didn't seem out of breath. She'd met plenty of officers like him, bringing up the rear when there was work to be done, but always the first in line for medals.

She leaned forward and tapped Kyle on the shoulder. 'Once Elliot is detained, you make the arrest,' she whispered.

Instead of looking pleased, his eyes widened and he appeared horrified. His gaze went straight to McCulloch, but before Kyle could argue the order came.

Go. Go. Go.

First strike with the door ram, and they were through.

Police! Show yourself!

The interior of the flat was as gloomy as the landing. Shona's view was blocked by the officers piling in after their sergeant, but she heard the shouts as the first two rooms were declared *clear*.

Suddenly, there was a commotion.

Show me your hands! Show me your hands! Get on the floor now! Move.

A few more seconds of scuffle then Shona's heart soared as confirmation came.

Subject detained.

'Yes!' Shona thumped Kyle on the back. 'Go on.' When he hesitated, she added, 'It's fine. Go now.'

With a last glance at McCulloch, Kyle went into the flat, pushing past the officers checking cupboards in the hallway.

Shona turned to see McCulloch close behind her, his face like thunder.

'Was that really necessary?' he said.

'I decide who makes the arrest.' She wanted to say that Kyle had been in McCulloch's shadow too long. Instead, she added, 'He could do with his confidence boosted.'

She raised her eyebrows, daring him to challenge her decision. McCulloch just shook his head, his scorn for her actions clear. Even though she knew McCulloch didn't rate her and regarded the CID operation as his personal fiefdom, Shona was shocked at the level of his petty jealousy. But, before either of them could say more, Shona felt a tap on her shoulder.

'All clear now, ma'am.' The constable stood back, inviting her and McCulloch to enter the flat.

McCulloch opened his mouth to say something then appeared to think better of it, putting out a hand indicating Shona should go first. She did, giving a nod of thanks to the constable, and pointedly ignoring her sergeant. No doubt McCulloch had been about to inform her that it was a breach of convention for a detective constable to make the arrest when a DS and DI were present. Or perhaps he'd give her a list of the operation's shortcomings so far – incorrectly focused on a low-level junkie, rather than an OCG. Either way, Shona didn't want to hear it.

Inside, the flat presented a whole new landscape of odours – sour sweat, unwashed clothes, and the rancid afterglow of fried food. The bedroom and bathroom on either side of the hall were uniformly dim. The green-and-blue curtains were closed and there was enough rubbish, mugs, crockery and drinks cans piled on the sills to indicate this was probably their permanent state. It was like being underwater. Black-clad shapes of the uniform team moved around the corners of her vision like creatures of the deep. In the recent sweltering weather, this top flat must be broiled by the sun all day. It might explain why, after the flurry of the arrest, a solid silence seemed to have settled once more amid the thickened air.

'You can start searching the bedroom, DS McCulloch,' she said over her shoulder.

Behind her, she heard a snap as McCulloch pulled on a pair of nitrile gloves and moved into the room to look for anything that would link Midge Elliot to Muir Maxwell's murder. As she continued to the living room, she fished her own pair from her pocket and did the same, relieved that protocol prevented her from ever touching any surface in here with her bare hands.

In the cramped living room, strewn with its own patina of poverty, the suspect was lying face down on the floor, his cuffed hands behind his back. He wore a T-shirt that'd once been white, and grey sweatpants cut off above the knee. An empty duvet cover was crumpled across the brown corduroy sofa and it looked as if he'd been asleep on it when the uniform crew had put his door in. Kyle stood over the prone figure, breathing hard, but otherwise calm.

In the corner was a massive TV screen and below it a games consol. As Shona crossed to it, the carpet, like every other surface in the room, felt sticky with grime.

'Kyle?' Shona beckoned him over. 'Did Midge Elliot say anything when you cautioned him?'

'Nothing, boss. Just asked what time it was.'

'Okay. Suppose we can't all be morning folk. See this TV and game thing? Does this look new to you?' In her experience, every man under forty knew more about these than they did about washing machines. Her hunch proved right.

'Yeah. Latest PlayStation. Top spec. Not long out.'

Shona crouched down and ran her gloved index finger first along the top of the games consul, then stood and repeated the exercise for the TV. She turned it to show Kyle. Her fingertip was completely clean.

'In this enclosed environment,' she began, 'I reckon it would take less than a week for these to become as mucky as every other surface.'

'Want me to bag them?'

She nodded. 'Check if they're stolen. How much d'you reckon they'd cost new?'

Kyle pressed his lips together, considering. 'Couple of grand.'

'And how much was the quad bike that was nicked worth?'

'Second hand? About four to eight thousand.'

'Well, somebody got a bargain then, unless we find a wad of extra cash in the mattress.'

Kyle surveyed the flotsam of scattered beer cans, empty vodka bottles, and telltale white smears on the glass coffee table. 'Looks like he's been celebrating something. No sign of his phone, though.'

Midge Elliot had been lying on the floor quietly, but now he'd begun to stir.

'Hey. Hey. Hey. Hey,' he shouted, but whose attention he was trying to attract wasn't clear.

'Get him out of here,' Shona said. As the adrenaline from the operation ebbed, she'd begun to feel nauseous. It wasn't just the filthy, stifling flat. The knowledge that Muir Maxwell's life had been traded for a couple of gadgets, and a booze- and cocaine-fuelled gaming binge, sat heavy on her stomach. Fresh air, a few sips of water and, hopefully, a murder conviction, and she'd get over it. She couldn't say the same for the Maxwell family.

Kyle tapped the prone Midge Elliot's arm. 'C'mon. Wakey, wakey. Time to go.'

A uniform officer hooked the other arm and together they hauled him to his feet. Midge swayed unsteadily for a moment then looked calmly around him.

'He's fine,' Kyle assured the officer, who promptly let go so that they could turn their suspect around in the cramped living room. 'Let's get him downstairs.'

It happened so fast that, for a fraction of a second, it seemed like time had skipped a beat. Midge threw off both Kyle and the constable. Still cuffed, he stepped nimbly between the strewn bottles and cans, moving away from the door. Ahead of him, caught by the movement in the air, a curtain flapped.

And then Shona saw it.

'Window,' she yelled. They were four floors up. 'Stop him.'

Kyle was quickest. He threw himself at Midge, catching hold of his shorts, but couldn't keep his feet. He crashed down on the strewn bottles, which gave way in a series of pops and cracks like distant gunfire. Midge staggered, but pulled free, one pale and hairy buttock exposed.

As Shona and the others in the room lunged towards their prisoner, one of the specialist officers drew his weapon.

'Taser. Taser.'

In nine out of ten cases, just the threat of fifty thousand volts was enough, but Midge Elliot wasn't stopping. The red dot of the laser sight glowed in the centre of his back. He put one bare foot up on a chair, his body tipping forward to the partially open window.

There was no time to de-escalate this situation. There was only one way Shona would take Muir Maxwell's killer out of here alive.

'Do it!'

The barbed probes struck him just below the hem of his T-shirt, square on his backside. He arched upwards and let out a yell of pain, before hitting the ground like a felled tree, scattering the contents of the windowsill onto the carpet.

'Grab him.' Shona shot forward, landing with one elbow on his shoulder and catching his right wrist with her free hand. The five-second burst had left his muscles rigid. It was like hitting concrete. He wasn't going anywhere now.

'Get the paramedics up here.' She glanced down to where the barbed probes stuck out of his rear end like a pair of fishhooks. 'No way I'm taking those out.'

-

When Elliot was passed fit by the ambulance crew and brought outside, flanked by Kyle and McCulloch, Shona saw clearly for the first time that he was surprisingly substantial for someone with his lifestyle choices. The handcuffed figure being put in a van was a strapping lad of twenty-five, six-foot tall, and with heavy muscles around his shoulders. The nickname 'Midge' – something small – was obviously ironic. The drink and drugs hadn't made much of a dent in Michael Elliot, yet. His size and the way he moved was a close match for the figure in the CCTV. Shona smiled to herself as she felt the familiar excitement of rising hope. At last, all their hard work – the phone calls, cross-checking interviews, trawling for hours through CCTV – was about to pay off. They had their guy.

Chapter 17

Shona and Kyle followed the van containing Midge Elliot, leaving McCulloch in charge of the flat search. So far they'd been unable to locate his phone, or the stolen GPS units, and both were priorities.

Kyle was more subdued than she expected, but live operations took cops in different ways. Some rode the high for hours afterwards, others just wanted to forget about it and get on with the next part of their day.

'You did well,' she said, eventually, stealing a glance at him as she made the turning onto the A75 which would take them back to Newton Stewart Police Office, half an hour away.

'Did I?' His wrinkled brow and flushed cheeks spoke not of triumph, but of self-reproach and shame.

As his senior officer, she could've given him the spiel about how policing was a *dynamic environment* within which he was bound to encounter *challenges*.

Instead, she said, 'Midge Elliot is a pure bampot. Four floors up? You saved his life.'

'Shouldn't have let go of him in the first place. And I wasn't the one that tazed him.'

'But you slowed him down. Gave them something to aim at.' She grinned and nudged him with her elbow. Being tazed on his bare arse was likely what Midge Elliot would be remembered for at the station, long after they locked him up for murder. 'Couldn't have happened to a nicer guy, by the way,' Shona added in a more serious tone.

Kyle just gave her a perfunctory smile.

'There'll be no comeback, if that's what you're worried about.' Each time a Taser was discharged, a report went to the Police Investigations and Review Commissioner for independent scrutiny. 'I was right next to you. You did everything exactly as you should've. You have my full confidence.'

At that, his shoulders relaxed a little. 'Thanks, boss.'

'Now, soon as we book Elliot in, the custody clock starts ticking. So, for the rest of the journey, I'd like to hear your interview strategy.'

Kyle swallowed. 'You want me to sit in?'

'I want you to lead.' Even though the road was mostly made up of long, straight sections, the custody van had tucked in behind a lorry and showed no signs of overtaking. Shona dropped back. It'd be a while before they hit the dual carriageway. 'Take your time. Remember, we're discussing the options. There are no wrong answers at this stage.'

'Well,' Kyle began. 'I'd start by aiming to build a rapport.'

Shona couldn't help herself. 'Is that what you were trying to do at the flat?' she said, before descending into a fit of giggles.

Kyle looked mortified.

'Sorry, sorry,' she said, composing herself. 'Honestly, you'll laugh about it yourself one day.'

'Aye, maybe,' Kyle responded, sounding unconvinced.

'Okay, I'm listening. Key points. Let's go.'

Once Midge Elliot was in the custody suite, Shona and Kyle went along to the CID office until the duty solicitor arrived, and a doctor passed their suspect fit for interview. When Kyle had led Midge from the van, Shona couldn't detect any ill effects from his arrest, but it was a favourite delaying tactic of suspects, despite the fact he'd been checked over by paramedics at the scene.

The corridor was sweltering. All the windows in the single-storey building were covered with security grills that prevented them opening more than a few centimetres, not nearly enough to banish the persistent heat that had no chance of dissipating in the short July nights. But Shona's spirits were lifted when she saw a familiar face was waiting.

'Jess, great to see you,' Shona said with genuine enthusiasm. She stepped aside to introduce Kyle. 'But you two know each other, don't you?'

'Aye, of course.' Jess extended her hand. 'How are you, Kyle?'

He looked momentarily disconcerted as many did when encountering DC Jess Johnstone. She was tall with pale skin and long dark hair. However, it was her eyes most people were struck by. True, they were an unusual colour – a deep blue, almost violet – but it was the intensity and nature of her gaze that was so unsettling. Shona herself had seen suspects shift in their seats and falter in their denials beneath Jess's persistent scrutiny. By contrast, she'd proved a compassionate and astute family liaison officer, with some victims' relatives even reporting to Shona that they felt their interests were now being protected by their very own Scots-Irish warrior princess. Shona fervently hoped Jess could work her magic on the Maxwell family and help make the remaining portion of the investigation into Muir's murder as painless as possible.

'Kyle, can you show Jess where everything is and bring her up to speed on the case while I have a chat with Ian?'

'Sure,' he said with a shy smile. 'Want to grab a coffee? Can I get you one, boss?'

She'd have preferred something iced, but after the early start, with a long day ahead, an office coffee was the only option for a pick-me-up.

'That'd be great. Black, no sugar.'

She caught Ian Smith's eye as he sat at his desk on the far side of the room and beckoned him to follow her into her office.

'Midge Elliot,' Ian began.

Shona pointed to the chair opposite and took a swig from her water bottle.

'He has access to a white van through his job.'

She paused, mid drink. Not only did this strengthen their case considerably, but it also potentially brought his boss into the equation. 'And?'

'Elliot's manager is currently trying to locate the vehicle. It doesn't seem to be in their yard. I've asked the Sherrif for a warrant, but if it's not there…'

Shona pictured the garages by the flat. Likely built in the 1970s. Not big enough to conceal the white Ford Transit Connect they'd seen on the CCTV footage.

'We need to find that vehicle as a matter of urgency,' she said. Three days had passed since Muir's murder. Enough time to make repairs. 'What about Elliot's associates? Family?'

'No father or siblings. Mum passed away.' Ian tapped his pen on his notebook, considering. 'He's got a couple of kids with his ex-girlfriend, Jodie Reid. She's in Stranraer. They're not on good terms, but it could be at her place.'

Shona replaced the cap on her water bottle. 'Ask DC McCulloch to go over there. Bring her in if necessary. And if his workplace can't produce the vehicle he has access to, I want all the white vans on their books checked for damage or recent repairs. That goes for any other companies across the group. In fact, I want details of all their vehicles, and confirmation they're accounted for.' She paused. 'I know Elliot drives and delivers for them, but what does the company actually do?'

'Elliot is on placement at a subsidiary maintenance company for the holiday parks. It's part of a rehab programme for addicts and offenders. Makes for good photo ops for their media image. But Graham McLean also owns a haulage business – GEM Haulage – transporting the caravans. Regular trips across to Northern Ireland and back and forward to the fabricators in Hull.' He gave her a conspiratorial smile.

To Shona his inference was clear. 'And what better way to transport stolen farm kit?'

Ian nodded. 'He has legitimate reason to be moving loads across most of Ireland, Scotland and northern England.'

'And beyond. Hull has a passenger and cargo ferry port sailing to Belgium and the Netherlands,' Shona added. 'And we know from Operation Raven that Eastern Europe is currently the most popular destination for stolen agricultural equipment.'

Shona steepled her fingers. The cold case file was in her bag on the floor by the desk. Here was a way to question Graham McLean. He needn't be the second man in the van, but he may have commissioned the theft, then covered up what Midge and his pal had done. That would open him to the serious charge of attempting to defeat the ends of justice, maximum penalty life imprisonment. With McLean locked up, witnesses in Ailsa's murder case might change their testimony or new informants come forward.

But was it possible that a multi-force investigation like Operation Raven had missed a key player right on their doorstep? And the last thing she wanted to do was throw doubt on the Manchester OCG convictions. It was risky. Any pressure she put on McLean might backfire. He'd claim that as a socially responsible, community-minded businessman, Shona was persecuting him over the actions of an addict he was trying to help turn over a new leaf. As her Superintendent Mark Davies might put it, that would result in *poor optics* for the force locally, and perhaps nationally if the media latched onto it.

Shona realised she was staring at the cold case file in her bag, and that Ian had followed her gaze. He gave her a questioning look, but she ignored it.

'I'm conscious that the custody clock is ticking,' she said, 'but let's give them a couple of hours to find that vehicle.'

Slasher Sue had been clear. There'd be a direct correlation between Muir Maxwell's injuries recorded at the postmortem, and the damage to the front of the van where it had struck him.

'And ask his manager if anyone there has a more recent number for his phone since the one they gave us is dead.'

Ian got up just as Kyle tapped her door and came in holding out a coffee for her. At Dumfries CID she had her own mug – a Charles Rennie Mackintosh design. She'd come to regard it as something of a talisman when it came to making strategic decisions. She knew it was purely the caffeine shot that mattered, not the choice of crockery, but the plain brown vessel she was now presented with was a reminder of how far she was from home. She could hear Murdo's voice – *getting superstitious in your old age, boss* – and perhaps Tommy the lifeboat helm would say the same. But cops and sailors had every right to their myths and customs. Both knew that no matter how hard you trained, how prepared you were for events, there was always the chance some ungovernable force – fate or the sea – would upset your best laid plans. Living with that knowledge everyday could make you either paranoid or blasé. She wouldn't class herself as the former exactly, but she hoped she wasn't the latter. Proceed with caution; *caw canny* as Murdo would put it. Though she'd reassured Kyle, Midge Elliot's near-fatal bid for freedom was evidence of how quickly things could go wrong, and she couldn't afford any mistakes.

'Let's see what Midge Elliot has to say for himself,' she said to Ian, who had paused in the doorway. 'We'll adjust our lines of enquiry with his workplace accordingly.' Nor was she passing up an opportunity to quiz Graham McLean, but she needed a legitimate reason.

'Sure, boss,' Ian nodded to Kyle as he left the room.

'Jess is reading through the case notes,' Kyle began. 'I've just had a message from DS McCulloch.'

'Any sign of Elliot's phone? The GPS units yet?'

He shook his head then turned the screen towards her. On it was a photograph of a bunch of keys.

'None of them match anything they've found in the flat yet.'

Shona glanced at it. 'Could be for an old property.' She studied the picture. 'The small one might fit a locker at work. Get Ian to ask his manager about it.'

Midge had been in work since the weekend and had been due there this morning. The GPS units would easily fit in a small space. The quad bike was another story, if he hadn't already sold it to fund his gaming requirements.

'Tell McCulloch not to worry about the key at the moment. Pull the carpets up and check in the loft. Ask the neighbours if there's anyone nearby he's friendly with. Bag any items of dark clothing and boots. What we really need is something that'll give us a timeline for his movements, like a smartwatch.' She paused as a question occurred to her, but the answer was woefully beyond her knowledge. 'Will the PlayStation tell us when he's been using it?'

'If he's signed in it'll track which games he's been playing, when and for how long. But you can partially disable it in settings and the game clock has a reputation for unreliability.'

'So, it's no use to us. That's what you're saying.'

Kyle reddened. 'Forensics might be able to help us get something.'

'Let's hope so,' Shona replied. 'Cos right now I'll take any help we can get to nail this guy.'

Chapter 18

Midge Elliot, now dressed in the custody uniform of grey sweatpants and top, sat placidly in the interview room. Next to him, the duty solicitor – a young woman in a neat black trouser suit, her fair hair tied back in a severe pony-tail – was making notes on her laptop. She introduced herself as Katie Pickles. An odd choice for a solicitor, Shona thought. Surely 'Katherine' sounded more serious. Did her name hold her back? The look she gave Shona suggested she was no pushover, so perhaps it was a useful bluff.

Shona scrutinised their prisoner. Midge's expression was blank and he showed no sign that he remembered either officer from his arrest. Or that he was suffering any ill effects from his recent acquaintance with fifty thousand volts.

When they'd all identified themselves for the recording, Kyle said, 'Mr Elliot, can I call you Michael?'

'Na. Only ma mother called me that when am gan tae be in bother.' He grinned, affably. 'Just call me Midge.'

Shona thought in the light of Midge Elliot's current situation he should reconsider his answer since he was, indeed, in a whole lot of trouble.

'Okay, Midge,' Kyle continued, smiling back. 'Do you understand what you've been arrested for?'

'Nae really. I've no' kilt anyone.'

Kyle placed the photograph of Muir that'd gone out with the public appeals on the table between them.

'Recognise this man?'

'Dinnae ken him.'

You'd need to have been living under a rock for the last three days not to have seen it. It had been on the national news and every shop and business in the local community had put the posters in their windows appealing for information.

'This is Muir Maxwell,' Kyle continued. 'You've been detained because we're investigating his murder at Eastcraig Farm. What can you tell me about that?'

Midge glanced at the picture, then looked straight ahead. 'Nothin.'

'Have you ever been to Eastcraig Farm?'

'A farm? Whit for? I'm nae a farmer.' He shook his head vigorously and grinned again.

Kyle shuffled through his papers. Finally, he pulled out a map.

'Let me show you where Eastcraig is. Maybe you don't know the name of the place. It's important that you think carefully. We're not interested in telling the tax folk if you've mibbaes done a bit of cash-in-hand labour, to help them out,' Kyle reassured him.

Midge peered at the screen, then shrugged. 'Dinnae ken it. Never been there.'

Shona couldn't decide if Midge, as an experienced interviewee, was playing the eejit – an alternative to the *no comment* route that falsely signalled compliance and therefore innocence – or was genuinely baffled by this morning's turn of events. Either way, being arrested on a murder charge should've prompted a bigger reaction.

'Why did you attempt to flee when we detained you?' Kyle said. 'Four floors up and you nearly bolted out the window. That's the actions of a desperate man. One who knows he's going down for murder. Don't you agree?'

It was a classic example of chaotic decision-making where cause and effect had become dissociated. Having witnessed the escape attempt, Shona could easily believe he'd have had no compunction about running over Muir Maxwell if the farmer stood between himself and freedom, then, having crossed that Rubicon, reversed just to make sure the job was done.

'I'm no' a killer. Wasnae awake this mornin'. Forgot where I wis.'

'Would you say you're a forgetful person?' Kyle pressed.

Midge's eyes narrowed as he spotted the trap laid for him.

'No' really. I wis asleep. I'd had a bit tae drink. Next thing youse is in ma hoose. Wis confused.'

'So, can you remember where you were last Saturday between ten p.m. and midnight?' Kyle said.

'At hame.'

'Anyone with you?'

'Na. Was gaming.'

'I saw your PlayStation. Had it long?'

'Nae long.'

'Expensive things, aren't they? Where'd you get it?'

'It's just borrowed, fae a pal.'

'Which pal?'

'Dinnae like tae say. His Mrs doesnae ken he has it.'

'Are you sure you didn't go out?' Shona said. 'Meet this pal of yours? Perhaps you'd like to check your phone for messages?'

'I lost it.'

'Where was that?'

'Cannae mind.'

Kyle gave him a sceptical look. 'There's that poor memory of yours again. You should see someone about that.'

A High Court judge, if Shona had her way.

'I lost it Saturday. Somewhere in toon.'

'What time? Evening?'

'Earlier.'

'We need a description and the number of your phone. It's possible someone has handed it in and we can reunite you with it.'

'Dinnae ken the number. Ye never call yerself, do ye?' Midge leaned back and folded his arms, visibly relaxing as his confidence grew that he'd walk out of the police office and be home for his dinner.

Katie the solicitor, who'd sat watching the exchanges, consulted her watch then leaned forward and tapped the desk once with her pen.

'If you have any evidence linking my client to this tragic incident, I suggest you put it to Mr Elliot.'

'Of course,' Kyle said mildly.

He'd done a good job putting Midge Elliot off his guard. It had gone as they'd planned. Shona sat back and folded her arms, mirroring their suspect's posture to create a false sense of safety. Time to shake things up.

'Midge, we've established that you have no alibi for Saturday night, and you claim never to have been to Eastcraig Farm.' Kyle took several photographs from his file and laid them next to Muir Maxwell's picture. 'Do you know what this is?'

Midge leaned forward and made a show of studying the image. 'A clarty tractor. Dinnae need tae be a farmer to ken that.'

'True,' said Kyle. 'But what I'd like to know is why your fingerprints are all over it.'

'Whit?' Midge jumped back in his seat. His solicitor shot him a look that said there'd been nothing in their pre-interview chat that'd predicted this.

'Also on a quad bike, a second tractor and a spreader.' Kyle dealt out the pictures like a winning hand of cards. 'The bike was abandoned by the thieves as they made their escape. But a second bike and GPS units removed from farm machinery were taken. Where are they, Midge? And were they really worth a man's life?'

'Wasnae me. It wasnae.'

'The thieves deliberately struck and killed Mr Maxwell, reversing over him, before making their escape,' Kyle went on in his reasonable tone. 'They were driving a white Ford Transit Connect van. You have access to such a vehicle through your job at GEM Property Maintenance.'

'So? Plenty o' them vans aroon.' Midge made a stab at defiance, but his face had reddened and sweat broken out on his brow. True, it was hot in the interview room. Shona had deliberately left off her suit jacket to maintain a cool demeanour. Katie Pickles was pulling at the neck of her blouse, either because of the heat or a rising sense that the interview was going badly for her client.

'Your van is currently unaccounted for,' Kyle said. 'Where is it, Midge? Did you hide it because of the damage to the windscreen and bodywork when you struck and killed Muir Maxwell?'

'Naw, I didnae. It's… it's no always me that drives it.'

'Where is it, Midge?' Kyle said, leaning forward, closing the distance between them across the desk. 'Where's the quad bike and the GPS units?'

'It wasnae me.'

Kyle seemed momentarily on the back foot, shuffling his papers.

'I'll ask you again,' he said. 'Where were you on Saturday night between ten p.m. and midnight?'

When Midge sat silent, Shona felt it was the right time to step in.

'Do you think we're messing about here, Midge?' she said. 'This is a murder enquiry. What you don't seem to understand is when you take another person's life, it sets a bomb off in yours. Nothing is ever gonna be the same again. If you want to minimise that damage, you need to talk to us.' Then she cocked her head as if an idea had occurred to her. 'We also know there were two of you. You just said, *it's no always me that drives it*. Your fingerprints show you were there. So, who was driving? Who was with you at the farm?'

He had enough previous experience of Scotland's criminal justice system to spot she was the good cop, offering him an escape route, a path of lesser responsibility for Muir Maxwell's death. DS McCulloch hadn't named any associates, but perhaps, backed into a corner as he was, Midge might recognise it as being in his interests. His co-conspirator had to be someone whose prints weren't on their records – a new face. Or someone smart enough to keep their gloves on. Colin from forensics had been right with his guess that Midge obviously hadn't been.

'I wis never there. I've no' kilt anyone. You're fittin' me up.'

He was breathing fast. Eyes roaming the room for an exit.

Katie Pickles put out a hand to calm him. 'I need to speak with my client.'

Remembering how quickly Midge could move, how disordered his thinking could be, Shona knew de-escalation was crucial if they were to continue the interview.

'Okay. We'll take a break,' Shona said, and Kyle paused the recording.

Outside in the corridor, Kyle raised his eyebrows, leaned forward with his hands on his knees and blew out a long breath.

'You did great,' Shona grinned, taking out her phone. She thought about Murdo's comment – how gamers, and addicts, lost sight of real life. Well, Midge Elliot had just experienced a massive wake-up call. 'Don't worry. I reckon that Katie Pickles is less *woodland creature* than *barracuda*. Mitch Elliot is facing a life sentence. We're offering him a life raft in exchange for full disclosure. If she's any sense, she'll tell him to grab it with both hands. And while I remember, there's something I need from you.'

Ten minutes later, the door of the interview room was opened and the solicitor signalled they were ready to resume.

When they'd restarted the recording, it was soon clear that Shona's optimism had been misplaced.

'My client will not be answering any more questions,' Katie began. 'I've prepared a statement on his behalf which I will read.'

Mitch had pushed his chair back against the wall and sat, legs extended and crossed at the ankle, an impatient frown on his face, as if the current proceedings were nothing to do with him. The statement was short, denying he'd ever been to Eastcraig, or was implicated in any way in Muir Maxwell's death. He'd fully co-operated with the police, even though the manner of his arrest had been heavy handed, resulting in him being tasered while unarmed and handcuffed. He had no explanation as to why his fingerprints were at the scene of Mr Maxwell's death.

'Mr Elliot suggests,' Katie Pickles continued, 'that the police examine the robustness of their evidence chain as he believes he is the victim of a potential miscarriage of justice. Should there be further proceedings against him, he will instruct his solicitor to deal with them accordingly.'

Kyle cast a wary glance towards his DI, blind-sided by the threat. But Shona just nodded.

'Thank you for making your position clear, Midge. I just have one more question for you.'

'My client has stated that, as is his right, he won't be answering any more questions.'

'It is his right, but I still have a duty to put questions to your client that are pertinent to my case.' Shona took out her phone and pulled up a photograph Kyle had just sent her. It was the one McCulloch had taken at the flat and showed a bunch of keys with the smallest one – the type used for padlocks and which looked new – extended. She turned the screen towards Midge. 'Do you recognise these?'

His eyes were directed at the ceiling, feigning disinterest, but curiosity quickly pulled them back. He blanched, the colour draining from his face so fast that Shona thought he might faint.

'I need an answer for the recording, Midge.'

'Nae comment,' he spat.

'So, if that is all, DI Oliver, I hope you'll be releasing my client?' Katie Pickles said.

Shona made a show of checking her watch. There were eight hours left on the custody clock. 'I'll be releasing your client when I'm good and ready. Right now, he's going back to his cell.'

Shona strode down the corridor with Kyle trailing in her wake. Midge had no alibi, and his fingerprints were at the scene. Would that be enough for the fiscal? She doubted it. And if she wanted to extend his detention for another twelve hours, she needed something more. She paused at the CID room door, turning back to Kyle, who looked thoroughly miserable.

'What's the matter?'

'I made a mess of it, didn't I.'

'No, you didn't. Did you see Midge's face when I showed him the keys?'

Kyle nodded, his eyes suddenly hopeful. 'He didn't like us having them.'

'Precisely. We find that bike and we'll nail him. Looks like the key, is the key to all this. All we need is the lock that it fits.'

'Maybe a shed?'

'Or a garage. There's a block of six opposite the flat. I noticed them when we pulled up. On an estate like that, there were probably dozens within walking distance. We checked with the local authority if Elliot has rented a garage nearby, didn't we?'

'I think we did,' stuttered Kyle. Then seeing Shona's expression he said, 'Yes, definitely we did. Could be under a mate's name,' he offered.

'True.'

This was the type of building that might pass from hand to hand, sub-let for a few quid, no questions asked. She doubted they'd find the van, but the bike was a possibility. The GPS units that had been lifted from the tractors were just a couple of small tablets and magnetic receiver units that could be stuck on the roof. You could easily hide them among other bits and bobs of technology and only recognise what they were if you were looking specifically for them. Shona checked her watch, conscious they didn't have time to waste.

'Right, we need to search the garages on the estate first. And if we don't know which one, it'll have to be a Cinderella job.' Shona smiled at Kyle's blank expression. 'C'mon, you know what I'm saying. Visit them all and see which the slipper, or in this case the key, fits. Tell McCulloch to put all the constables he can spare on it. Rule out any with combination locks first and let's hope our very own fairy godmother is watching and gets us a result.'

Chapter 19

When Shona and Kyle came back into the CID room the others looked up expectantly from their desks. She shook her head.

'Not playing ball then,' Ian said, as Shona stopped by his desk.

'We need that vehicle. Any sign?' She could feel the start of a headache building.

'I'm just off the phone to Midge's manager. Claims they don't know where it is.'

'Not good enough,' Shona spat. 'If one of my vehicles was involved in a brutal murder of a local farmer, I'd be falling over myself to get it handed over to the police ASAP, d'you not think? Fucksake, Graham McLean should be on the phone himself assuring us of his employees full co-operation. Does he think cos Dalrymple's not here he can take his own sweet time. Ian, where's that bloody warrant?'

'It's just arrived, boss.'

Erin had sunk down behind her desk. Kyle was staring at her. Ian eyed her like she was about to explode in his face, which Shona had to admit was a fair assessment. Only Jess retained her composure, sitting on the edge of Kyle's desk with her arms folded.

'Want us to pay Graham McLean a wee visit, boss?' she said, evenly, but still managed to convey sufficient threat in her tone to make the others glance at her and look quickly away.

'Damn right,' Shona said. 'In fact, we'll all go. Round up every uniform who isn't on search duties with DS McCulloch. You two,' Shona pointed to Jess and Kyle, 'are coming with me.' With a plan of action came the reassurance that the case wasn't losing momentum.

'And I could come if you like,' Ian said. 'I know the background.'

'I appreciate the offer, but you're not a warranted officer.' She could see the former detective had the bit between his teeth, but a returners role was strictly in support. His disappointment was obvious, and Shona immediately regretted her sharp tone. 'But I do appreciate the work you've done on this, Ian.'

'Sure. No bother. We're all behind you on this.'

She gave him a nod of thanks.

'Okay, Kyle, Jess. I'll see you outside as soon as we're ready.'

–

Half an hour later, Shona sent Kyle to confirm the target with the uniform officers and she and Jess left the CID office and headed for the carpark. Uniform had been unusually swift at assigning officers and Shona took this as further proof the whole of Galloway's police operation was intent on catching Muir Maxwell's killer.

As they made their way along the corridor, she fell into step beside Jess.

'I'm sorry I've dragged you over here as FLO, just as we've detained a suspect. If we charge him tonight, there won't be much left for you to do.' They could bring someone in from Kilmarnock to keep the family updated through the trial. 'But there's one thing I'd like to know that might prove sensitive. It came up at the postmortem and it's still bugging me.'

'How did Muir Maxwell get his bruised knuckles?' Jess replied. 'Aye, I saw that. Probably farmwork, but I agree we need to be sure. Your fella Ian Smith said there were no domestic violence call-outs on record, but that's not surprising. Most farms don't have close neighbours and if a member of the family, especially the husband or father, gets locked up, that might be the end of your home and your livelihood.'

Shona opened the back door to the carpark, wincing at the blast of heat. 'I was hoping we could match the injuries to Midge. Sue said they'd happened a day or two before Maxwell's death, but it'd really strengthen our case if we could show the two men had an acrimonious history.'

'No luck?'

They stopped in the small patch of shade thrown by the building and Shona shook her head.

'I checked with the police doctor when he passed our suspect fit for interview. No bruising on Midge's face where he might have taken a punch. No defence injuries on his hands. He just has a few fresh scrapes and bumps from his attempted high dive from the window.'

'I heard about that,' Jess smirked.

'The worst of it is Kyle thinks he bungled the arrest.' Shona sighed. 'I told him that he probably saved Midge Elliot's life, but it didn't seem to help. McCulloch gave me grief for letting Kyle make the arrest in the first place, but you know I've no time for petty jealousy in my team.'

'Kyle's a good cop,' Jess said. 'I guess he must still carry some guilt.'

'What d'you mean? Guilt? Over what?'

'You know, the wee bit of bother he had?' When Shona still looked mystified, Jess continued. 'When I called in at Stranraer they couldn't talk about anything else. Back of last year, during his final week in uniform, he did a traffic stop. The fella was way over the limit, getting physical. Kyle managed to handcuff the suspect, but he got away. Ran out into the road and was hit by a lorry.'

'Killed?' Shona couldn't help sounding shocked.

'Aye, he was. Kyle and his partner were cleared of any blame. He was on leave for a bit, so he's only been in CID a couple of months.'

'Oh shit.'

'Sorry, boss. Thought you knew. Guessed you were trying to boost his confidence. That was why you had him sitting in on the Midge Elliot interview.'

'Sitting in? I had him lead it.'

'Oh.' Jess looked taken aback. 'How'd he do?'

'He did fine, mostly.'

'There you go, boss. No harm done.'

Shona remembered Kyle's nervous behaviour before they'd gone into the flats, how subdued he was afterwards. No wonder. Another suspect bolting on him and nearly coming to grief. Why had she bullied him into leading such an important interview? He was clearly out of his depth at times. Had her dislike of McCulloch, who knew Midge Elliot, but discounted him as the killer, led her to make a poor strategic decision? A wave of heat rolled over her that was nothing to do with the weather. The idea of a lost opportunity to solve this case – that with McCulloch as lead interviewer Midge might've given them more – stung like a slap.

Stop it, she told herself. You were there to back Kyle up. Everything went as they'd planned. It was Katie Pickles who'd thrown a spanner in the works. A different solicitor might've advised their client to take the deal that was being offered and name the other culprit. Perhaps, even now, as Midge Elliot sat in his sweltering cell, he was having second thoughts. She knew she was fashioning herself a lifebelt that she could cling to through the rest of the afternoon. What happened when the time on the custody clock ran out was another matter.

'So, Mitch Elliot's work,' Jess began when they'd both got in the Audi and Shona had pushed the air-con to max. 'What's the deal here?'

As Shona headed for GEM Maintenance's offices, she considered whether she should tell Jess about the cold case. But their primary objective was tracing Midge's vehicle; that took precedence over everything. So instead, she relayed what Ian Smith had found and the possible complication for Operation Raven.

'Maybe they weren't involved before. Just saw the gap and stepped into it,' Jess said. 'Have you met the boss fella? What's he like?'

'Wealthy. Domineering. Finger in every pie.'

'So, he's a risk-taker because, more often than not, he gets away with it.'

Shona thought of the way Graham McLean had escaped a teenage murder charge. There'd been a very public argument at a dance the night before. His alibi of being with his creepy best pal, Bruce Campbell, backed up by Campbell's girlfriend, was uncorroborated by any independent witness.

'Yep,' Shona said. 'That just about sums him up.'

Chapter 20

At just after eleven a.m., Shona pulled into the carpark off the industrial estate on the edge of town. Behind her came three patrol cars, then Kyle bringing up the rear. Shona had barely killed the ignition when the door of the portacabin opposite opened and Graham McLean himself strode out. There was something faintly comical about this short man taking long strides, like he was a toy that someone had wound up and set loose, but the speed of his response hinted that perhaps his business contacts stretched to the fiscal's office, and he knew they were coming.

As McLean got closer, he switched on a smile like a high-beam searchlight and fixed it on Shona.

'DI Oliver, how lovely to see you,' he said, extending his hand like she'd turned up with a bottle of wine and some flowers for Sunday lunch, not a pack of constables and a warrant.

'Mr McLean.' She gave him a respectful tilt of the head. 'You're very hands-on. Didn't expect to find you here at this time of day.' Flattering him – like he was the Duke of Galloway who'd been discovered mowing his own lawn – was the effect she was after, and it seemed to be working. McLean looked suitably gratified by this mix of deference and admiration of his work ethic.

'No matter how high you climb up the business ladder, it's important to stay in touch with the grass roots,' he said.

Shona thought it was a bit of a mixed metaphor, but he seemed pleased with it, and that was the main thing.

In the portacabin, Shona was aware of shapes moving behind the grubby windows. She couldn't afford to allow them the time to conceal anything they might wish to.

'Anyway, back to today's business,' Shona said, mildly. 'We have a warrant to search these premises.' McLean opened his mouth to protest, but Shona cut him off. 'Let's go.'

Jess and Kyle were already moving past Shona, along with five constables and a supervising sergeant, fanning out to the adjacent buildings. McLean made to follow Kyle to the office, but Shona caught his arm.

'If you could stay here, sir. There's a couple of questions I'd like to ask you.'

McLean took a step towards her. 'What d'you want, DI Oliver?'

It would be easy to underestimate, to ridicule, this jumped-up wee numpty, but there was real menace in the man that stood just inside her personal space. Shona resisted the urge to step back. De-escalation wasn't appropriate here. She didn't need to forge any kind of working relationship with this wee shite. C'mon pal, push your luck.

'What I want, is what we've been requesting since first thing this morning. Where is the white Ford Transit Connect that Midge Elliot has been driving to jobs, for you?'

'Not for me, DI Oliver. For my company. I don't know him personally.'

'Yet here you are. At the grassroots. Mr Elliot is part of your community rehab scheme. You never check in person that you were getting value for money?' His connection to Midge wasn't close enough to haul him in for an interview, not without more evidence that he was wrapped up in agricultural theft. But she could rattle his cage. 'Let me show you a picture. Jog your memory.'

She pulled up Midge's photograph on her phone and turned the screen towards him.

He made a show of studying it, then shook his head. 'Don't know him.'

'What about this?'

A row of men in GEM branded sweatshirts. In the middle, Graham McLean shaking hands with Midge.

McLean's face darkened. 'I can't be expected to remember every…'

'Boss?' Jess was waving from the steps of the portacabin, a sheet of paper in her hand. Kyle was holding up a set of keys.

'Excuse me. If you could wait here a moment. We're talking murder, Mr McLean. Maybe have a wee think if there's anything you want to tell me.'

Shona joined Jess and Kyle. 'What've we got?' Jess handed her the sheet. 'This is Midge's van? What took them so long?'

Jess shrugged. 'Maybe this wee visit concentrated their thoughts.'

'But they should've known which vehicle was signed out to Midge, even without index number details. Where is this van?' Shona said.

'This way, boss,' Kyle replied, pointing to a nearby warehouse.

Inside, the van stood gleaming from a recent wash. On the side, the blue letters 'GEM Maintenance' and a logo against the white bodywork. Shona felt a jolt of uncertainty. There'd been no lettering in the video. But when she examined it closely she saw why. Working her thumbnail under one corner, the sign peeled away.

'Magnetic,' she said to the others who'd gathered round. 'Why?'

'Guy in the office said it was efficiency,' Kyle said. 'They switch vehicles between parts of the company.'

'How convenient.' Shona moved around to the front. There was no sign of any damage, in fact much of the bodywork and windscreen looked suspiciously new. Either they'd managed a quick fix of what would've been extensive damage, or this wasn't Midge Elliot's van. They only had the company's word for it after all.

'You did the original DVLA checks, Kyle. How many white Transit Connects?'

'Forty-five, across all the subsidiaries,' he replied.

'Shit.' Shona mentally calculated how far the forensic budget would stretch. Not far enough.

When Shona came out into the carpark once more, McLean was pretty much where she'd left him.

'Perhaps you'd like to wait in your vehicle, sir.'

'How long is this going to take?' McLean said, making a show of checking his chunky Rolex.

Shona stared at him, expressionless. He needed to know that, for once, he wasn't running the show.

'We'll let you know when we're done.'

-

An hour later, during which Shona had been in the Audi sifting through what evidence they had against Midge, and what else they might need to convince the fiscal he could be charged, the uniform sergeant approached. 'Ma'am?'

'Well?' Shona said.

He shook his head.

'Nothing? No quad bike, or agricultural kit? No GPS units?'

Graham McLean was watching her intently from the driver's seat of his BMW, a supercilious smile on his ratty wee face as Shona saw him read the body language of the conversation. He'd parked in the shade, while she'd been forced to endure the heat. But if he thought she'd be driven out of his yard before she was ready, he'd another thing coming.

'Sorry, ma'am,' the sergeant continued, 'but you mentioned earlier checking vans for damage? Two of my constables have forensic RTA experience.'

Here was the flickering possibility of salvaging the whole debacle. 'Forty-five vans. How long?'

'Depending on where they are, a couple of days.'

'Thank you, Sergeant.' It wasn't ideal, but it'd have to do. She could extend Midge's detention and pray they got a result sooner rather than later. She got out as Kyle and Jess came towards her across the yard, the search team in tow. From the corner of her eye, she saw McLean follow suit. To gloat, no doubt.

'Kyle, get the details of all the vehicles and their locations pinged across,' Shona said. 'Everyone else can get back to the office.'

When McLean drew level, she said, 'Thank you for your co-operation but we'll be here a little longer. I want to see all of your vans.' When he looked outraged, she continued, 'I know you're used to dealing with DI Dalrymple. He'd be just as thorough with this horrific murder case that has caught the public's sympathy, as I'm being. Especially since you're an old friend of the family. Well, Isobel's sister Ailsa, to be precise.'

His gaze was on Kyle on the steps of the portacabin with a wad of papers and two constables, but the muscles were twitching in his jaw.

'Oh dear,' Shona murmured. 'Looks like trouble.' She locked eyes with McLean. 'And trouble just seems to follow you around. Doesn't it?'

For a fraction of a second there was nothing.

'For the record, Inspector, I loved Ailsa, and was devastated by her murder,' McLean replied softly, never taking his glassy eyes off Shona. 'If you've any allegations to make, I'll be answering them in the presence of my lawyer.'

Despite the heat, Shona suppressed a shiver. It would be easy to treat McLean as a joke, a pantomime villain, but for the question that had hung over his head for forty years – had he picked up a rock and beat his girlfriend to death with it, then gone about his life with the swagger of a man who knew he'd got away with murder? Was he helping Midge Elliot to take the same path. Looking at him now, Shona believed absolutely that it was possible.

When Shona reached the Audi, she turned and saw with satisfaction that her gamble had been worth it. McLean was staring at her, his face scarlet from more than the unrelenting sun. He knew what she wanted. He understood Shona was here for more than the van.

-

Halfway back to the office, she pulled into a filling station and grabbed the last ice-cold cola from the chiller, convincing herself her thickening headache was down to dehydration and caffeine-deficiency. The can felt good against her burning forehead and cheek. She had to get a grip on things. Work was engulfing her personal life and vice versa. She was snappy with Becca, short with Simon, telling him she didn't have the time or the headspace to think about moving to Glasgow. She'd neglected to visit Isobel, avoided the local lifeboat station, who'd extended plenty of invitations, because of her suspicions around Roddy. Any thought of her mother Angie sent her brain into an immediate code red.

Already she regretted her words to Graham McLean. What an idiot she'd been to let him rile her. Her comment about Ailsa had been a mistake. Not only had she pissed off probably the most connected man in Galloway, but she'd also forewarned him. *Be careful*, Dalrymple had said. *Keep a low profile*, had been her Super's orders. Jeezo, Shona. Why not just paint a big target on your back and be done with it. What she needed now was a miracle. *This land of the saints*, Isobel had called her part of Galloway. She had to talk to Isobel again, get more of a fix on Graham McLean and his relationship with Ailsa. St Michael the Archangel was patron saint of police officers, but she wasn't sure he had jurisdiction over the local lads and lassies – St Ninian, St Patrick and the rest. She should copy them all into her prayers to be on the safe side.

McCulloch's name flashed up on her screen. She took a deep breath. If anyone was likely to tip her over the edge it was this eejit.

'DS McCulloch, how's the search going?'

'You'd better see for yourself.'

Shona rolled her eyes. 'Drop me a pin.'

Twenty minutes later she pulled up beside a block of garages, the red paint peeling from their doors. One set gaped open. McCulloch stood before them, his expression blank behind sunglasses. He was jacketless and had his sleeves rolled up, arms folded like a bouncer at a car boot sale. Two squad cars blocked off the entrance and exit of the parking area, and police tape held back a small group of sun-striped women and toddlers, beyond which older kids half-heartedly orbited on bikes.

A constable raised the tape for her to duck under and Shona fought the urge to tell the women to get some sunscreen and a hat on their weans if they wanted to get any sleep tonight, or better still – just go home.

McCulloch held his stance until Shona reached the garage.

'Well?' she said. There was no sign of the stolen quad bike. She pushed back her hair and perched her sunglasses on the top of her head, squinting into the dim interior. Racks ran down both sides. On one, a lockable metal chest stood open. Next to it were Ziploc bags stuffed with bank notes, and a set of scales. With a start, she realised what she was seeing. She stared at McCulloch. A haul, and a big one at that. 'You've got to be kidding me. Drugs?'

'Looks like I owe Midge Elliot an apology,' McCulloch began. 'I said he was a plodder. Didnae ha' the brains for anything else. Seems he's proved me wrang.'

It was as close to an admission that he'd been wrong as Shona was going to get.

She replaced her sunglasses. 'Tsk, tsk, DS McCulloch. You promised me a quad bike. But I guess this will have to be enough to be going on with.' She could've punched the air – the substantial drugs bust and a reason to keep Midge Elliot in custody, until they worked out how the murder of Muir Maxwell fitted in with this. 'Called forensics?'

'Aye. On their way.'

The saints, it seemed, had come up trumps after all.

Chapter 21

That evening, once Midge had been charged and was on his way to Dumfries jail, Shona called Anna Maxwell and her mother-in-law, before they saw the news on TV. She apologised for not coming in person. She'd visit tomorrow afternoon and introduce their FLO, DS Jess Johnstone, who'd answer any questions, and see them through to the trial. Recognising the complexity of two cases Shona had changed her mind; she needed Jess on this and Jess for her part seemed happy to be here.

By the time Shona left the office in Newton Stewart, the high of the arrest was ebbing. They'd all been on the go for over sixteen hours, a rollercoaster of a day, and she'd be glad to get back to Coldharbour Cottage. But first, she owed Dalrymple and Isobel a visit.

'Here she is,' Dalrymple beamed when he opened the front door. Shona blushed, suddenly overwhelmed by his greeting. 'Well done, Shona.'

'It was down to your team,' she said, moving past him into the hall.

'No doubt,' he said, with a mischievous smile. 'But at least half the credit is yours. Midge Elliot? Who would've believed it. I bet George is scratching his head on how we missed that. He'll be pleased though.'

The arrest had indeed signalled something of a truce in Shona and McCulloch's relationship. He gave her grudging credit for pursuing Midge in the first place, and she acknowledged his dogged determination to find the correct lock for the mysterious key.

'I don't think you did miss anything.' Shona was anxious that he didn't see her success as his failure. 'Looks like we've nipped a new county line operation in the bud.'

He nodded. 'Even more reason to celebrate.' He tapped Shona lightly on the arm. 'Well done. I mean it.' The evening light from the doorway caught the lines on Dalrymple's face and he looked exhausted.

She saw that any good news was a lifeline for him at this troubled time and, tired as she was, her spirits soared at the idea that she'd provided one.

'Isobel has been asking for you,' he said in a low voice.

They were still standing in the hall. Reflexively, Shona glanced up the stairs to the landing, all the while knowing that the days when Isobel could move from her bed unaided were long gone.

'I've read through all of Ailsa's file now,' she whispered. 'I saw Graham McLean today. As Midge's boss I think he could be tied to an agricultural theft ring. He's got the means to transport big stuff quickly with the caravan operation. And I'm sure he's withholding Midge's vehicle from us, if it hasn't already gone to a chop shop. The van they provided was both undamaged and pristine. I've seen how Midge lives. It'd take a team of valets a month to get it that immaculate. It's crucial for the murder charge. I've Kyle checking GEM Maintenance's records and two volunteer constables going over the whole fleet.' Shona paused, weighing up what she was about to say next. 'I want McLean off balance. So, I goaded him about Ailsa.'

Dalrymple's eyebrows shot up. But instead of a warning or telling her off, as she expected, he merely nodded. 'How did he react?'

'Didn't say anything, but he looked fit to explode,' Shona said.

'McLean's connected. He could make life awkward for you.'

Join the queue, Shona thought.

'It's why I said to be careful,' Dalrymple went on. 'But maybe you did the right thing. I'm not sure how much time Isobel has left. If she's to get her dying wish of justice for Ailsa, perhaps we need to rattle a few cages. Is there anything I can do to help you?'

Shona thought for a moment, glad of this vote of confidence. 'What I'm struggling with are the dynamics of the relationships around Ailsa. Teenagers' emotional worlds can be governed by their peer group. Can I ask, what's your honest opinion of Graham McLean?'

'You'll need to ask Isobel about that time. I came here from Ayr as a young constable. But he was throwing his weight around even then.' He paused. 'I've known him for thirty years. Never been charged with anything, or even formally interviewed. But there's a ruthless streak in Graham McLean a mile wide. He's driven competitors out of business. Bought up land that no one knew was for sale. Thirty years back there was an ex-wife. He made the divorce process as tortuous as possible until she settled for far less than she was entitled to. Shortly afterwards she drove her car off a bridge in the highlands. He didn't even attend the funeral. If you were to ask me what I thought he was capable of? Under pressure, I'd say he's capable of anything.'

-

Upstairs, Isobel looked much the same as Shona's last visit, her attention fixed on the rosy evening glow now bathing the lighthouse. But her movements were slower, her expression less animated, as if the barest actions – blinking, breathing – were now taking a heavier toll on her.

When she saw Shona, a fire kindled in her eyes. Isobel reached out and took Shona's hand. 'Hello, dear. I'm so glad you came back.' The grip was surprisingly strong.

'How are you today?' Shona sat down as Dalrymple tactfully left the room.

'I'm getting there,' Isobel replied, as if her sights were now fixed solely on the road ahead, a place Shona couldn't even imagine. For a moment she looked fearful, as if time was short. 'Ask me. I'll tell you everything.' If Ailsa was waiting, then it was clear Isobel was anxious to bring her both justice and answers.

'What was Ailsa like?'

'Talented. Ambitious. She was going to make the world sit up and pay attention.'

The irony of Isobel's words wasn't lost on Shona.

Suddenly, her mother Angie's revelation at their meeting came back to her. The age gap between Ailsa and Isobel was two years. For Shona and her lost older siblings it would be about the same, yet she had no memory of them.

'So, what was it like having an older sister?' Shona began. 'Were you close?'

Isobel pressed her lips together as she considered. 'She stood up for me at school.' She smiled at the memory. 'I miss that. It's good to have someone who's always on your side. No matter what. I didn't see that then. I should have loved her more. I didn't understand that I annoyed her too.'

'Isn't that what wee sisters are for?' Shona smiled without any idea if it was true. 'Did you confide in each other? Ailsa and Graham had an argument at a dance the night before she was murdered. Do you know what that was about?'

'Who the other one was seeing, I think. They argued a lot. I think Graham wanted to control Ailsa.' She gave a rasping laugh. 'There was no chance of that.'

'The file mentioned it could've been another girl they argued about.'

'He had girls flocking around him. Surprising, isn't it? We all thought he was the bee's knees, cos he had a car and lived in a posh house. You know what it's like at that age. And every little thing is a drama.'

Shona nodded. 'What about McLean's pal, Bruce Campbell?'

'Always followed Graham around like a dog.'

'What did Ailsa think of him?'

'She mostly ignored him. Graham is the kind of person who always needs a sidekick.'

Shona thought of the way psychopaths could operate as a killing team – one partner dominant and the other submissive. Did Graham McLean have a sadistic desire to dominate, degrade and control Ailsa? If she objected to his womanising, he could've killed her in a fit of rage, or in tandem with Bruce Campbell. She'd have expected sexual assault to have featured in that scenario. Having visited the hollow, she knew it wasn't as exposed as you'd think, though it was still on a public footpath in the height of the tourist season. And why pose the body as if it had been a fall? In Shona's experience psychopaths were proud of their actions and wanted them to be seen, their power acknowledged.

'What about Bruce's girlfriend?' Shona searched her memory for the young woman's name, but it wouldn't come. She'd provided the alibi for both McLean and Bruce Campbell. 'Were she and Ailsa mates? Might she have confided something in her?' There was nothing in the statement, but she was still alive and forty years could've shaken something loose.

'Jan?' Isobel supplied. 'They weren't pals.'

'What about her art teacher? Jeremy Young?'

'God, we all thought he was ancient,' Isobel smirked, and Shona caught a glimpse of the lively, confident young woman she must've been before her sister's killing had overshadowed the Scott family's lives. 'We laughed at him then, but later I understood how dangerous men like that can be. I saw his type throughout my teaching career, and I made damn sure they were reported,' she said, her expression now serious. 'Obsessed with themselves and their power over the girls. Leveraging their position for sexual favours and promising them the world.'

'Is that what happened with Ailsa?' Throughout their conversation, Shona had the sense that Isobel was holding something back, waiting for her to unravel a truth carefully guarded since her only sister came to grief on the cliff path. Could Ailsa's affair with her teacher be it? Attitudes now were more enlightened than in the 1980s. But since the beginning of human history, girls learned early that they could carry the blame for the actions of others. Ailsa's reputation would've been trashed forever, and Jeremy Young might still have gotten away with it. Isobel's parents might easily hold her responsible. Ailsa, the promising artist in life, now in death the teenage temptress who'd ruined a man's marriage and career and ultimately driven him to *accidently* kill her. 'Whatever happened, it's safe to tell me,' Shona said gently. 'I'm not here to apportion blame.'

But something had shifted; a cloud rolled in. The lighthouse was no longer bathed in pearly light. The vivid paintings on the wall were fading, the room filling up with shadows as if it was Isobel herself that had illuminated them.

'Roddy was my friend,' Isobel said, at last.

Shona felt her pulse quicken.

'We were in the same class at school. Neither of us were popular. Do you think we carry our childhood self inside us all our life? If not, at what point do we abandon it? Be someone different, someone better?'

If Isobel had asked that question a year ago, Shona would've answered her confidently. We cannot escape our history, but what you choose to do now is what matters. Since Angie MacDonald had appeared like a revenant, Shona was less sure. Past, present and future were jumbled up and she could no longer see the compass points of her life.

Their conversation had led them to a place Shona thought was better suited to a priest than a police officer. But the mention of Roddy had sent alarm bells jangling. *Roddy was my friend*. Did that mean he wasn't any more, and when did that break occur? Forty years ago, perhaps.

'Would you like to see Roddy?' Shona asked. The lifeboat coxswain had, after all, mentioned a visit.

Isobel had closed her eyes. It seemed she didn't expect an answer from Shona after all. For a moment, Shona thought Dalrymple's wife was beyond questions and felt a wave of panic. She took Isobel's hand, but it was warm and her chest rose and fell softly.

Dalrymple himself came in quietly and beckoned Shona from the room.

'It's okay. She'll sleep now for a bit. Did you have a useful chat?'

'Yes, thank you, we did.'

She'd forgotten to ask Isobel who she thought had killed Ailsa, since she still seemed to have all the suspects in play. But it was a moot point. After forty years, if Isobel knew for sure, she'd have told the investigation at the time, or her husband, who she knew needed so badly to find Ailsa's killer, for her and for himself.

Chapter 22

It was after nine p.m. when Shona finally made it back to Coldharbour Cottage. She'd stopped halfway up the track and made a call to the mobile number art teacher Jeremy Young had given her when they'd met that first day. When it went straight to voicemail, she left a vague message about discussing ideas for his community project. When they met, she'd ask him straight if he'd had an affair with Ailsa. The lassie was dead; he'd nothing to fear from a prosecution. If he fobbed her off she'd say she was quietly reviewing the cold case. If it was found he'd withheld any evidence once it was officially reopened, he'd be for the high jump.

Graham McLean could be hauled in for an official chat for Muir Maxwell's murder – as a witness to Midge Elliot's movements for his company, obviously – but she'd need to work out how to get to Bruce Campbell.

Roddy was the problem she knew she was avoiding. That he'd been Isobel's friend, a close one by the sound of it, was not in the file. This implied Dalrymple had no knowledge of it. *He used to be my friend.* What had he really been doing on the clifftop when her sister was killed, and why had Isobel protected him with her silence? Whatever had severed their connection was profound and long lasting.

It would be light for another hour but the sting had gone from the day. On the western horizon, the sun hung low over the waves, like a burning coal already meeting the quenching power of the sea.

The wind had dropped and when Shona got to the cottage, she stood for a moment taking in the call of gulls and bedtime twitter in the hedgerows. Her head ached and her limbs felt heavy, but it was with the glow of accomplishment as much as the weight of the day. Midge Elliot was safely behind bars the fiscal having had no hesitation in approving both the supply of drugs and murder charges. There was plenty of work still to do but now, with double the intel, they had a clear sense of the road ahead. The connection between the two cases was sure to become clear as they investigated.

Becca had been sitting in the window seat reading when Shona pulled up. Now she came out of the cottage's open front door and greeted her mother.

'Have you eaten?' Shona said as she hugged her.

'At Jack's. Have you?'

'Had something at the office.' It'd only been a slice of slightly dubious pizza, but tiredness had robbed her of any appetite. Still, it was too lovely an evening to be indoors, and she knew if she went to bed now, the light and her still racing thoughts would conspire to keep her awake. 'Do you want to go for a quick walk?' Shona thought it'd be a way to wind down, but her ulterior motive was to get Becca to tell her about her day without her complaining she was being interrogated. Often that was easier on the move.

'Sure. D'you want a drink first? No coffee for you but I have herbal tea.'

Before Shona could answer her phone rang. She glanced at the screen.

'It's the Super,' she told Becca. 'It'll be a quick call.'

'I'll make you that tea,' Becca whispered, as Shona answered.

Shona gave her daughter a thumbs-up. 'Evening, sir.'

Detective Superintendent Mark Davies sounded upbeat as he congratulated her on the arrest and charges. 'Great result, Shona. Not bad for your first week.'

'Thank you, sir.'

While they chatted through the next stages of the investigation, Becca came out with a mug of herbal tea and placed it on the bench by the door. Shona mouthed a thank you and sat down. Davies's home life was something of a blank to her, but surely he had better things to do. Most of this could wait until morning. She stifled a yawn.

'By the way, Shona, it's come to my attention that you're looking at a cold case, the Ailsa Scott murder.'

Shona was suddenly wide awake. 'Who told you that?'

'It's my job to know what's going on in my division,' was his typically cryptic reply. 'Anyway, budgets are so tight, we have enough problems funding current investigations never mind old ones.'

It had to be that wee shit Graham McLean. Dalrymple had warned her, but she hadn't paid sufficient heed.

'Obviously my interest is purely theoretical,' she said lightly. 'I'm always curious about other areas' cold cases. Useful lessons to be learned from studying past procedures.'

'Really?' He sounded unconvinced. 'I just worry that it brings past police failings back into the light. If the family hear about it, that is. Wouldn't want to give them unjustified hope. Leave all that to the true crime conspiracy theorists, eh?'

Dalrymple could've said something, particularly since he had a family connection. He was scrupulously honest and the Super might even have okayed it on the quiet but had now got cold feet. One of the reasons for sending her to Galloway was to make her lie low. True, a cold case breakthrough would result in the opposite of that. But since he'd never mentioned it before, it felt like it was something Davies had just become aware of.

'Sir, Galloway's last outstanding murder case finally solved. That'd be a boost for the force.' Shona thought he should consider it an opportunity. 'People are drawn to cold cases because they hold a particular power for the public. Folk understand that the families have had to endure not only the pain and shock of losing a loved one, but everything that follows. The years of not knowing what happened and who was responsible.'

'I'm aware of that, Shona. Which is why I don't want hopes needlessly raised.'

Shona heard the warning in his tone. Perhaps it was the tiredness, or she was still riding the adrenaline wave of a successful day locking up a bad guy, but she pressed on even as the alarm bells were sounding in her head.

'DI Dalrymple talked about the idea it was someone still within the community,' she said. 'Someone he'd shaken hands with. If we can make a breakthrough, it'll be a good thing for police officers and the public.'

Becca had come to stand by the front door and Shona realised she was speaking loudly enough to be overheard, even if it was only herself and her daughter here. But still, she couldn't stop.

'The public will understand how important that is for the family, share a little in their sense of release from limbo. Knowing the facts, knowing who was responsible, gives the whole community something that matters deeply.'

'Enough, DI Oliver,' Davies snapped. 'May I remind you I backed you when the National Crime Agency wanted you suspended. You're in Galloway to lie low, not ride in on a white horse waving a flag.'

It was as if he'd emptied a bucket of iced water over her. She shuddered at the renewed realisation of all that was at stake for her professionally and personally.

'I realise that sir.'

In the doorway, Becca frowned.

'Good. Well done for today. Keep me informed.'

Aware that Becca was watching, Shona slumped back on the bench and rolled her eyes. 'Bosses, eh? You wait until you're out of university and in your first job.' She downed the cooling contents of the mug and tried not to wince. 'That tastes so awful I'm sure it's doing me good.'

'Camomile. Makes you calm.'

Better bring me a bath-full, Shona thought. Instead, she said, 'Right, let's get out before the sun sets. Shall we walk along the coast path for a bit?'

When they'd returned the mugs and locked the door, Becca said, 'Anyway, I'll be fine. Archaeologists always have good bosses, because otherwise they get buried in a trench.'

Shona grinned and put up a hand. 'Don't tell me any more. I've had enough of work for one day. Let's just enjoy the sunset.'

-

It had only taken Shona and Becca fifteen minutes to walk from the cottage to Black Point. Below, the calm sea purred fire-tipped waves onto the smooth sands.

'In the early days of its operation,' Becca began, 'if the lighthouse keepers saw boats in trouble on the busy Liverpool to Belfast route, they'd fire distress rockets to alert the Portpatrick lifeboat crew.'

'How d'you know that?' Shona turned to her daughter in surprise. 'Was that the book you were reading when I got home?'

'Roddy told me.'

'He talked about the lighthouse?' Shona stiffened. 'What else did he say?' Had their conversation on the quayside unearthed old memories? Perhaps they'd never really been buried.

'He said a girl from Portpatrick had been murdered here, and they never found out who did it. Is that true?'

'Yes, it's true.'

Why had Roddy mentioned this to her daughter? They were staying in a cottage in full view of the lighthouse and no near neighbours for one thing. Becca, whose imagination could sometimes run riot, might have nightmares, or feel unsafe there on her own while Shona was at work. Or was there a darker reason for him bringing it up. Was he quizzing Becca in case her mother had said something about re-opening the investigation?

'It was forty years ago,' Shona said eventually. 'At the time, police concluded it was someone walking the Southern Uplands Way, but they never found out who.'

'Is that what your boss was giving you a hard time over?'

'You know not to listen to work calls,' Shona said. 'It's for your own protection.'

'I could hardly not hear,' Becca pointed out. 'Is it a famous case?'

'Don't go googling it,' Shona warned.

'I won't.' Becca sounded indignant, which told Shona she probably already had, as soon as Roddy had mentioned it. 'But are you investigating it?'

'You know I'm not going to discuss that. But I don't want you walking this path on your own. Not because of a forty-year-old case; it's just a dangerous place.' She gave what she hoped was a reassuring smile. 'Are you planning some interesting trips out with Jack? How is he, by the way?'

'He's good. I was reading about the archaeology and history of the area when you came home. D'you know these bays were where the locals drowned sailors whose ships they'd lured onto the rocks, so they could steal their cargo.'

'Oh, for goodness' sake,' Shona muttered. 'Did you know the lighthouse is a holiday cottage now?' she said, attempting to lighten the conversation. 'A place to relax and enjoy the scenery. They've managed to put together a very nice brochure with no mention of murder at all.'

'Okay.' Becca rolled her eyes at her mother. 'Can I ask you something?'

As Shona looked at the cottages, she was sure the same man who she'd seen watching her the first evening was there again. When she shaded her eyes from the low sun, he moved into the shadow by the front door. She looked again but couldn't be sure what she'd seen.

'Mum? Can I ask you something? Promise you won't get mad?'

'Is it about a crime or does it involve a corpse?'

'No.'

'Okay, go ahead.' The sun was about to dip below the horizon. Shafts of light spread out across the grey surface of the sea. Above the clifftop, the first stars were visible.

'Now you've had some time to think about it,' Becca said slowly, 'how do you feel about Angie?'

Shona almost wished it'd been a question about serial killers. She'd intended to grill Becca about Jack, but it looked as if her daughter had turned the tables on her.

She blew out a long breath. 'If I'm honest, I don't see how any good can come of it.'

'What? You won't help her find your brother and sister?' Becca looked shocked and deeply disappointed, though Shona had given her no cause to think her reaction would be otherwise. 'You know you're depriving yourself of the opportunity to be a daughter.'

It sounded like something Becca had picked up in therapy. Shona bit back her reflex reply – I can live with that – and interrogated the question. She'd been a wife; granted that hadn't gone spectacularly well. She'd been a mother; hopefully better. Did she even need to feel like a daughter? What could she gain from cultivating a relationship with someone she already didn't trust, didn't like and whose actions might easily have killed her as a child? Nothing.

'I'm sorry, Becca,' she said carefully. 'I know this is important to you. Meeting her once was enough for me. Perhaps, if you've never had a mother or father growing up, you don't feel you're missing out on being a daughter.'

'Mum, I just think if you don't take this opportunity to get to know Angie, *properly*, you'll regret it later.'

'I really don't think I will.' Earlier, she'd argued the case for resolution and closure with Detective Superintendent Davies, now here she was denying it was something she needed for herself. 'If you're not going to judge Angie for her choices, please don't judge me for mine.'

'What about your brother and sister? What if they're out there needing help?'

'Well, in case you haven't noticed, I'm out there every day trying to help folk. I don't require shared DNA to do that.'

It was perhaps Shona's calmness that did most to confound Becca's argument. Shona herself was only aware of it once she'd finished speaking.

Becca didn't look happy, but she shrugged her shoulders. 'Okay, if that's how you feel.'

'And another thing. Why don't you bring Jack up to the cottage more?'

'Why? Do you want to keep an eye on us? We were living together in Glasgow so if you're worried about my virtue, that ship has sailed.'

Shona flushed and Becca looked amused at having shocked her famously unshockable mother.

'It's not that,' she answered truthfully. 'Roddy works from home sometimes and I don't want you getting under his feet.'

'He's fine about it. And some of Jack's cousins are coming over at the weekend. Roddy's happy about having his family around,' Becca said and marched ahead.

The sun had gone. They walked back to the cottage in silence through the soft twilight. It should've soothed them both, but when they reached the front door, Becca said she was tired and was going to bed, and Shona could think of nothing to say that would ease her daughter's disappointment.

Shona forced down another herbal tea and sat in the front room without turning on the light. Thoughts of

Ailsa's violent and lonely death filled her mind, piling question upon question. Now she'd visited the site again, a new question had arisen. Why was she posed as if she'd just fallen? If the killer wanted to make it look like an accident, why didn't they just push her body into the sea? There were many possible answers – panic, a lack of planning, chaotic thinking – all things that'd likely contributed to Muir Maxwell's death. But in Ailsa's case, Shona still couldn't make the pieces of the jigsaw fit. For a start, what'd been the motive? Not theft. Not sex. Revenge? If so, for what?

Enough, she told herself. You need to sleep.

When Shona went out to check she'd locked the Audi, the golden fields were now full of deep blue shadows and the faint rustling of the wind and the night creatures. She had the creeping sense she was not alone, that something was moving in the dark beyond her vision. She shivered. It was ridiculous. There was nothing and no one here that could harm her.

But even when she hurried inside and turned the key, the feeling of unease followed her. She leaned her back against the front door in the darkness. After the day's events, she should've felt a sense of accomplishment, completion. But now all she had was a sour aftertaste and the belief that, somehow, she'd left important things undone.

Chapter 23

When Shona arrived at Newton Stewart the next morning, any elation of yesterday's success had completely evaporated. It was already hot and she wasn't looking forward to the long drive to Dumfries jail for Midge Elliot's interview. The pink cotton blouse and linen trousers she'd chosen were a compromise between being smart and staying cool. Whatever Midge told her this morning, assuming he said anything at all, would have to be put to the Maxwell women. Asking if Muir was connected to a drug operation wouldn't be easy and she'd be glad of Jess's support.

On her desk, she found a note. Midge's solicitor, Katie Pickles, was apparently already waiting for her in the interview room along the corridor. Shona went back out to the CID office and held the paper up between two fingers. Kyle was out with Jess, following up on a loose end, leaving DS McCulloch, who Shona would be taking with her to the interview in acknowledgement, to herself at least, of her previous poor choices, and the two civilian support staff.

'When did this come?'

Their appointment with Midge was fixed for eleven a.m. She and McCulloch would be heading out the door shortly. Was this a delaying tactic by his solicitor? Or had something happened to Midge in prison overnight? Surely she'd have been informed if it had.

'Came from reception,' Erin supplied. 'About ten minutes ago.'

Shona turned on her heel, retrieved her notepad and phone, then beckoned McCulloch to follow her.

'Any guesses what this is about?' Shona said, but McCulloch just shook his head.

In the stuffy interview room, Katie Pickles was pacing the floor. As Shona and McCulloch entered, the solicitor held out her hand, bracelets jangling, and they shook. Shona's attention was already on the other occupant, a young woman in her early twenties.

'Jodie?' McCulloch said, sitting down. 'What are you doin' here? You okay?'

Shona took in the cut-off denim shorts and strappy top. Her streaky blonde hair piled on top of her head and secured with a scrunchie. She was biting her nails and shooting nervous glances at Katie Pickles, who'd taken a seat next to her. This had to be Midge's ex-girlfriend, Jodie Reid.

When the young woman didn't answer McCulloch's enquiry, the solicitor said, 'Jodie has something to tell you.'

Shona folded her hands on the chipped table and waited. Either the young woman knew something that'd help the father of her kids – which individual had put pressure on Midge to steal the quad bike – or she knew who the second man might be. It was the opening shots in the next round of the investigation, a trade off. Jodie had a record herself for drug offences. Had she been in on either the farm raid or the operation at the garage? Perhaps she wanted immunity in the future, in exchange for co-operation now.

Eventually, Jodie sighed and pulled her phone from the rear pocket of her shorts and opened up a photo. She turned the screen towards Shona and McCulloch. It showed a glassy-eyed Midge crouching next to a buggy with a baby festooned in pink. On his other side was a wee boy, no more than a toddler, holding a piece of card coloured in black and white, which Shona thought was supposed to represent a Belted Galloway cow. In the background, beyond a fence, turkeys were visible in fields.

As if the picture had just come into focus, Shona felt a jolt of recognition.

'Where is this?'

'It's thon farm place.' Jodie gave her a look that said she was an eejit. 'It's Midge and the weans at thon farm.'

Katie the solicitor took the phone from Jodie's hand. 'This is evidence that my client Midge Elliot was at an Eastcraig Farm open day, three weeks before Mr Maxwell was murdered.'

Next to her, Shona felt McCulloch stiffen. Shit, she thought. Shit. Shit. Shit.

'And this is how Mr Elliot's biological markers, including fingerprints and DNA, were found at the scene.' There was a gleam in the solicitor's eye, certain she held an ace.

'Jodie?' McCulloch said with such force that the young woman jumped. 'Is this right? You were oot for the day wi' Midge. You telt me yesterday that you two weren't pals any more.'

'Aye, well, we're no' thegether.'

'This trip to the farm,' Shona said, her heart thumping in her chest as she processed the ramifications of what they were hearing. 'How come we're just learning about it now?'

'My client didn't remember the name of the farm when you questioned him.'

'So now, he's admitting he does know the farm?'

'He wis pissed,' Jodie cut in. 'An' he'd had some pills.'

'Model father, then,' Shona replied. She turned back to the solicitor. 'Ms Pickles, if these pictures are indeed genuine, you're claiming they prove your client's innocence. I'd say this is evidence of pre-meditation. Midge went there in the guise of a family trip to scope out the farm and plan the theft of the quad bike and tractor GPS units, which ultimately led to Mr Maxwell's murder.'

'It's no true,' Jodie spat. 'It wis a family day oot. He's got parental access he has.'

'We picked Midge up early yesterday morning,' McCulloch said. 'An' yer just tellin us noo?'

'Aw, right. So? I just needed some peace,' Jodie replied, slumping back in her chair and folding her arms. 'Whit?' she said, seeing Katie's shocked look.

'Jodie, are you saying you deliberately withheld evidence in a murder enquiry because Midge was getting on your nerves and you wanted him locked up?' Having spent time in an interview room with him, Shona could sympathise with the impulse, if not the execution. 'Do you know that the penalty for attempting to defeat the ends of justice is a big fine or a prison sentence?'

'How am I goin tae jail? I havenae done anythin'.' She turned on Katie. 'You said he'd get oot.'

'Jodie,' Shona said. 'Do you know anything else about Midge's involvement in Mr Maxwell's murder, or who was with him that night?'

Jodie shook her head. 'We just went for a day oot. That's all.'

'What about this drugs operation Midge was running?' Shona said.

'Oh no,' Katie jumped in. 'If you want to question Jodie, you'll need to arrest and caution her. She's here voluntarily, as a gesture of goodwill, to provide evidence as witness in the case of Muir Maxwell's murder.' The expression on Jodie's face said that goodwill was in short supply.

Shona considered doing just that. The lassie looked like she'd a temper on her. Could she have been the second man? It was possible. She was short and lightly built. A hoodie and balaclava would add bulk. Midge might keep quiet to protect her and stop his kids ending up in care. But they already had her DNA on file. There was no evidence, forensic or otherwise, to link her either to the murder or the drugs operation.

The solicitor got to her feet. 'So, I'll be making a bail application for my client, Mr Elliot, this morning.'

Shona stared at her, incredulous. 'I'll remind you that your client is currently being held on a murder charge *and* a big-ticket drug operation, so I admire your optimism. He's going nowhere.' She reached across and took Jodie's phone from where it lay.

'Haw you, wait.' Jodie tried to snatch it back, but Katie put out a restraining hand. 'I need ma phone.'

'Thank you for bringing this evidence to our attention,' Shona said. McCulloch frowned at Jodie as he placed the device in an evidence bag. 'You'll get it back as soon as forensic tests are complete.'

After their visitors had been escorted out, Shona stopped in the corridor on the way back to CID and turned to McCulloch.

'What d'you think?'

'That Pickles wummin is right aboot the forensics.'

'Those photos are a problem,' Shona agreed. 'We need to nail down more on Midge Elliot. No luck with checking the other vans for damage?'

'Uniform guys were at it all night. Nothin.'

Shona pointed to the phone he was carrying. 'Let's see what we have and take it from there.'

When they reached the office, McCulloch handed the phone over to Erin.

'Tell me as soon as you've got anything,' Shona called as she headed for her office.

Once inside she threw herself into her chair, leaned forward and rested her head on the desk for a moment. She was holding back the creeping sense of dread that threatened to overcome her, but only just. Juries often put the principal weight of their verdict on the strength of forensics. All it took was for the defence to offer an alternative reason to introduce doubt in their minds. Whatever she may have said to Katie Pickles, Shona knew that their murder case against Mitch might now be in serious risk of collapse.

Shona sat up and smoothed her hair back from her face, lifting it away from her neck and allowing cool air to clear her head. What she needed now was to hold her nerve and make sure the other officers in CID did the same. She would have to call the fiscal but to do that she needed to be armed with alternative reasons why Mitch should still face the murder charge. She opened her laptop and began scrolling through the case-management programme looking for the outstanding actions that might signal that the tide could be turned in their favour again. There was little in the way of forensics that did not relate to the van. If they had that they could check tyre tracks and the paint samples taken from the gate and most significantly any damage or repair work that had been done to the front bumper area and the windscreen.

The drugs case had advanced quickly with damning evidence of the kind juries preferred – forensic traces on the burner phones, the drugs themselves, and the associated equipment including the scales and small plastic bags that Midge had been in the process of filling. There were even a few witness statements from neighbours overlooking the garages. Many had refused to speak, but those that did complained of comings and goings at all hours. To cap it all there was even CCTV from a doorbell cam of Midge arriving and leaving. Whether these witnesses were prepared to stand up in court would be something they'd deal with later. That rested on who he was connected to. There might come a point when they needed to hand this over to a major crime team because, undoubtedly, this would connect to a large-scale drugs operation in a city somewhere in Scotland, or even the north of England. That might lead them full circle to Muir Maxwell's murder. But Shona knew in her heart they had a long way to go and much to prove before they could tie both those loose ends together.

Shona opened her emails and scrolled through for any outstanding updates that she'd missed. She was halfway down the first page when she stopped dead. An email from her mother Angie stared back at her. It was dated last Wednesday, two days after the disastrous pub date. Shona's finger hovered over the delete icon. She thought she'd made it clear at their meeting that there was no point in further contact. Remembering both Angie's and Becca's faces, she didn't think she could be accused of not being clear on that point.

Should she read it? What did she have to lose. She could always delete it afterwards. It would only confirm that she'd made the right decision.

> Dear Shona,
>
> I realise how shocked and unhappy you were at our meeting and I am sorry for that. I just wanted to let you know I've decided to press ahead with looking for your brother and sister. They may not want to have anything to do with me, and that's fine, but I think it is important for them to have the option of a relationship with each other, after my death, if that's what they want. I'm not asking for your help as this is something I need to do for myself. I know that I can never undo the pain that I've caused you all but I hope in time that you will see this is my gift to all your futures.

Shona read the email twice, then deleted it. She couldn't explain why, but it felt like her mother had cast her aside all over again. Didn't work out with Shona, let's have a go with the others. Would she keep going until one of them let her back into their lives? Why had Shona expected any better? It felt predictably cynical on Angie's part, but it still stung.

'Boss?' McCulloch was at the door, holding it open for her to come.

In the CID room, Kyle and Jess had arrived. By the look on their faces she knew they'd heard the news.

'Well?' Shona folded her arms and leaned forward to stare at Erin's screen. The others gathered round. There were a series of pictures of Midge, Jodie and their children in various locations which were undoubtably Eastcraig Farm. They showed them outdoors with lambs and chicks, faces screwed up in the bright sunshine. Midge's expression was largely blank, though he was smiling in some. It felt to Shona that her heart couldn't sink any further after the morning she'd had so far, but when Erin scrolled down to the final pictures, she realised it could.

Midge leaning on a tractor. Midge holding his son who was seated on a quad bike. Her mind ran like a rat through a maze looking for ways out.

'We're sure these photos haven't been tampered with?'

'No variable lighting,' Erin said. 'The metadata is clean. No mixed compression levels across the image. The original thumbnails are embedded and they're a match for all the top-level photographs.'

'And the dates check out?'

McCulloch nodded.

'There's something else you might like to see, boss,' Jess said, holding out her own phone. 'There was an off-licence receipt in one of the bags we found in Midge's flat from just before ten p.m. on the night of the murder. Obviously, plenty of time to get up to the farm. Kyle and I just went to chat to the shop owner, in case there was anyone with Midge in the shop.'

'And?'

'He was alone,' Kyle said. 'Thing is, Midge came back to the off-licence later, after it was closed. Banged on the door, demanding to be served. It was caught on CCTV.'

Jess set the video going. Sure enough, there was Midge thumping the shutters.

'What's the time stamp?' Shona asked, knowing she probably wasn't going to like the answer.

'Quarter to midnight,' Jess said.

Shona looked around the group of faces and saw they'd all made the leap too. No way could Midge have been in Stranraer and at the Eastcraig Farm in that time frame. It was like all the air had suddenly been sucked out of the room.

'Midge Elliot,' Shona said. 'He's not our man.'

Chapter 24

Shona sent everyone out for decent coffee while she processed precisely what had gone wrong and what they could do to salvage things. Worse, they were heading into a weekend with nothing to show for their graft, a guaranteed dampener on momentum.

When she came back into her office, she saw a missed call from Freya. Hitting redial, she told herself that this wasn't because she needed a hit of home and normality to stall the spirally panic about their imploding murder case. When the call was answered, Shona heard background chatter that told her Freya was in the kitchen of the Royal Arms prepping dishes for lunch.

'Freya? Everything okay?' Shona took a sip from the extra-large cup of coffee Jess had brought her.

'Aye, Shona. Hello. Just wanted tae check a High Pines cancellation an' rebooking. The Robsons, fae Bolton. Should I bill them the usual fee o'er the change of dates?'

'Have they been before?' Shona couldn't picture them.

'Oh aye. Twice afore. Mrs Robson got a cancellation for her hip operation.'

'Oh, right. Tell them it's fine. I'm glad we could accommodate them and I hope everything goes well with the op.'

'Okay doke. Mrs R says she's excited tae get doon intae the garden this time. Hasnae managed it afore.'

Shona grimaced. While the self-catering units had level access, the garden was steeply terraced and had run rather wild lately. 'I better get someone in to tame it before she comes.'

'Ach, it's fine,' Freya said. 'Sounds like she's up for an adventure. But I could get Derek to have a peedie look at it for ye?'

Derek was Shona's regular handyman, gardener and supplier of firewood. At the thought that the life of the house and garden was going on without her, Shona suddenly felt a longing for home. Coldharbour Cottage's visitor book contained glowing praise from travellers drawn to Portpatrick from across the world for its picturesque harbour, beautiful scenery and friendly locals. So far, she hadn't found it as relaxing as she'd hoped but perhaps a brutal murder, and the knowledge that a cold case had happened on your doorstep, took some of the shine off.

'Thanks Freya. Be great if Derek could give the place a tidy-up. Everything else okay?'

'Aye. Fine.' There was a pause, and the background noise seemed to lessen. It sounded to Shona as if Freya was looking for a quieter spot. 'Are ye planning on coming back home at all this weekend?'

Shona had no intention of leaving Becca alone at Coldharbour Cottage. And the previous weekend, her return to Kirkness had caused Dalrymple to be hauled from his dying wife's bedside. She couldn't risk a repeat of that.

'I'm sorry, Freya. I'm staying here. I've got Becca with me now, and Simon's coming down on Sunday.' In truth, she doubted she'd see much of her daughter, who'd be with Jack. But although she wouldn't insist the rest of CID came in – not after the week they'd had – she hoped to do some catching up on paperwork herself on Saturday before Simon arrived on Sunday. She missed him so much it was a physical ache. They'd hardly had a chance to talk in the last few days. If anyone could help her make sense of everything it was Simon. And after last night she wanted to smooth things over if she could with Becca, who'd scarpered before her mother was up this morning – maybe help out if she and Jack needed a lift anywhere. 'Is it the changeovers that's the problem?' There was a new set of guests arriving at High Pines on Saturday afternoon.

'No, no, yer grand. It's just...' Freya paused again. 'Tommy's having trouble raising a crew. Had to tak the lifeboat oot of service for a couple of days this week, cos there wasnae enough folk on call. Doesnae want tae ask ye again. He knows yer busy.'

'Oh,' Shona replied, shocked. She obviously knew he'd been having continued trouble with crew numbers – it happened occasionally – but in the years she'd been at Kirkness, it'd never led to the *Margaret Wilson* being withdrawn from service. 'I'd love to help, Freya, but short of splitting myself in two, I can't see how I can. Promise I'll try and make it the weekend after.'

'Aye, yer fine,' Freya replied hastily.

'Freya?' Shona said. 'Really, thanks for everything. I'd be lost without you.'

'Nae problem. I'll let ye go. Cheery bye the noo.'

It was the quick sign-off that convinced Shona of the true gravity of the situation. Perhaps Freya felt it was disloyal to discuss further the lifeboat's lack of support with Shona if Tommy himself wasn't about to. She racked her brains for any way in which she could help but came up empty. The coastguard would task other assets to cover the gap left by Kirkness, but no station wanted to do anything less than their best.

And she hadn't forgotten Simon's proposal that she moved to Glasgow. If the lifeboat station closed, it would be another nail in the coffin of her reasons for staying. People joked about their *lifeboat family* and the number of times they'd responded to a shout by leaving their real family behind at weddings, christenings, anniversary dinners. It wasn't just that she wanted to maintain her years of training and skills, being part of the crew gave her the kind of unconditional support that she'd find impossible to replace. And she really wasn't sure she was ready to give that up.

-

Shona led the constable carrying two whiteboards into the CID office and showed him where to prop them on the two empty desks at the back.

'Five minutes, everyone,' she said to the curious faces.

They were just beginning when Jess Johnstone arrived, mouthing a *sorry, boss* apology. George McCulloch gave up his seat and went to fetch another chair. It seemed she had charmed, or intimidated, even the detective sergeant. Erin Brown was watching her from the tail of her eye. Jess smiled at her, and Erin's cheeks flamed scarlet, though she did manage to smile back. When everyone was seated Shona passed on the Super's and her own congratulations for all the hard work they'd done so far.

'Now we need to reset and go again. Review what we know about Muir Maxwell's murder.' She pulled the cap off her marker and tapped the nearest board. 'I know we're in the era of an online case-management system but humour me. This is an addition aide-memoire.'

She wrote *DRUGS* on one board and *MURDER – MUIR MAXWELL* on the other.

'We know that Midge Elliot has an alibi for the time of the murder and a plausible explanation for his bio markers being at Eastcraig Farm. But we also know he was involved in the setting-up of a major county lines network. Where might those networks originate? Anybody?'

'Glasgow and the central belt?' Kyle said.

Shona added it to the board.

'Manchester?' offered McCulloch.

'With Stranraer's proximity to the ferry, we should consider Belfast,' Jess said.

Shona added both names. 'Two serious crimes in Galloway within a close time frame doesn't feel like coincidence to me. County lines operations rely on youngsters, mainly teenagers working on the ground.' She thought about Murdo's comment about young lads, particularly those with a drug habit and poor impulse control, finding it hard to differentiate between real life and online gaming. 'It's important to keep in mind that we may be talking about the same individuals in both cases, or we may not. It is for that reason I've decided to run our evidence gathering in parallel, rather than hand one over to another team.'

The line of faces in front of her looked both pleased and apprehensive. She'd considered asking the Super for a second unit or even co-opting anyone she could get her hands on from Dumfries but settling them in might cause more problems than it solved if they were understaffed and a major incident occurred.

'It will mean extra work for everyone,' she acknowledged. 'I cannot stress this enough – it's important that you share intel and work closely together. This is your chance to land two major cases. I know you can do this.'

In that respect, the small team, already used to working with each other would be to their advantage.

'Do we have any idea how the drugs operation might connect to Muir Maxwell's death?' Jess said. She was used to Shona's working methods and knew she didn't need to wait to be asked to contribute.

'Maybe it doesn't, directly,' said Kyle. He stopped and eyed Shona in case he'd spoken out of turn but she nodded for him to go on. 'Supply of drugs is a business like any other, and businesses have cash-flow problems.'

'And Midge is no criminal mastermind, right DS McCulloch?' Shona said.

McCulloch nodded, which Shona took to mean the frost between them had indeed thawed in acknowledgement of the other's usefulness to the investigation. She required a professional working relationship, that was all. They didn't need to be pals.

'Operation Raven was all over the news last year,' Jess added. 'Maybe that gave our assailants the idea. Even wee villages have their share of CCTV. Country roads not so much. My da used to tell me that in Belfast in the old days, if you needed ready money for drugs or guns, you just went out and stole a car or two. That's why motor insurance was so high. Thieving cars is hard these days. Farm kit is an easy ten grand, as long as you've a customer lined up. And the idea it might be youngsters, lads down from the city, would fit with these so-called campers they had trouble with.'

Shona nodded. 'Okay. Good. So, we have a working hypothesis that might connect the two cases. Maxwell's murder is part of a single incident because someone needed ready cash for their drugs operation, possibly connected to the campers. We didn't find any of the associated low-level criminality that you might expect – shoplifting, petty theft – but maybe that's because they had the support of a network. Previous gangs have used Airbnb to park their dealers, but they'll know it's the first place we'll look. Camping might be their thing, initially till they get set up. And it may be that the pictures of Midge and family at the farm did constitute planning, even if he didn't carry out the raid. It's a question we can put to Midge, if he'll talk to us.'

There were nods around the room as the team spotted a new quarry to pursue.

'We prioritise the murder,' Shona said. 'That's where the greatest threat to the public lies, especially since the drugs merchandise is off the streets. We still need to find the quad bike and the GPS units. And where is the van on the CCTV? We know it's not Midge's. I still want a chat with GEM and Graham McLean about any potential involvement with the drugs operation. And not forgetting we still don't have Midge's phone.'

'Records confirm last calls around Saturday lunch time,' Ian said. 'Nothing after that.'

'So, he could've dumped it,' McCulloch said. 'But he also could've had one we dinnae know aboot yet.'

'True,' Shona agreed. 'Now in terms of Muir Maxwell's murder, I walked the route from the byre to the road, but I want it searched again, this time a strip five metres back from either side of the track. Jess will be FLO. Can you organise that and tell the family?'

'Sure, boss.'

It'd be something positive to offer the family when they broke the news that Midge was no longer in the frame for

Muir's murder. And Shona had a feeling they were going to need it.

With all the action agreed and in motion, Shona returned to her office. On the desk sat Ailsa's file. She checked her phone again. She'd left several voicemails for Jeremy Young but heard nothing back. And Becca hadn't responded to any of her messages. Isobel's words about Roddy were still going around in her head. She couldn't help but connect Ailsa's death with her fears for Becca. Similar age. Same step on life's ladder. While Jack was in Becca's life, Roddy would be there too and Shona was powerless to stop it.

Shona stared at her phone. She could chalk it up to a poor signal, but right now, that wasn't enough. She dialled again. The call went straight to voicemail.

'Becca, darlin', I appreciate you are still processing what I said last night. I just need to know you're okay.'

She opened Ailsa's file. Outside, the main CID room was a hive of activity. As she looked at the photographs, the burbling office chat became the rushing of the waves. A body laid out under the open sky. Suddenly Shona wasn't a detective but a mourner holding not questions but flowers for the grave, reaching in to touch the face of her daughter.

She jumped as Ian tapped her door and came straight in. He must've seen something in her expression. His eyes darted to the file open before her.

'Sorry, ma'am. I can come back?'

'No Ian, it's fine.' She moved around the desk, perching on the edge to block his view of the file, a jarring paper artefact, incongruous amongst a sea of technology.

'GEM Maintenance?' he began. 'The van checks uniform were doing?'

He kept his eyes on her face but she could see the effort it was costing him to remain where he was and not manoeuvre himself back into a view of her desk.

She could lean around and flick the cover shut; but that would be admitting she knew what he was doing. What she didn't know was why.

'Did they find anything at all?'

'Nothing, boss. GEM's procedures are shoddy. We can maybe refer them to the Traffic Commissioner for Scotland and the Driver and Vehicle Standards Agency. Put a bit of pressure on them to co-operate with us. And as Midge Elliot is their employee, I could ask the fiscal for a warrant to search all the caravan sites in connection with the drugs.'

'That would certainly shake them up.' It was an original thought – one Shona might have devised herself given what was rapidly turning into a personal loathing for Graham McLean.

When he lingered, she pushed off from the desk. A detail from the file that'd snagged in her memory began to float free.

Before she could grab it, her phone buzzed.

> Sorry Mum. With Jack all day. See you later. X

A cool wave of reassurance swept over her. But while she lacked answers for Ailsa's case, the relief would only be temporary.

'Right, I'm going to see the Maxwell family,' she said. 'Let the others know they can call if they need me.'

She closed the file, picked up her handbag and jacket, and followed Ian out into the main room. Jess wasn't at her desk, which made what she was about to do easier.

Stepping out into the corridor, she walked ten steps then stopped. After a minute, she turned and retraced her route. The door to her office was closed. Her team were busy, either on the phone or concentrating on whatever was on their screen.

Quietly, she turned the handle and edged open her office door.

A figure stood with their back facing her, outlined against the window.

'Is there something I can help you with?'

Ian Smith jumped.

So, she'd been right. And despite all her years in the job, she'd never seen anyone look half so guilty as he did at that moment.

Chapter 25

Shona closed the door, walked around her desk. She placed her hands on either side of Ailsa Scott's file and leaned forward to look Ian dead in the eye.

'Why did you tell the Super that I was investigating Ailsa Scott's murder?'

He looked like he was mustering himself for a denial, but in the end saw it was pointless.

'I'm sorry, boss. Mark Davies was my DI at the end of my career when I worked out of Kilmarnock. I thought the case had been reopened and I wanted to offer my support.'

Shona gave him a sceptical look. 'Sure you weren't offering to keep an eye on me?' She flipped open the file to a scene log, detailing who'd been at the clifftop immediately after Ailsa was found. 'Constable I. Smith. That's you.' The name had meant nothing to her at first glance, being so common. 'And witness statements. Signatures on evidence sheets. You were a busy boy. I appreciate that you're loyal to DI Ross and the original investigation, but going behind my back…'

'Look, that's not what happened.' Ian clasped and unclasped his hands as if summoning resolve. 'I only investigated a few murders in my career. Ailsa Scott was the one that stuck with me. I was just a young uniform plod guarding the scene. I didn't know the lassie, but she was about the same age as me. Her parents were distraught. I had to stop her mother throwing herself onto her daughter. I can still remember that scream. The sister, Isobel, had to hold her back too. I've met Mrs Dalrymple a few times since. I'm thankful she doesn't remember me, but it brings it all back.'

'Does DI Dalrymple know about this?'

'No. My wife and I are from Paisley, originally. He knows I worked here for a bit at the start of my career. That we retired to Galloway cos we liked it so much, which is true. I guess I didn't think it would bring back such bad memories.'

Shona straightened up and made an effort to relax her shoulders and slow her breathing, to process all the possibilities and avoid a rash decision. She held out her hand indicating the opposite side of the desk.

'Sit down.' Until this moment, she'd wondered if she'd been imagining Ian Smith's interest in Ailsa's folder. He was lucky the Super had called her. At least now she was sure it hadn't been Graham McLean pulling strings, which begged the question – why hadn't he? Was he so desperate to keep a low profile that he'd let Shona practically accuse him of murdering his teenage girlfriend right there in his own yard?

'Ailsa Scott's father was white as a ghost,' Ian said, as he pulled out the chair. 'He kept shaking his head like he didn't believe what was happening.'

'And you were involved throughout the investigation?' He'd only been a uniform constable, not part of the CID team.

'Yes. We were short-handed. I mostly did fetching and carrying.'

'But you were present at interviews?'

He nodded.

'Is that why you brought Graham McLean's business to my attention?'

He looked uncertain for a moment, then nodded.

'You think he killed Ailsa, don't you? Why?'

'He and Bruce Campbell were each other's alibis, and I trust either of them as far as I could throw them.'

Shona frowned. 'I thought it was Bruce's girlfriend, Janice, the bakery worker, who said they were both at lunch with her – sandwiches she'd smuggled out of the bakery.'

'That was never corroborated by a third party…'

'…because the manageress chased anyone she found hanging around, cos she thought, quite correctly, that the girls were giving free stuff to the lads they fancied.'

'We picked both lads up due to the argument at the dance. Ailsa had accused McLean of seeing another girl. McLean in turn accused Ailsa of spending too much time with her art teacher, Jeremy Young. He admitted to all of that but said it was no big deal and they'd made up.'

'I read that in the file.'

'Aye,' said Ian, edging forward as he became caught up in the memories. 'Thing was, Isobel, Ailsa's sister did think she'd seen McLean at their farm on the afternoon Ailsa died. But her mother contradicted her by claiming she'd come back for a flask of tea, and Isobel had already gone to muck out the horses, so if Graham was there it must have been earlier. For his part, McLean denies he went anywhere near Ailsa's that day.'

Shona had also read both Isobel and McLean's statements and noticed the disparity. The investigation hadn't pursued it at the time, choosing to give more weight to Ailsa and Isobel's mother over the timings. It was odd though that during both of Shona's visits to Isobel she'd never pointed the finger at Graham McLean if she believed he'd been at the farm that day.

'McLean could've claimed he'd come to see Ailsa but she wasn't around – we know she went out early to paint and was expected to be gone all day. That'd cover any chance sightings.'

'Probably thought it was too risky. And he already had an alibi from Bruce and Janice. But no one else in town saw him. Since the farm was so near the cliff path, it was assumed that the man Isobel saw was the unidentified walker. If McLean admitted to being there at any point, we might say they did meet, she rejected him, and he killed her in a fit of rage.'

'Good point.' When she'd first arrived, she'd marked out Ian Smith, the retired detective who'd returned as a civilian investigator, as probably the canniest of the bunch. He was proving her right.

'What about the art teacher?'

'The case against Jeremy Young was mostly hearsay, though his alibi was shaky too and these days, the way he behaved with his female students would definitely be seen as crossing the line.'

She remembered raising an eyebrow when she'd read the file – gifts of soft toys, artificial flowers and suggestively shaped cactus, which he'd claimed were all drawing assignments. The risqué nicknames – he'd dubbed Ailsa, *Angel Pie* – should've got him suspended if not sacked.

'Did you have much interaction with Graham McLean?'

'Oh aye. He tried to lodge a complaint against me. Said I'd been listening in to his chats with his solicitor. I'd denied him water. Said it infringed his rights.'

'And had you?'

'God, no. The custody sergeant was a stickler for procedure. Couldn't have, even if I'd wanted to. McLean was just throwing his weight around. Entitled. When his solicitor told him to calm down, I thought he was going to punch me.'

'Interesting. So, he's a man with a temper who reacts violently when he's denied what he wants. From the little I've seen, I don't think he's changed much.'

She'd thought Ian was a spy for her Super, or worse, for Graham McLean. She'd also thought there were no new witnesses she could speak to. She'd been wrong on both counts. There was a witness sitting right in front of her. The best kind. One from right inside the investigation itself.

'What are you going to do now?' Ian said. 'I'd really like to help. It feels like for most of my career, Ailsa Scott's murder has been unfinished business. You're a good cop, boss. I know the original investigation was flawed by an unwillingness to go up against local powerbrokers like the McLeans. Us working together will be the best chance of bringing her killer to justice.'

Shona scrutinised Ian's face for flattery, for guile, but saw only a man desperate to right a wrong that had haunted him and would go on haunting him for the rest of his life.

'I'm going up to Eastcraig Farm,' Shona said, evenly. 'When I come back, you and I are going to sit down and have a wee talk.'

Chapter 26

Shona let Jess drive. It was important that they informed Maggie and Anna before they heard about the charges against Midge being dropped from the media. The temperature was climbing as it had done yesterday, but there were ominous clouds out over the Irish Sea and a breeze that promised to deliver them to Galloway within the day.

Muir's mother's response was what she was dreading, partly because she knew it would be explosive but mostly because the woman was entirely justified in her opinion. They had messed up. Ultimately it had been the fiscal's decision to charge but Shona felt the failure keenly. And it was Shona and her team who'd have to face the aggrieved relatives, soak up whatever shock and disappointment they hurled at them, then dust themselves off and get back to work.

Dalrymple had offered sympathy when she'd called him, but she got the impression his only interest now lay in what she had to say about Ailsa Scott's killer. In the first moments of the call, she must've raised his hopes that there was some progress, only to dash them again.

'You all right, boss?' Jess said when they turned off the main road and began weaving through the narrow lanes bordered on all sides by farmland. Shona had been silent since they left Newton Stewart and she realised she'd neglected her role as SIO, which was to motivate and support her team as much as to guide the investigation.

'Yes thanks, Jess. I'm just wondering how Maggie Maxwell is going to take this.'

'Much of her anger will be because she's scared. They've lost a crucial member of the farm team, as well as the personal bereavement.'

Jess pulled over onto the verge to let a Land Rover hauling a trailer full of sheep pass.

'I meant to ask, are you still planning to go home this weekend?' Shona said.

'I am, if that's okay?' Jess rolled her eyes. 'You'd never believe the fuss my brothers, Drew and Ben, can make over the smallest decision.'

'It's fine. You go. Don't your brothers get on?'

'Oh, well enough. Most of the time they're thick as thieves, but, like any siblings, they argue about trivial stuff.'

Shona, having grown up an only child in her grandmother's care, always felt a twinge of discomfort when people assumed she'd know exactly what that meant. Up ahead, Shona saw the Belted Galloways and realised they were nearly there.

'What sort of stuff did they argue about?'

'Chores mostly. Who'd do the mucky stuff. Whose job it was to cut the hedges. They'd defend each other to the death, but I've seen them come to blows over whose turn it was to wash the tractor. My mother tells them she's getting me home to sort them out, and it's mostly all over before I arrive. I'm the oldest, see. You know there's a line your parents won't cross, but with your big sister coming at you, all bets are off.'

They pulled into Eastcraig, wheels kicking up dust from the gravelled parking area.

'So, d'you think domestic violence is something we should spotlight in our rural crime strategy?' Jess said. 'You mentioned one of the aims of your secondment was to expand our engagement outside urban areas.'

'What?'

'Domestic violence. Rural crime,' Jess said.

'Oh, yeah. Yeah. Good idea.'

'Was there anything other than Muir's bruised knuckles that made you think it was an issue with the Maxwells?'

Shona scrolled back through her memory to the interview with Maggie and Anna.

'Muir's brother, John, said they'd ongoing aggro with wild campers. But when I asked Maggie and Muir's wife, they couldn't remember any incidents with campers.' Shona paused. 'And there was a look that passed between them too. It made me think there was something that they weren't saying.'

'There's two wee girls, isn't there?'

'There is,' Shona said. If there had been domestic violence, Muir's death put an end to any threat, though Jess was right in thinking the family might need additional support. Across at the kennels, she heard the dogs bark and the sound of hammering was coming from the thirty-metre-long shed where the tractors and quad bikes were stored.

Up here, it felt fresher, not so claustrophobically hot. As she got out of the car, the breeze raised goosebumps on her arms, but it also raised her spirits a little. Across a hillside cloaked in summer green, Billy with a feed bag in hand and a couple of Border Collies close by, was leading the girls – six-year-old Olivia and five-year-old Ava – among this year's crop of lambs. Even from this distance, Shona could hear the girls' squeals of delight. He must've noticed the car arrive for he turned and gave Shona a wave. Here was a glimpse of the future of Eastcraig, resting as much on the next generation of Maxwells, as it did on the bloodlines of the animals all around her.

'Nice set up,' Jess said, surveying the buildings and the Belted Galloway cattle with their calves. 'That the butchery operation?' she said, pointing to the metal shipping container as they crossed the yard to the farmhouse.

Shona was about to quip that maybe Jess should keep her voice down in front of the mammies and their bairns, when she saw Maggie.

'Mrs Maxwell, Maggie, this is DC Jess Johnstone. I wanted to come and introduce her. She'll be your family liaison officer for the remainder of the case. She'll be able to answer any questions you have.'

Maggie stood on the threshold of the kitchen door with folded arms, her posture one big frown. It was impossible to tell if she'd already heard the news about Midge as this seemed to be her habitual greeting. Behind her, in the kitchen itself, Shona saw Anna in an apron, with her hair tied up, standing over a food mixer.

As Jess and Shona walked towards her, Maggie never took her eyes off them, stepping backwards into the kitchen only when they reached the door.

'Hello, Maggie, may we come in?' Shona said.

Maggie nodded. Anna switched off the mixer and gave them a cautious nod of welcome.

'Out wi' it then,' Maggie said. 'I can see from yer faces it's no' good news.'

'Maggie, Anna, would you like to sit down?' Jess said.

'Ma son is already dead, the other is in the shed for all the good he is, and the tow wee lassies are out wi' Billy. There's nothing ye can tell me that needs a chair.'

It looked as if Anna was of a different opinion. She stared from one officer to the other and back again, her face as white as the flour she was mixing. 'What is it? Tell me.'

Jess went past Maggie to Anna's side, resting her hand gently under the woman's elbow in case she should need physical support. Shona thought Anna, slim as she was, had lost weight in the days since she'd last seen her up at Moine Farm. There were dark circles under her eyes. Tiny flurries of flour fell from her hands like snow, and she held them tightly together in a futile attempt to stop the trembling.

Maggie had made it clear she despised any attempt to cushion the blow. Best then that Shona got it over with.

'I'm sorry to have to tell you both that the charges against Midge Elliot for the murder of Muir are being withdrawn.'

Anna let go a great sob, as if she'd been punched, her legs going from under her. Jess manoeuvred her back to a stool which she'd pulled out from under the kitchen countertop. Maggie stared blankly ahead as if she'd been turned to stone.

It wasn't the reaction Shona had expected from Maggie. If anything, this near-catatonic state was more worrying than any outburst.

Jess indicated with her eyes that Shona should switch the kettle on.

'We'll have some tea, yes,' Jess said. It wasn't a question.

Shona flicked the switch and stepped forward to touched Maggie's hand. Despite the overpowering heat of the day, the flesh was ice cold. The action seemed to bring Maggie back to life. She jerked her hand away and glared at Shona.

'Is that a' you've got tae say for yoursel?' she shouted. 'Coming here, makin us relive it a' again. Polis everywhere an' it's a' for nothin?'

Anna's eyes were squeezed shut, her hands clamped over her ears. Jess wedged her firmly against the corner of the worktop.

'We will catch who did this, Maggie,' Shona said, her voice firm and her face calm, though her heart rate had leapt.

The woman took a step towards her, her face twisted with grief and anger and brandished a fist in Shona's face.

Jess crossed the kitchen in two strides. 'Calm yourself down, Maggie. It's only you that stands between this farm and disaster. You'll not let your granddaughters suffer that, will you?' Maggie blinked at her. 'Now you take Anna through to the wee parlour there. We'll sit down, have some tea, and DI Oliver here will tell you what's got to happen next. We're not about to abandon you. We'll see you through this.'

Maggie stood defiant for a moment, but somewhere inside the fire had been quenched. She nodded, then gathered up her daughter-in-law and took her through to a small conservatory off the kitchen. She set her down in a cane armchair, surrounded by wellies, dog leads and cast-off jackets and together they both wept.

'We'll give them a minute,' Jess said quietly.

'I thought she was going to clock me one,' Shona said under her breath.

'I thought she was too,' Jess replied.

'Jeezo, I wonder if there's any brandy in the house?'

'D'you think it safe to give them alcohol?'

'I was thinking more for me,' Shona replied.

Chapter 27

While Jess made the tea, the two girls came skipping in, stopping short when they saw their mother and grandmother weren't alone. Jess gave them a biscuit and a glass of milk each and they escaped into the front room. Moments later, the sound of cartoons on the TV drifted through.

Shona went out to the shed to fetch John Maxwell, since he had a right to hear what had happened, and she'd rather not explain it twice. The hammering had stopped but she could hear a radio on somewhere. She followed the sound and saw John sitting on a bale of straw with his back towards her. He had his arm around one of the Border Collies, his face burrowed in the fur of its neck. The dog met her eye but didn't move. It only took a moment for Shona to see John Maxwell was crying.

For a moment she wasn't sure what to do. Half an hour would make no difference to what she had to say. Shona turned and walked quietly from the shed.

-

When it was time to call John in, Shona sent Jess. It wasn't an act of cowardice. It was why they had family liaison officers in the first place. Jess's role was to act as a bridge between the Maxwells and the investigation, and Shona thought she'd never seen an officer more suited to a particular case than the investigation they found themselves in now.

When they were all seated around the kitchen table, Shona said, 'There was something that came up at the postmortem that I need to ask you about. Muir had injuries to his hands, likely from being in a fight. Have you any idea how he came by them?'

John and Anna shook their heads. Maggie just glared at Shona.

'These campers? Are you sure you don't remember anything about them? Could one of the confrontations have happened in the days before he died?'

When there were shakes of the head, Shona said, 'I have to ask you. Were Muir's injuries the result of domestic violence?'

Maggie scoffed. 'So now our Muir wis a wife-beater? You saw whit happened? How is that domestic violence?'

'We saw what happened, but not why,' Shona said gently.

'Thought it was a crime gang stealing machinery?' John frowned. 'Theft. You said so.'

'What about drugs?' Shona began. There'd been no narcotic substances identified in the PM screening, but that rarely told the whole story. Smart dealers didn't touch their own merchandise.

Maggie gave out a shriek.

Anna flinched, practically jumping out of her chair.

'So, my son was a junkie now n'all.'

'I'm just ruling out lines of enquiry.'

'Clutching at straws, more like,' Maggie spat.

'Look,' John said, putting out a hand to quieten his mother, which was swiftly batted away. 'That doesnae make sense. It was a theft. Cannae be anythin' else. Muir hadnae came oot the hoose…'

'Oh look, for God sake. Just tell them,' Anna burst out. When everyone turned to stare at her, she said, 'Muir was in a fight the day before he died. A brawl in the pub.' She turned to Maggie. 'That was your precious son. That was who he was.'

Maggie looked pale and shocked. Shona reckoned it wasn't what was being said, but who was saying it that was the biggest upset.

'A company used one of our buildings for storage,' Anna went on, 'then didn't pay us. I wanted to take them to court, but Muir insisted he could sort it out himself.'

'Why didn't you tell us this before?' Shona said, frowning.

'I didn't think it mattered,' Anna insisted. 'We only tried it once. Just storing plumbing supplies. It was one of our diversification threads that we didn't pursue. More bother than it was worth. If I told you he'd gone after someone who owed us money, that he'd been in a fight, you'd have thought he brought it on himself, and he didn't. I don't see what it has to do with Muir being murdered in that awful way.'

But Shona could see. A bad debt with the wrong kind of people. Tempers on both sides running high and it could quickly turn violent.

Shona looked from John to Maggie and back again. 'Just plumbing supplies? Nothing else? Either of you know anything about this?'

'It wasnae drugs if that's wit yer saying,' Maggie growled. 'I knew there'd been an argument, but no' who it wis with.'

John just shook his head.

Shona turned back to Anna. 'Do you know where this fight happened?'

Anna nodded miserably. 'In the White Horse in Glenrock. But he wouldn't tell me who the fight was with.'

The pub was likely covered by CCTV. If this was the dispute that led to Muir's murder, there might even be images of the vehicle, complete with index number.

Shona caught Jess's eye and signalled it was time to go.

On the doorstep, once they'd said their goodbyes. Maggie took Shona's arm and drew her aside. If Shona had expected an apology she was disappointed.

'Dinnae come back until you're sure you've got them. I dinnae want tae end up like Ailsa Scott's parents. Aye, you know what I'm talkin aboot. Constantly in the papers and on TV. Lost their farm, lost everything.'

'Did you know the Scott family?'

'Aye, and I kenned those two lassies. Chalk 'n' cheese they were. Forty years ago this month.'

'What d'you mean?' Shona frowned, but Maggie just waved her away.

'Dinnae come back tae you find my son's murderer. Got nothin' else tae say to ye.'

-

As they drove down the lane from the farm, the clouds obscured the coast, and fat raindrops began to splatter on the windscreen.

'Let's head over to Glenrock and see if they've any useful CCTV at the pub.'

'Do you think there is a connection to Muir's death?'

'Maybe,' Shona replied. 'Right from the start, everything about the murder has been overdone. You'd have to really hate someone to run over them repeatedly like that, yet Muir doesn't seem to have confided in his wife, brother or mother, despite the fact they all live so closely. What's your assessment of the family dynamics?'

Jess blew out her cheeks. 'Both women denied domestic violence. But today when Maggie came at you, I wondered if it was a reaction to years of powerlessness and fear.'

'Anna didn't seem surprised or shocked at her mother-in-law's outburst. She went straight to duck and cover.'

'Maybe because she'd seen it before,' Jess replied. 'It could recall childhood trauma, not necessarily anything recent. D'you think there is a connection to Midge Elliot's drug operation?'

'I'm not ruling it out, but none of the Maxwells have any previous. And despite what Anna said about the storage business not working for them, the farm is doing well, so what was the incentive to get mixed up in something like that.'

Jess nodded. 'Doesn't seem worth the risk.'

'What did Maggie mean about John?' Shona went on. '*The other is in the byre for all the good he is.* From her tone, I don't think it was a joke.'

'Muir was the favourite child, no doubt about that,' Jess said, overtaking a campervan that had stopped in a passing place.

'How do you know that?' Shona said, genuinely intrigued. 'Is there a favourite child in your family?'

'It's me, of course,' Jess joked. 'Naw, for my da it's me, only daughter, following in his footsteps by joining the police. For my mother, it's definitely Ben. He's the youngest. That's usually the way it works with mothers.'

By that logic, I should be the favourite, Shona thought. What if I am? The way she treated me, God help the other two. Her husband Rob was definitely his mother's favourite. The golden child. Everything he wanted, he got. That road led to HMP Brixton, so it didn't work out so well for him either.

'What d'you think this tells us, in terms of the case?' Shona said.

'Well, from what you said about John in the shed, and the way Maggie talks about him, I'd say he grew up idolising his older brother and being the scapegoat for his mother. Muir protected him like a second father, and now he's lost that and the full weight of the farm has fallen to him, giving Maggie even more opportunities to criticise him. In fact, he might be the one who needs the most support of all three of them. Don't want him getting to the stage where he feels he has no options left, like his father did.'

The rain was pounding the windscreen in earnest now, blurring the fields and hawthorn hedges, recognisable only for fractions of a second between the sweep of the wipers. The same features, but each a subtly new permutation of the old. It was what Shona had to do now. Assemble all the elements of the case in every possible combination until the answer emerged like the sun behind the clouds and illuminated the truth.

-

When they arrived at the pub it was a squat, old-fashioned building painted white with window frames picked out in blue. Its carpark was huge, but Shona had already spotted two cameras covering the main areas. She prayed Muir and his defaulting business associate hadn't gone off anywhere more secluded.

The landlady, a stylish woman in her sixties, greeted Shona and Jess with a smile as they came through the door, immediately picking them out as non-locals.

'What can I get you, ladies?'

Shona flicked out her warrant card. 'DI Shona Oliver from Galloway CID. I'd like to have a look at your CCTV.'

The woman eyed them and Shona thought she was going to demand a warrant, but after a minute of scrutiny, she said, 'I'm the landlady, Moira Brown. This about the fight?'

'How did you know?' Shona replied.

'I've been here ten years. Never had a sniff of trouble till ten days ago when the Chuckle Brothers decided to have a square go in my carpark.'

'What happened?' Shona said.

'See for yourself.' Moira inclined her head to the end of the bar and showed Shona into a cramped room with two TV monitors stacked on top of each other. Each had its screen bisected and showed two views from inside the pub, and two outside. Moira shuffled through a stack of files on a third screen on a laptop. 'There you go, ladies.' She set the video rolling and stepped back out of the way. Two evenly matched figures stumbled into shot, each having hold of the other's clothing. The taller of the two, immediately recognisable as Muir Maxwell, grabbed his companion's polo shirt and landed a punch on his jaw. Both men went down, scrabbling for control until polo shirt managed to get to his feet first, just as Moira could be heard yelling that she'd called the polis. Muir was up now too and they exited on either side of the frame. Muir had his hand to his face, but polo shirt looked straight into the lens.

She'd only met him once, and on that occasion he'd been wearing a suit.

'You know him, boss?' Jess said.

'I certainly do.' She touched the frozen frame gently with her pen. 'Unless I'm very much mistaken that is Bruce Campbell.'

Bruce Campbell. Petty thief. Arsonist. Voyeur. Torturer of animals, one of the prime suspects in a forty-year-old murder case. About to discover he's the prime suspect in another.

Chapter 28

The unrelenting cloudburst forced Jess to slow down. Back on the A75 things weren't much better, the spray from lorries creating a thick haze that reduced visibility to a few metres. On a long straight, Shona saw the outline of two cars hitched up onto the verge. It looked like a breakdown or perhaps a minor shunt, yet the rear car, a blue VW Golf, didn't have its hazards on.

As they grew nearer she could see two figures who appeared to be struggling with each other. Closer still, she realised it was a man in shorts and a T-shirt and a woman in a long print dress.

Jess was already slowing, alerted by the cars' precarious position on the single carriageway with no hard shoulder.

'Pull in, Jess. And get backup.'

Shona was out of the passenger side as her DC got on the phone. The grass verge was slippery and uneven. The man was grasping the woman around the neck while she tried to push him away. Shona couldn't see a weapon, but there was a real danger both would stumble out into the busy road.

'Hey,' she yelled at the two figures. 'Stop. Police. Let her go.'

Jess was coming up on Shona's right in an attempt to prevent the struggling figure reaching the road. Lorries thundered past sending thick curtains of spray over them.

An image flashed through Shona's mind. Kyle Wilson witnessing the man he'd just detained crushed beneath their wheels. The mental scars he still carried. That wasn't going to happen here if she could help it.

'Let her go,' Shona shouted again, coming up behind the man and grabbing his collar, to both choke and destabilise him. He staggard backwards, releasing his grip as the momentum and his victim's weight began to topple him.

At the same time, Jess had reached the woman, dragging her away from both her attacker and the roaring traffic, before looking back to check on her boss.

Shona had him on his back, her knee pressing into the joint of one shoulder, his other arm pinned down where she gripped it. She reckoned he must be in his early sixties but fit.

'Lie still,' Shona yelled. 'Show me your hands.'

She'd primed herself for more of a struggle, but once he hit the grass the fight seemed to go out of him. He did as he was told. Keeping the pressure on him, Shona scanned the surrounding area for any dropped knife or other weapon, but the long summer grass made it impossible to be sure. She couldn't see any blood on either the man or the woman, but with rain this heavy it was hard to make an accurate assessment. It looked as if the blue VW Golf had rear-ended the silver Honda, though she couldn't tell who owned which car.

'What's your name?' Shona said. The man had his face turned to the sky, longish grey-blonde hair plastered across his forehead. His eyes were closed as the rain ran down his cheeks, but she knew better than to relax her grip on him.

'Okay, boss?' Jess had pressed the woman up against one of the cars, holding her by the shoulders.

'Get her in the car. And get my cuffs,' Shona shouted back. 'What's your name?'

'You've got this wrong,' he said. 'She's my wife.'

'That how you normally treat your wife?' Shona said. 'Name?'

But he didn't answer, his jaw clenched as he shook his head. 'Let me go. I haven't done anything.'

She could feel the tension returning to his muscles. The shock of his detainment had ebbed and he was starting to struggle again.

Her own soaking hair had fallen across her face. She tried to shake it away but it was stuck fast, obscuring her vision. She dug her knee into his shoulder and was rewarded by a yelp of pain, just as Jess arrived with the handcuffs. Together they rolled him over onto his front and cuffed him.

'I'm arresting you for breach of the peace,' Shona said, then cautioned him. It would keep him in custody till they heard from the victim the full story of what had happened.

'Is she okay?' Shona said, getting to her feet.

Jess nodded. 'She's shaken up but just cuts and bruises.'

'Did she say what happened?'

'Can't get much out of her, but she definitely knows this fella.'

Just then they saw the blue lights of an approaching patrol car. Shona pushed back her hair from her face squeezing out the water, even while she knew it was a futile gesture. Her pink cotton blouse was sticking to her and her linen trousers were covered in mud and grass. Jess had fared better, but together they hardly represented the professional face of modern policing.

Together they hauled the man to his feet and began marching him along the verge to where the uniform unit had pulled up behind Jess's vehicle. Two cops came and relieved them of their charge. It was only when they backed him against the patrol car to search him, that Shona got a clear view of who they'd arrested.

'What name did the woman give?' Shona said.

'Alison Young. D'you know her?'

'No, we've never met. But I know him. His name's Jeremy Young. And he's not been returning my calls. Dalrymple introduced me when I arrived. Runs a community arts programme helping *at risk youth foster good relations with the police and other authority figures*.'

'Needs to work on that, doesn't he.'

It was on the tip of Shona's tongue to tell Jess that forty years ago he'd also been in the frame for the murder of Ailsa Scott. Instead, she said, 'Can you give uniform an update on what happened while I have the word with Mrs Young?'

'Sure, boss.'

A second patrol car had arrived. They'd need officers at the scene to manage the traffic until they could tow the two cars. Paramedics were already on their way. Shona wanted a quiet chat with the woman before she went off to hospital for further checks. It wasn't strictly by the book – the traffic cops should be getting a first account from the victim now – but Shona had the sense that fate had dropped this opportunity in her lap and she'd be a fool not to take it.

Shona got in the back seat of Jess's car and introduced herself.

'Are you okay to talk for a minute?'

The woman was smoothing down her ruined dress. The rain had flattened her dyed brown hair, showing the grey at the roots. Shona reached into the front seat for her handbag and pulled out a packet of paper tissues. She handed a couple to Alison, and began dabbing herself down with another, smiling ironically at the futility of the operation. It was enough to break the ice. Alison Young smiled back.

'D'you want to tell me what happened?' Shona said.

Alison's response was halfway between a sigh and a sob. 'I've finally left him, and he didn't like it. I was on my way to my parents. They're in their eighties. Goodness knows what it'll do to them to see me like this.'

'Don't worry. We'll make sure you get cleaned up.'

'I didn't know he was following me until the car ran into me. Then I saw it was him. I just think he was trying to stop me. I don't think he meant any harm.'

Shona was sure he had meant her harm but kept it from showing on her face.

'What'll happen now?' Alison looked fearful, as if it was somehow all her fault and she was already preparing herself for the anticipated retribution.

Shona sidestepped the question. 'Why were you leaving? Were you worried about your safety?'

'Oh no.' Alison looked shocked at the suggestion. 'He's never been violent. He just wanted to talk to me, but when I tried to get back in the car he wouldn't let me.'

'It looked very much like violence when we pulled up.'

'It's frustration.' She fixed Shona with a weary stare. 'He's getting old and he doesn't like it.'

'I met your husband recently. I've been leaving messages for him, but he never calls me back. We met at a police community partnership get-together. He told me you'd moved back here so you could support your parents, and for the arts project.'

'I did want to come back for my parents, but the arts project was an afterthought.' She sighed. 'We left because Jeremy got a seventeen-year-old girl he was teaching pregnant. She had a termination. The school never knew the details and he opted to retire before they found out. It would probably have been the same outcome if they had. Anything to avoid a scandal. In the end, Jeremy paid the lassie off with a car. The odd thing was, I found I was disappointed she'd settled for so little.'

It certainly fitted with what Shona knew about Jem Young. What angered her most of all was the chances missed to hold him accountable for his behaviour. For four decades, he'd prayed on vulnerable young women. Those in authority had known, but they'd actively chosen not to act.

'I see,' Shona said. 'I'm sorry you had to go through that.'

'So am I.' Alison looked and sounded exhausted.

Ahead of them, two constables were looking over Alison's car assessing the damage. One tried the boot, which had been badly dented and wouldn't open.

Behind them, the patrol car carrying her husband pulled out and headed east towards Newton Stewart Police Office. Shona hadn't consciously been waiting for it to leave, but she saw Alison's posture relax a little and knew she had felt constrained by her husband's proximity.

'There's something else I need to ask you.' Shona paused. None of what they'd discussed would hold up in court. What she needed now was an honest answer from Alison. She'd find other ways to make it stick. 'It's about Ailsa Scott.'

There was a flash of something in Alison's eyes. Anger? Fear? Shona couldn't tell what for sure. Alison turned away, her gaze on the road ahead. The rain had stopped though there was enough water still lying on the road for the passing cars to throw up rainbows of spray. The silence stretched between them. Just when Shona thought she'd gambled and lost, Alison turned back to her.

'What do you want to know?' she said quietly.

'You gave your husband an alibi on the day of Ailsa's murder. You said he was with you at home. There was no one else who could verify that.'

'Ever since we came back, I've been waiting for someone to ask me that.' Alison's shoulders fell and she put a hand to her mouth for a moment, steadying herself. When she looked up again there were tears in her eyes.

Shona felt a fluttering in her stomach as the seconds dragged on. All she needed was a nod and she'd find the evidence. Any trial probably wouldn't be until after Isobel Dalrymple's death, but the knowledge that justice was speeding towards Ailsa and couldn't now be stopped might be enough for the Dalrymples.

'Did I give my husband a false alibi?' Alison repeated, swallowing hard. 'I'm sorry to say I didn't.'

For a moment, Shona thought she'd misheard. 'You're saying he was with you that day?'

Alison nodded. 'I'm afraid so. Many times, I have wondered if I'd just said he wasn't with me, how different my life would've been. I'd have saved all those girls the pain and heartache he brought them.'

Shona looked down at her hands still clutching the tissue she'd shredded in the expectancy of a confession from Alison. The constables had given up on trying to open the boot of Alison's car and were lifting bags from the rear passenger door.

'You could've lied and he might've still got off,' Shona said, eventually. 'And if he had been falsely convicted, you'd have left a monster out there to kill other women. So, hard as it may have felt, you did the right thing.'

Jess was standing at the front of the car, behind her the haze of rainbows glowed. Her navy-blue top had deepened to black by the rain, and her long dark hair was loose and drying in the sun. She turned her piercing gaze on Alison and seemed to understand there was more at play here than a marital dispute. Not for the first time, Shona thought there was something otherworldly about her detective constable. She came around to the passenger side and opened Alison's door.

'Mrs Young, we've a squad car ready to take you up to your parents. We've managed to get your bags out of your car. There's a petrol station just up the road. We can stop and let you get cleaned up.'

'What will happen to Jeremy now?' Alison asked Shona.

'He'll be processed at Newton Stewart.'

'Will I have to press charges?'

Shona considered. 'We'll be doing that. Dangerous driving, breach of the peace, assault, there'll be quite a charge sheet. You may be called as a witness, but frankly, attacking your wife on the public highway in front of two police officers will be enough to be going on with. And if you ever feel unsafe, call us.'

It hadn't been the conversation she'd expected, or wished for, but it removed one suspect from her list for Ailsa's murder. Graham McLean and Bruce Campbell had remained stubbornly at the top and cracking their alibi would be the most difficult, and she wouldn't be this lucky again. Bruce Campbell's wife, Janice, had stuck to her story they were both with her for forty years and Shona couldn't see why she would change it now.

Shona got out of the car and tried to tidy her appearance, shaking out her hair, which had become a mass of wavy curls, rather than the straightened bob she'd set out with this morning. The mud stains on her trousers wouldn't budge, but her pink shirt was drying quickly. Jess came back from the patrol car, and together they watched Alison Young being driven away. Shona had a sense it was into an unknown but certainly safer future.

Chapter 29

When they got back, Shona washed off the mud, changed into the spare clothes she kept in the boot of the Audi, and reapplied her make-up, all while eating a sandwich since she'd missed lunch by a mile. In Shona and Jess's absence, the final forensics from the garage had come through, along with two DNA hits flagged. Peter Christopher Lynch and Niall James Cawardine, both small-time dealers in Ayr, fifty miles further up the west coast, had been detained by local cops. McCulloch had travelled up with Kyle to question them, but they'd gone no comment. McCulloch texted that the local DI would extend their detention by another twelve hours if necessary, and he'd call her later once the initial search on their homes had been done.

'Okay,' Shona said as she stood in front of the whiteboard. 'Muir Maxwell's wife Anna has just told us he was in a fight over an unpaid bill the night before his murder.'

Shona had given Erin a memory stick containing the video file from the pub, and now she had a blown-up still of a tall man in his fifties with prominent cheekbones and receding dark hair.

'This is Bruce Campbell. He runs a plumbing business and is a close associate of Graham McLean, Midge Elliot's erstwhile employer.'

'D'you still think McLean is behind this somehow, boss?' Jess said.

'The way his company dragged their feet on the van… maybe he was helping his mate Campbell out. His premises aren't too far from McLean's.'

'Is Campbell a physical match for either of the assailants?'

Erin ran the footage from the pub, then the farm CCTV.

'He's tall enough,' Jess offered.

'What I can't understand,' Erin said, 'is why we haven't picked the van up on CCTV anywhere near the farm, going in or out, other than the one on the barn.'

'Where's the nearest camera?' Jess asked.

'About half a mile away.'

'They came in the front gate,' Ian said, 'which I understand wasn't closed at night. It's the quickest access. But you also pass close to the farmhouse, and its camera.'

'And the dogs,' Jess added. 'But they left by the field track.'

Shona frowned. There was something out of alignment with the evidence they had, but she couldn't put her finger on it.

'The field track is rough,' Shona said, 'and it was dark, so it's slower and riskier.'

'Which also points to planning,' Jess said. 'Or local knowledge.'

'So, first thing we need is a further appeal to the public and a sweep of properties. Are there any CCTV sources we've overlooked. Get the press office onto that. But I also want backroad routes and tracks. Erin can you digitally plot us some search routes?'

'How far out from Eastcraig?'

Shona crossed to the map pinned on the wall, tracing her finger across the interconnecting lines of backroad.

'Forget the area between the farm and the A75. If they're avoiding traffic cams they'll be smart enough not to head for a main road.' Where were they going? Either they had a base in the area or they were heading out. 'I want a sweep towards Stranraer. Stop when you get to the first of our cameras. Houses, pubs, garages, shops, industrial estates. Appeals for doorbell cams. It's July. Folk could've been away on holiday and just got back. And I want a sweep in the other direction. Same thing.' It was more rural, more sparsely populated, but that might mean strangers sleeping in their van or renting out a caravan were less likely to go unnoticed.

'I was thinking,' Jess said. 'If we're talking planning, then d'you think it's possible the thieves did what we thought Midge Elliot did?'

'You mean scope the place out on an open day? It's possible. But if Bruce Campbell or his guys are behind this, then they already know the layout of the farm from storing stuff there. But it'll strengthen our case if we find premeditation.'

'I'll ask Anna if they've any footage from a month back we can go through.'

Shona was gratified to see no one looked downcast at the prospect. She folded her arms, then cupped her chin in her hand as she paced before the whiteboard.

'We should rule out the county line campers. That needs another look.' Maybe that's what was bugging her. 'John Maxwell said there was a bothy further along the Southern Upland Way, off their land, that they "encouraged" troublesome hikers to use. Jess? Any thoughts?'

Her DC was the expert, part of the Police Mountain Rescue team. She'd gone out during her time in Highland division to look for missing walkers and had now settled in with their southern counterparts.

'It's something walkers might warn each other about. An unfriendly farmer or lads causing trouble,' she conceded. 'And bothies have visitor books. Has anyone been up to check this one?'

Shona looked at Erin and Ian.

'Can't recall that as an action,' Ian admitted.

'Can I leave that to you, Jess?'

'Sure, boss. Do you still want a search team out at the farm checking the van's exit route?' Shona consulted her watch. It was getting late and she felt she'd worn out her welcome a bit with uniform, and a weekend overtime bill would be considerable.

'Stand them down. Let's concentrate on Bruce Campbell and the wild campers for now. When are you off home, Jess?'

'I can go to the bothy tonight, and see who's there, before I go.'

'That'd be great, thanks everyone.' As the briefing broke up, she added, 'Ian? Can I have a word?'

When they'd gone into her office and closed the door, she updated him on her encounter with Alison Young and her confirmation of her husband Jem's alibi.

Ian leaned forward, elbows on his knees. 'Do you believe her? I mean the way he behaved today puts him more in the frame for Ailsa Scott's murder, not less.'

'That's just it,' Shona said. 'I think if she could drop him in it, she would. She almost regrets that it wasn't him, that he wasn't caught and locked up forty years ago. I think there's no doubt she enabled him in many ways and she sees it now and it's eating her up.'

'Okay, so what now?'

'I had Jess phone Bruce Campbell's office and he's not been in for a few days. I'm gonna put out a general alert on him. Can you get me all the index numbers of vehicles registered to him?'

'There is one place he might go we haven't tried,' Ian said. 'What about his wife's work. He used her for an alibi once and it worked. Why not this time?'

'Good call.' Shona went to the door and yelled, 'Hang on, Jess. I need you to come with me first.'

Then she looked at Ian. 'C'mon then, since it was your idea.'

-

Janice Campbell's hairdressers was in a prime spot in Newton Stewart's main street. The sign on the door said closed but when Shona tapped the glass Janice herself pulled back the blind and frowned. Her hair was a perfect up-do and the make-up looked freshly applied. She eyed Shona, Jess and Ian. After a moment's consideration she unlatched the door and stuck her head out.

'I ken who you are, so let's keep this short and sweet. What'd you want?'

'I was hoping for a wash and blow dry and perhaps a little chat.'

'Sorry. No can do.'

'Is that the hair or the chat?'

'Both, where you're concerned.'

'Why won't you talk to me Janice? I can help you out of this mess.'

'What mess is that? I know that you're sniffing around my Bruce and Graham McLean's too. You cannae keep anythin' quiet here. Think you're the first to come after me? If it's no' the cops, it's the papers offering me cash tae come clean. I've got nothing tae say because there is nothing to say about Ailsa Scott. Graham is better off without her, but it doesn't mean he killed her. It doesn't mean Bruce killed her, and the sooner you get that into your heads then the sooner you can get out there and look for the real killer.'

With that, she attempted to slam the door, but Shona got her foot in quick.

'Where is he Janice? This is not like last time. There's CCTV of Bruce knocking Muir Maxwell about. Next day he's dead. And I've got some questions for him.'

Jess was moving past Shona while Ian stayed by the main door.

'Where is he, Janice?' When again there was no reply, other than a stoney stare, Shona muttered, 'Bet your clients don't leave many tips.'

Suddenly, a curtain at the back was pushed aside and a tall figure stepped out. 'It's all right, Jan. I've got nothing to hide.' He held out his wrists and Jess cuffed him.

Shona's phone rang. She groaned when she saw the Super's name. He'd warned her about the cold case and she'd ignored him, bringing Jim Smith on board to compound the defiance. She stepped away, out of Jess and the Campbells' hearing.

'DI Oliver,' he said. 'I need a word with you.'

Shit. Her only option now was to throw herself on his over-stretched mercy.

'Yes, sir. I know what this is about. I understand the priorities and I'm happy to step back.'

'You are? Well, that's excellent news and much appreciated. I'll tell DCI Stephensen he can pick up Lynch and Cawardine and bring them to Kilmarnock. It makes sense to combine all the drug operations under one team. We'll be questioning Midge Elliot again as well, but I'm sure anything relevant to Galloway will be shared. DS McCulloch and DC Wilson will be back with you soon. I'm expecting a quick result on the Maxwell murder, Shona. Don't let me down.'

Shona stared at the screen. What had just happened?

'We've been pulled,' she said to Ian, who'd joined her and was studying her reaction for clues.

'From Ailsa Scott?' he murmured.

'No, from the Midge Elliot drug operation.' She had to admit it would take the pressure off them. Midge Elliot's phone still hadn't turned up, and she was beginning to think his tale of losing it was the one bit of truth that'd come out of him. Well, that was someone else's problem now.

When her phone rang again, she knew who it was without seeing the name. McCulloch's voice was an angry growl.

'I've just heard,' she said. 'I'm so sorry. There's nothing we can do. But things are moving in the Muir Maxwell case. I need you back here, George. Quick as you can.'

Chapter 30

Not long after Shona got back to the police office, Bruce Campbell's lawyer turned up with Graham McLean in tow. At reception McLean stared at Shona as if he was ready to tear her head off but said nothing. In return, Shona glared back, convinced he understood her message – take a good look, cos it'll be me putting you both in the jail.

Campbell appeared calm, only the slight nervous tapping of one foot gave away any anxiety. But Shona didn't underestimate how tough a suspect he'd be to crack. He may look like a respectable businessman now, but Dalrymple's notes in Ailsa's case file told a different story. Junior crimes – some pursued, some not. Arson. Petty theft. Voyeurism. Animal cruelty.

The lawyer was from Connelly, Repton and James, a firm happy to be a constant thorn in the side of Police Scotland's Greater Glasgow Division but also willing to branch out. McLean must be paying them a packet to make the two-hour trip to Galloway but then there was a lot at stake. His own and his pal's liberty for a start.

'Shall we get on?' said Gus Connelly, a patrician whose senior partner status obviously didn't rest purely on the alphabetical. 'I'd like to get my client home as soon as possible to his family.'

As far as Shona was concerned, that was Jan and a couple of Jack Russells who'd probably relish more space on the sofa. A glance at McCulloch's face told her he wasn't about to be pushed around by some fancy Glasgow brief either.

'We'll be sure to do what we can,' Shona replied. 'If you'd both like to come this way.'

Once they were settled in the interview room, Shona said, 'Did you arrange to meet Muir Maxwell in the White Horse in Glenrock?'

'No. It's my local. I don't make a secret about it.'

'That's a nasty bruise on your jaw, Mr Campbell. Can you tell me how that came about?'

'You know how it happened. Muir Maxwell threw a punch at me.'

'So, he was the aggressor? You didn't start it?'

'Course not.'

'That must have upset you. I've some pathology photos of Mr Maxwell's hands that would fit that bruise pattern to a T.' Shona placed the pictures on the table. Despite Campbell's gruff façade, she saw him flinch. 'Is that why you killed him? Ran him over, then reversed to make sure, in front of his elderly mother, to pay him back for what he did to you?'

'No, I didn't,' Campbell said, the colour that had drained from his face returning to flush his cheeks. 'And if Muir Maxwell was still alive he'd be facing an assault charge, and probably fraud as well.'

Beside Shona, McCulloch shifted in his seat. What had they missed? They'd seen the books for Eastcraig. Jess, with her particular experience of what farm accounts should look like, had also gone over them with a fine-tooth comb. There wasn't a lamb or a bale of straw unaccounted for.

'Care to explain that?' Shona said, her interest quickening. Campbell was building the case for them. If he had another reason to feel aggrieved by Muir Maxwell, then so much the better.

Campbell shot a look at his lawyer, who nodded for him to go ahead.

'I like to support local businesses,' he said, pompously, a line he'd surely picked up from his pal McLean. 'But there was damage to the stores at Eastcraig Farm. Boxes opened, bits missing. No way was I paying Maxwell after that.'

'And you blamed Muir?'

'Who else would it have been?'

Shona stared at him in disbelief. 'Did you not check with the courier?'

'It was my guys who took the stuff up there.'

'And you don't think they may have been skimming stuff to do jobs for family and friends?'

'They said they didn't.'

'And you believed them?'

'Aye. I did. They've been working for me for years.'

Shona shook her head. 'Wasn't it the case that you saw a way of getting out of paying *a local business* what you owed them?'

'No.'

'How much did Muir want from you?'

Campbell looked as if he was about to make some excuse, but eventually he said with an air of righteousness, 'It was nine hundred quid.'

'Small change to a guy like you,' Shona said. 'Hardly worth a man's life, wouldn't you say?'

Gus Connelly leaned forward and tapped his fountain pen once, lightly, on the table between them. 'Really must stop you there, DI Oliver. If you have any more *pertinent* questions to ask my client, I suggest you ask them now.'

Shona nodded to McCulloch, who took his tablet and turned it around to show Campbell and his lawyer the CCTV from the farm. This time, Campbell was primed and didn't flinch.

'Is that you in the video?' Shona said.

'No.'

'Do you know who that is?'

'Course not!'

'I couldn't help but notice you were quite uncomfortable when I showed you the forensic photographs, but not when watching this...' she paused, searching for the correct term, '...this frankly horrific video. But then you like to watch, don't you?' Campbell frowned. 'Or is that because you knew what would happen? Did you send someone to teach Muir a lesson? Perhaps you never intended this. Perhaps your *messengers* went too far?'

'I wasn't prepared for the photographs. You don't often see dead bodies.'

'Just dead animals?' Shona shot back.

At that, Campbell's cheeks flamed and he glared at Shona. Gus Connelly looked from Shona to his client and back, aware there was a subtext being exchanged that he wasn't party to.

Before the lawyer could raise an objection, Shona pressed on.

'Where were you on Sunday, the night Muir Maxwell was killed?'

'I was at home, with my wife. Asleep.'

'And we know she'll give you an alibi, don't we?'

'I know what you're up to,' Campbell said, pointing a finger at Shona. 'I didn't kill Muir Maxwell, why would I? If he wanted to go to court over a bill, I've lawyers coming out of my ears to handle stuff like this. My pockets are deep. I didn't need to slug it out with a farmer to get my kicks.'

'Oh, your youth record is quite clear on how you get your kicks, Mr Campbell.'

Gus Connelly looked set to intervene, but Campbell put out his hand to stop him. 'I didn't have the best start, but I turned my life around.'

'So, in the spirit of your new law-abiding self, is there anything you'd like to tell me about the murder of Ailsa Scott?'

Campbell sat back and folded his arms, a look of triumph in his eyes. 'Absolutely nothing.'

'On that note, DI Oliver,' Gus Connelly said emphatically, 'I suggest we bring this interview to an end.'

–

Shona had no choice but to release Bruce Campbell. Without forensics connecting him to the farm, without the identity of the assailants, nothing could be linked back to him. She felt sick to her stomach that although she'd had a suspect linked to both Muir Maxwell's and Ailsa Scott's murders, she couldn't charge him with either.

McCulloch stopped Shona as they made their way back along the corridor to CID.

'Why's the boss got you looking at Ailsa Scott?'

'He wants a review for Isobel, before it's too late.'

'He's been goin' over that case for years. What makes you think you'll find somethin' he hasn't?' he challenged.

'Nothing.'

'So why are you doin' it?'

Shona stopped and turned to her DS. 'Because I didn't feel like refusing a dying woman's request, George. That's all. We're all tired. Go home. We'll start fresh on Monday.'

He stared stubbornly back at her for a moment, then turned and stalked off down the corridor.

Shona had just got back to her office and sent anyone who was still there home, when Murdo's name flashed up on her phone screen. Until she saw it, she wouldn't have admitted to anyone, even herself, that this was precisely what she needed.

'Boss. How ye doin'?'

She'd texted him when Midge Elliot was released and received his commiserations. Now she recounted the latest developments on Muir Maxwell's murder. How McLean and Campbell were both potentially connected to it, but she didn't have enough on either to make it stick and was running out of options.

'I think you're right aboot it being personal,' Murdo said. 'You've got tae have been off yer heid or really hated the fella tae act thon way.'

Shona rubbed her eyes. 'If this had happened in a town, I feel like we'd have so much more to go on. When I first saw that CCTV of the actual murder – good quality, sourced quickly – I thought, not that we'd necessarily solve it straight away, but we were off to a flying start at least.'

'These cases can be like that, boss. The breaks come when ye least expect them. Just gotta keep goin'.'

'You know what Muir Maxwell's mother, Maggie, said to me? *I don't want to end up like Ailsa Scott's family.* She saw how an unsolved murder destroyed their farm and their lives.'

'Aye. It's no' ideal,' said Murdo, with classic understatement. 'I've been lookin' at what you sent me, an' having a wee think aboot the boyfriend and his pal. Wi' a crime like that, thon lassie Janice that gave them both the alibi… well, that's a big secret tae carry aw this time. If either, or both lads, killed Ailsa Scott, Janice might wonder if they'd do the same tae her eventually, just tae make themselves safe.'

'She's been visited by the media over the years,' Shona considered. 'Maybe you're right. If she's been offered money to sell her story, and ensure her own long-term safety, why wouldn't she do that.' Part of her didn't want to believe what Murdo was saying, but she knew in her heart he'd have considered all the options. 'I suppose every marriage has its moments, even if it's just an argument that escalates over whose turn it is to empty the dishwasher.' She and Rob had plenty of rows about that and more. But whatever Rob's crimes, she knew he wasn't a killer. How would you even sleep in a house with someone who'd murdered a young woman. And Janice Campbell didn't strike Shona as a victim of coercive control. 'So, who d'you think killed Ailsa?'

There was a pause and Shona sensed Murdo was building up to something she wasn't going to like.

'Well, I think the original investigation, though no' watertight by oor standards, likely landed on the truth.'

'The walker they never traced?'

'Aye, that's who ma' money's on.'

Shona paused, taking what he'd said and letting the idea settle. 'Okay, Murdo. Thank you.'

She was sure where that left her, with both cases. All she knew was she wasn't ready to give up on either.

–

When Shona got home she didn't sleep. Becca had been out with Jack all day and was exhausted. She took one of the local history books from the bookcase and said she might read for a bit, but when Shona looked in half an hour later, to ask if she wanted to watch some TV, Becca was fast asleep, the open book resting on her chest. Shona eased it from her hand. Placing a thin blanket over her daughter, she switched off the light and tiptoed out.

When she'd arrived at Coldharbour Cottage, she'd thought that you could never tire of the view. But now, as the sky turned a deep violet and the land became only shadows, she felt as if the lighthouse was taunting her. It had stood there as a symbol to saving lives, but it had also witnessed death, both at sea and at the hands of men and women, driven by greed, fear, desperation or a desire for revenge, and it seemed to Shona that it would never give up its secrets.

She began a final sweep through her emails before a bath and bed. She was feeling the exertion of the day in her muscles. She remembered her dirty linen trousers and pink blouse were still in the car. She should bring them in and wash them. What was it with Galloway? Why was it intent on ruining her wardrobe?

There was an email from a Helen, at an address she didn't recognise, but Angie's name was in the tagline. As soon as she opened it, she felt a surge of panic. The letter explained that Angie had uploaded her DNA to a website and found an immediate match.

Helen was Shona's sister.

She apologised if contact was unwelcome but wanted to write a letter that expressed how she felt. She'd had a good adoption and was married with three children, aged twelve, ten and eight. She only became interested in tracing who her mother and father were when her adoptive parents died, and she had children of her own. Finding out who she was felt like the last piece of the puzzle She could remember very little about their father or mother when she was young and nothing about Shona. She did have a sharp memory of being hungry. Her one happy memory was finding a margarine wrapper in a bin in the house and licking it clean. She remembered her brother, but not much. It was likely he was dead, as a social worker had said that he was *gone and never coming back*, when her adoption was being finalised. How else do you explain death to a six-year-old?

Shona thought for a moment, then sent back a cautious reply. She explained that she'd need time to think about what Helen had told her and would be in touch. She felt curiously calm. Now that what she'd dreaded happening was real, it seemed less terrifying than she'd imagined. Already she was wondering if they shared any interests or had experiences in common. Isobel had missed Ailsa all her life: the family gatherings, the shared memories. Knowing there was someone who always had your back. Maybe Shona had missed her sister just as much but hadn't known what it was until now. Becca would be thrilled. She had cousins. Shona had a big sister. What had Isobel said? The relationships with your siblings were the ones that really mattered, not your parents, since they were the ones that lasted longest. What had happened to her big brother? He'd been taken from Angie by that point so

Shona couldn't hold her responsible for his death. She thought of all the positive relationships she'd had with the men around her – Tommy, Murdo, Ravi were all like brothers to her.

She had a choice now. So far she'd let this happen to her, but it was her life too. It had gained the momentum of a runaway train. The only way she'd have any control was to engage with the process, but she knew she could only do it on her terms. No uploading DNA to websites, but maybe there were other ways she could search.

There were places Shona could look without going anywhere near the Police National Computer. Forums, websites, street directories. It wouldn't take her long once she put her mind to it. If she didn't follow this thread to its end, it would always be hanging there ready to unravel her life. And one thing she knew for sure: if her brother was still alive somewhere, any contact they might have would be on her terms.

Chapter 31

When Saturday morning came, Shona made a dash into the office. She would steal a march on the day and be back before Becca went out. Jess had already reported in that her trip to the bothy yesterday evening had been interesting. There were a few seasoned walkers lamenting young folks' behaviour and poor grasp of bothy etiquette, but it was more general than specific. There'd been no reports of drug paraphernalia on the Southern Upland Way route in general. This morning Jess was heading across to her parents' farm in County Antrim. *My brothers are fighting over something stupid* she'd told Shona, and she needed to go back and knock their heads together.

Shona paced the carpet in front of the whiteboard but fresh ideas about Muir's murder wouldn't come. Jess had tactfully asked Maggie and Anna about being pressured to store items by anyone, and deliveries they weren't expecting, before asking them again – had they seen any drugs on the farm? If they had, they should say now and let the police protect them. From the vigorous denials, it was clear that in all the ways the farm had diversified, narcotics wasn't one of them.

In the afternoon, Shona thought a walk out to the lighthouse would clear her head, but it had the opposite effect. The day was grey with a sharp wind, which suited her mood and kept other visitors away. She walked and re-walked the sections of path on either side of the lighthouse to check for any vantage points where potential witnesses could've been overlooked but found nothing new. Once more she had the sense of being watched. She'd taken the binoculars from the cottage with her, stopping regularly to sweep the path for anyone following her, but there was no one.

By Saturday night, Shona's head was full to bursting with work and she was desperate to think about anything other than forensics, alibis or possible hiding places for stolen farm equipment. However, any attempt to bundle work into a mental cupboard and slam shut one door resulted in her mother Angie spilling out of another. A succession of snapshots – the roof terrace, her mother's disappointment, Becca's shocked disapproval – still spun through her mind's eye whenever she dropped her guard.

Roddy had suggested she come with Becca for dinner on Saturday night. They had some family visiting. But she'd pleaded a headache, which wasn't far from the truth. Isobel's phrase, *Roddy was my friend*, still echoed in her head and she was desperate to know what it meant but could see no way of broaching it in company. She'd had a bath and a glass, or two, of wine, called Simon, then fallen asleep in front of some trashy TV, knowing that tomorrow would bring him in person, a pub lunch, and maybe, if she was lucky, some clarity.

-

On Sunday morning, the wine-fuelled early night hadn't left Shona as groggy as she'd feared. Below Coldharbour Cottage, Portpatrick harbour sparkled in the early light.

The clouds of yesterday had been carried away by the stiff winds which had now moderated to a gentle breeze, barely enough to push the few early yachts across the calm of the North Channel. It'd be busy on the water today. That thought inevitably led her back home to Kirkness, to Tommy and the lifeboat, the precarious position they were currently in and the long-term viability of the station itself. She felt bad about letting him down. The whole operation depended on volunteers. Without them, the RNLI might be forced to merge neighbouring stations, which would lengthen response times, which could, ultimately, result in more fatalities. It really was a matter of life and death.

'Mum? Are you doing porridge?' Becca called from the kitchen, then appeared in her pyjamas, mug in hand. 'You're not out here waiting for Simon, are you?' she teased. 'He'll be ages yet.'

'It's only two hours' drive.' Shona consulted her watch. 'Might be here by nine.'

'Oh my God, you've only an hour to do your hair,' Becca said, clutching her mother's arm in mock horror. 'I better make the porridge. You've got work to do.'

'Cheeky besom.' Shona pushed her daughter before her into the cottage, trying – and failing – to hide her smile.

–

At the sight of Simon coming up the track to the cottage a little after ten a.m., Shona's spirits soared. The hug he gave her when he got out of the car cemented them in place.

'Where's Becca?'

'Gone to Jack's. They're coming to the pub later. Come in. Tea, of course?'

'Yes, please.'

It was a running joke between them. Simon put it down to his time in the army. Never refuse a tea, you don't know where the next one is coming from.

'Honestly,' Shona smiled, 'Becca's running that lad ragged, determined he'll be fit for uni this year. She always wanted a dog as a kid, but we never got her one. I think she's redirecting all that pent-up disappointment. She'll have him chasing after a ball next.'

'Most lads don't need much encouragement for that.'

Shona laughed. 'How was Gabe's hockey match yesterday?'

'Bearing in mind I did my basic training with the Scots Guards, the way those lads hack at each other with sticks…' Simon shook his head. 'I'll be glad if Gabe makes it through university without getting all his teeth knocked out or losing an eye.' He came up behind Shona and put his arms around her, kissing her neck. 'So, what've you got planned for me today?'

'I thought we could have a walk. Lunch at the pub.'

'Walking is very overrated,' he whispered. 'Does that front door lock?'

'It does.'

'Good.'

-

The pub on the seafront was busy, but they were led to a quiet table in the corner. When they'd got their drinks, Simon folded his arms and gave her a piercing look.

'So, are you going to tell me what really happened when you met your mother?'

'Nothing.'

'There are times when you are remarkably opaque, but this is not one of them.'

Shona sighed. 'Okay.'

Once she'd told him what had really happened, including the email from her sister, and her reservations about meeting her, she said, 'My siblings are strangers. My brother died. I've nothing in common with my sister. What if I've arrested one of her friends? That'd be weird. I mean, why didn't my gran tell me all this? She must've had a good reason. Then this Angie comes along and it's like my whole life has been a fake. I think that's why I lost it with her. Who'd want to reunite with your family after a lifetime apart?'

'So, you don't feel any connection to your siblings?'

Shona thought for a moment. 'No. Is that bad?' she said, suddenly unsure.

'No, it's very natural. And you may blame them as well as your mother.'

'How? They were just kids too.'

'They are older. People you would have looked to for guidance or protection?'

Shona took a moment to process that thought. Rationally, she wouldn't ever blame them. But subconsciously, in her heart? It wasn't just a lack of warmth. She'd felt empathy for people who'd done terrible things. So why not her brother and sister?

'Did your sister know about you?'

Shona shook her head.

'One thing I do understand,' he said quietly, 'is no matter how old or successful, we never truly escape the things that happened in our formative years. Maybe you have more in common than you know.'

Simon had spent most of his childhood in Germany, where his mother had been one of the few female military police officers. He rarely talked about it, but from the little he had said, she knew the statement was heartfelt.

'Right.' He picked up a menu and handed it to her. 'No more discussions on an empty stomach.'

When they'd finished their fish and chips, ordered dessert, and Simon had made her laugh with tales of military incompetence, of which he had an endless store, he asked how her secondment was going.

'It's been interesting. Had a bumpy start with some of the team. The murder of the farmer is proving tricky. Murdo reminded me you have to keep going with a case. Hunt out new leads.'

'He's right. And what about the cold case?'

She sketched in the background and her encounters with the main suspects. Jeremy Young, she'd dismissed from her list. She'd found no fresh evidence on McLean and Campbell. She bit her lip. 'It's Roddy Rutherford who's giving me sleepless nights. He doesn't know I'm looking at Ailsa's death, but he brought it up with me and separately with Becca. I can't tell if it's residual anger at the way he was treated or if he's throwing up a smokescreen of indignation to divert from the fact he knows more than he's saying.'

'You don't really think he did it?'

Shona scrubbed her hands through her hair. 'That's it. My heart says no, of course not. But my head says, look at the evidence and don't let your judgement be clouded.'

'Seems to me that being questioned over a girl's murder would have quite an effect on a teenager, no matter how it was done. It's triggering him even now. Could be it tainted his reputation locally for a while. Might still be whispered in corners, since no one's ever been charged. Rather than thinking of him as a suspect, you could try treating him as a witness. Ask for his help. It'll be awkward, but I think he'll appreciate you being straight with him.'

Shona nodded, considering. 'Yes. That's worth a try.'

'Anyway. Enough work talk.' He reached out and took her hand in his. 'Have you thought about what I said? About coming to Glasgow?'

The pub door opened and Becca and Jack took off their sunglasses and scanned the pub, blinking as their eyes adjusted to the gloom.

Shona waved, and they waved back. 'I will think about it, Simon.'

Becca and Jack made their way through the busy tables.

'Jack,' Simon half-rose and offered his hand, then hugged Becca.

As Shona watched them, she remembered they were bonded in a way that left her on the outside. In those dark days after Jack had been stabbed in a mugging on the way home from a night out, it was Simon who'd stepped up. He'd supported both Jack and his father Roddy, cutting through red tape and hospital delays. Keeping Becca's spirits up through the long weeks when Shona, detained by work and separated by two hours of motorway, couldn't always get there. She'd forgotten this when she'd shared her doubts over Roddy. Now she felt guilty that she'd put Simon in a difficult position, one of potential disloyalty to a friend.

'What are you two plotting? Hope it's not a big walk. We've just had one.' Becca flopped down on the sofa beside Shona.

'I'm trying to persuade your mum to move to Glasgow.'

Shona stared at Simon. It was underhand, recruiting her own daughter to his cause. But Becca wouldn't want her mother to leave High Pines. While she might never return full time, she cherished it too much as a refuge from the pressures of university and the world and often brought her friends down for a weekend by the sea.

But instead of being shocked by the prospect, Becca just nodded.

'You wouldn't want me to leave Kirkness?' Shona said.

'I like Glasgow,' Becca mused. 'Being there makes me think I might be a city girl at heart. I miss the buzz of London, our old house in Camden. I wouldn't mind working there. I've looked at internships that'd help me get a job in archaeology. Maybe move into forensic archaeology for post-grad. There's good courses at University College London and King's.'

'Oh. Okay.' It was the first Shona had heard of this. 'I'm blaming Slasher Sue for being a role model and putting ideas into your head.' She tried to laugh it off. But everything made sense and she wondered why she hadn't considered that Becca's plans for the future might take her far from the Solway. She didn't need Shona's permission to dream. Shona had been just the same at that age, rushing to join the City of London police. But she'd always assumed it was the push from the grim conditions and zero prospects of the Glasgow scheme she'd grown up in, rather than the pull of ambition.

'I'll get us some drinks. Come with me, Jack.' Simon got up, tactfully leaving Shona and Becca alone.

'What d'you think, Mum. Glasgow? You'd be going home.'

Shona had hoped for a day to process all the events of the past week. Instead, she'd acquired a set of new and potentially life-changing things to think about.

'I don't know, darlin',' she said, feeling embarrassing tears prick her eyes. 'I really don't.'

Chapter 32

The next morning Shona was woken by her ringing phone. It was already light, but at this time of year the sun rose unreasonably early and wasn't a useful indicator of the hour. The screen said it was just after seven a.m. It also told her that the caller was DS Dan Ridley, once of Cumbria CID, but now settled in at the Met in London.

'Shona, I'm sorry. I'm so, so sorry.'

Shona sat bolt upright. 'Dan? What is it?' She threw the sheet back and stumbled to the chair she'd thrown her clothes over the night before.

'It's Thalia. I wasn't sure if you'd heard. Shona, I'm afraid she's taken her own life.'

'What? Oh no. No, no, no.' Shona collapsed into the chair. Now, after all this time. After all they'd been through together. 'I thought things were getting better the last time we spoke.' She bit her lip, not sure how long she could hold back the tears.

'There's something else I have to tell you. She left a note for the police. I've been away. I just picked up my post; she sent me one too. Did you get anything?'

'I'm sorry, Dan, I'm in Galloway for a couple of weeks on secondment. What does it say?'

'In it she says that she killed Defont and why, and that she did it alone and no one helped her. She added that the NCA had been putting pressure on her and she knew she would never get justice. A neighbour with a spare key was worried about her. They found her at her flat late last night. She'd taken an overdose. Shona, I really don't think there was anything you could have done.'

Shona put her hand over her mouth to hide her sobs. She hadn't pulled the trigger herself, but she'd made sure Thalia got away. She'd done it for Becca, for Rob and for herself, to know that Delfont was never coming back. Protecting Thalia was protecting them all.

'Are you okay? Are you on your own?' Dan said.

'No, Becca is here. I'll be okay. It's just the shock. How, how are you?' She sniffed, searching the jumbled clothes for a hankie.

'I'll be fine. Listen, you know this means you'll probably get another call from the NCA? You and Thalia worked together at Bishopsgate, she visited you at High Pines, that's all they've got.'

'I know. Will they call you do you think?'

'As far as they know I was part of the original Cumbria CID investigation into Delfont's death; that was all. They know we're friends, but that's not so unusual between neighbouring police forces. Everyone knows everyone to some extent in countryside policing.'

'True,' she said reassured.

'Listen, I've got to go. I'm so sorry. I know she was your friend. I hope she's at peace now.'

'Yes,' said Shona, struggling to hold back another wave of tears. 'Thanks, Dan.'

Shona went to the sink in the corner of the room and washed her face. She didn't want Becca to see her like this. It would be too hard to explain. Pushing the window up, she took long slow breaths of the fresh morning air.

'Why, Thalia?' she said out loud. But she already knew the answer. Thalia had struggled more than Shona did when the CPS had dropped the case against Delfont because they thought there was little prospect of a conviction. She'd been an excellent police officer but had never returned to work. In her heart of hearts, Shona had feared Thalia's story was always going to end this way.

Shona took time to compose herself. In the shower, the tears had almost started again but she knew she had to tuck them away for later. They were due to have a proper review of Muir Maxwell's murder this morning, and she'd need to inspire the team to dig deep and go again.

As soon as she came into the kitchen, Shona heard Becca calling her from the front room.

'Mum, what's going on?'

She couldn't know about Thalia.

But then Shona remembered she'd left her laptop open on the coffee table. Had Becca seen the email from her sister Helen?

'What is it? Coming.'

Shona hurried in. Becca might be annoyed Shona hadn't shown her the email already, but she'd understand it had all happened so fast and ultimately things were moving in the direction she wanted.

Becca was indeed standing by the coffee table, but it wasn't the laptop that held her attention. In her hand was a page from Ailsa Scott's case file. She held it up for Shona to see, her face pale with anger.

'What's this?' Becca hissed.

Shona pointed a finger at her. 'You, lady, should not be looking through work files.'

'Jack's dad is a suspect in a murder case? You don't think you should have told me about it?'

Shona came towards her, but Becca held the sheet out of her mother's reach.

'I thought Roddy was your friend too. You don't really believe he did this do you?'

Becca was angry, but Shona also detected a note of fear in her voice.

She stepped back from her daughter and held up both her hands in a conciliatory gesture.

'Becca, please put that down and we can talk about this.'

Becca looked taken aback. She'd obviously expected her mother to tell her she was mistaken or flatly refuse to discuss it. She placed the page on top of the file and Shona closed the folder over it.

'The reason I didn't tell you about this is because, yes, I don't want the fact that I'm looking at the Ailsa Scott murder case to get back to Roddy. He was fourteen years old at the time and I think it was a very rough period in his life. He was treated as a suspect. My interest is in talking to him as a possible witness but only when the time is right. Do you see the difference?'

Becca nodded.

She didn't add that it had been Simon's idea, that she herself had struggled with the idea Roddy wasn't involved in some way. Now, with Becca aware, she couldn't delay any further.

'And you won't talk to Jack about this will you? Because I think that it's something between him and his dad, and you could cause a great deal of hurt on both sides by bringing it up before Roddy is ready to talk about it. Okay? Come here.'

She beckoned her daughter towards her. Becca rested her head on her mother's shoulder and let herself be hugged. Then she stepped back and scrutinised her mother's face.

'There's something else. I heard you on the phone. What is it? What happened?'

Keeping Roddy's involvement in the cold case from Becca had nearly blown up in her face. Shona realised she had to come clean about everything that might impact on her daughter.

'If I told you I didn't know where to start would you believe me?'

'Yeah,' said Becca, cautiously. 'Is it about Dad? Is he okay?'

'He's fine. I've a couple of things to tell you.'

'Something good or something bad?'

'One of each, I think?' Shona said. 'But let's get some breakfast first and I'll tell you on the way to Jack's.'

-

By the time they got to the Rutherfords' granite townhouse, a little way up the road from the harbour, Becca was for once stunned into silence as she took in the implications of her new aunt Helen's email.

'I've got cousins?'

'You have,' Shona said. 'Are you pleased?'

'Yeah, I think so. I wasn't expecting them to be younger than me.'

'Is that not a good thing?'

'I suppose it is. Does that mean you won't ever be able to find your brother?'

'I don't know. And don't be so greedy, lass.' She gave Becca a playful poke. 'An auntie and three cousins is enough for starters surely?'

Becca gave her a wide smile, then her face became serious again.

'I'm sorry about your friend Thalia.'

Shona looked down at the car keys she was turning aimlessly in her hand. 'Thank you, darlin',' was all she managed.

'Are you coming in?' Becca said. 'I think Roddy is working from home today.'

The subtext was obvious. Though Becca believed what her mother had told her about Roddy, here was an opportunity to prove it.

'Yeah, why not. Just for a minute, if he's not busy.' It was Shona's way of saying that her daughter shouldn't get her hopes up. Resolution wouldn't be easy or quick for a hurt that had lasted forty years.

Becca led the way. Jack opened the door, and they hadn't been in the hallway more than five seconds when Becca blurted out that she now had three wee cousins. To his credit Jack, whose family stretched out on both sides into the dozens, tried his best to look impressed.

'Is your dad around?' Shona asked and was directed to the study at the back of the house.

Shona tapped the door. When she heard him say *hello*, she stuck her head round, hoping he wasn't in mid conference call. The room was square and neat with filing cabinets on one side. An old wooden desk sat at a right angle to the window, through which she could see a neat garden with a lawn and borders overflowing with flowers. Like Dalrymple's study, there were family photographs everywhere.

'Thought I'd pop in and say hi. I hope I'm not disturbing you.'

'Come away in, Shona. I was beginning to think we'd never get to see you.'

He got up from his desk, pressing his Paisley pattern tie against his immaculate white shirt, and gave her a quick professional hug.

'I've a meeting in half an hour, but you've got time for a coffee, haven't you?' When Shona nodded, he said, 'Great. Come away out into the garden. If I don't make the effort I'm stuck in front of a screen all day.'

It was already hot enough in the sheltered garden for them to choose a table in the shade. When they settled with their coffee, Roddy reminded Shona that they'd love to see her down at the lifeboat station, when she had a minute.

'But I don't think that's why you've come to see me this morning,' he said, shrewdly.

Shona knew there was no point in trying to put this delicately.

'Kenny Dalrymple asked me to review Ailsa's case, unofficially. Isabel doesn't have long left and she wants to know what happened to her sister, before she goes.'

Roddy nodded. 'I thought as much.'

'I've looked at your statement and thought about what you told me and I believe you were treated very badly by the investigation. I'm not going to make the excuse of different times. You know as well as I do that it should never have happened. I'm sorry, and I'd understand if you wanted to put in an official complaint.'

But Roddy waved the suggestion away. 'You know when you asked the other day if that early encounter with the police had influenced my choice of career? I'd never thought about that. I guess it did. So, you could say they did me a favour.' He gave her a wry smile.

'Thing is, I believe that by treating you as a suspect from the start, they overlooked your potential as a witness.'

Roddy pressed his lips together and nodded.

'This isn't an official inquiry, but if there is anything you can tell me about that day, I'd like to hear it.'

Roddy thought for a minute. 'I was up in the lantern room for most of the morning. It was still Trinity House back then, an operational installation. I was there to learn what I could because, believe it or not, I really fancied a job as a lighthouse keeper, cos I was really into bird-watching. I'd spent all morning scanning the cliffs, and that's why I can't understand it.'

'What was it you saw?'

'It was what I didn't see. I didn't see the walker, the one the old couple say they passed on the cliff path.'

'Couldn't you just have been looking in another direction?'

'No, I don't think that's it. There'd been some trouble with folk stealing birds' eggs. I'd have noticed anyone on their own, acting suspicious.'

'Do you think the elderly couple were mistaken?'

'Must have been. Maybe with a shock, they were confused. It was someone, a tourist, they'd met closer to Portpatrick, just out for a wee daunder. Only person I saw that day was Isobel.'

'She said something strange to me the other day – "*Roddy used to be my friend.*" What d'you think she meant?'

Roddy pushed out his bottom lip, thinking. 'I don't know. We were pals when we were younger, but things change. I got really into my studies. I was interested in photography and birds. She was mad about horses, and they scare the living daylights out of me. I was chased by a Shetland pony as a bairn. Never got over it.' He grinned.

'Isobel and I didn't fall out, but by that time she was hanging around with an older crew. Tagging along with Ailsa. In fact, I'll be back in a minute.' He got up and went inside, reappearing shortly afterwards with a snapshot of Ailsa and Isobel with their arms around each other, ponies in the background. It was from a slightly different angle to the one in the case file and had likely been taken at the same time. 'Think I did that for a school art project.'

'It's a lovely picture,' Shona said, handing it back. 'And you didn't see Graham McLean or Bruce Campbell that day on the cliff?'

He shook his head again. 'Sorry.'

'Thank you, Roddy.'

Here was one explanation why the outsider, this mysterious walker, had never been found. His presence hadn't been corroborated by any other witness. Sometimes, an investigation would light on a particular scenario and remain wedded to it until the whole operation ran out of steam. Unfortunately, it didn't help Shona come any closer to the answer she knew Dalrymple wanted.

'I better let you get on with your meeting.'

'Grand. So, we'll see you here again? Maybe for dinner?'

Shona smiled. 'Thank you. I'd like that.' It struck her that Roddy must be lonely, even with the lifeboat operation and his busy job. Sometimes it was just nice to have a fresh face to talk to.

She'd said her goodbye and just reached the Audi when her phone rang.

McCulloch. Probably wondering where she was.

'I'm on my way in,' she said.

'Boss, we've had a call. Another farm's been targeted.'

'What? Is everyone okay?' If there'd been another assault she'd never forgive herself.

'Yes, boss. Farmer and his wife slept right through, thank God.'

Thank God indeed. 'Much taken?'

'Same as before. An all-terrain vehicle and GPS units. Thing is, they've got good CCTV. There's something you better see. I'll send it over now.'

Her phone pinged and she leaned into the Audi's passenger seat and fished her glasses from her handbag, then realised it was too bright out here to see the screen. 'Just give me a minute. I'll ring you back.'

She jumped into the passenger seat and pressed play.

Two figures in black balaclavas, hoodies and gloves. One tall and stocky. One shorter and of lighter build, just like before. The vehicle was different but that stood to reason. They could hardly drive around, even at night and through the lanes, with the damage that the Ford Transit Connect had sustained clearly visible. This time they had a battered pickup but they also covered its number plate with tape. They'd loaded the ATV into the back, let the handbrake off and coasted back down the hill and out of the main gate without turning on their ignition. They were so quiet, not a word had been exchanged, and they were obviously practised as a team, which made it all the more sinister that even after a murder, they'd continued with the same MO.

When they reached the gate the pickup had stopped, checking that their exit was clear. It was then she saw it. This clip wasn't from the farm CCTV, it was from a front-door-type motion-activated video on the gate. The passenger had pulled off their balaclava. Without knowing it, they'd looked straight into the lens. Shona's hand flew to her mouth. Even in infrared there was no mistaking that face.

Billy Fraser, Eastcraig's sprightly farm hand.

Only then did it come to her, the problem with the original Eastcraig CCTV, a disconnect that had been tugging at her brain since that first day.

'The dog that didn't bark,' she said out loud.

Maggie Maxwell had been woken by the sheepdogs, she'd said, Muir not hearing them because he had headphones in. But there'd been no barking on the CCTV even after enhancement. They didn't bark because they recognised the vehicle.

A sick feeling was growing in Shona's stomach. She replayed the video, concentrating on the larger man – the way he walked, held his head – until she was sure.

The driver of the van who killed Muir Maxwell could only be one man.

It was his brother, John Maxwell.

Chapter 33

Shona's first instinct was to go straight to Eastcraig Farm and arrest John Maxwell and Billy Fraser. She would be completely justified in taking that action because having killed once there was a real danger it would happen again if they felt under threat. But it wasn't as simple as that. There were so many questions unanswered, and she couldn't risk another hasty arrest after Midge Elliot.

She gathered her team together at the second crime scene – a small family farm about six miles south of Portpatrick – while they waited for forensics to arrive. Shona thought the choice of target had been made because of the lack of CCTV on the backroads between the two properties.

In a quiet corner of the barn, Kyle, McCulloch, Jess and Ian stood in a loose circle. Kyle had propped his phone up on a hay bale so Erin could listen in from the CID office. Above their heads, swallows swooped in and out, feeding their chicks, oblivious to the human concerns that were going on below them.

'Okay,' Shona said, 'these are the problems we have. Firstly, and crucially, we have no forensic evidence from Eastcraig that will stand up in court because the defence will claim it was deposited in the course of their farm work, not the murder.'

'What we get here might establish a pattern to their crimes,' Kyle said.

Shona shook her head. 'Beyond the gate camera, I think they were careful not to leave much. And we'd have to prove they'd never been here in the course of their business.'

'They could easily claim,' Jess began, 'that they staged a copycat raid because they feared Eastcraig was in financial difficulties after Muir's murder. I mean, stealing from your neighbours is bad and you'd probably have to leave the country. But you could do your time, sell up. Plenty of farming work abroad. Better than a life sentence in jail.'

'We need tae find thon van,' McCulloch said.

'Exactly, that's a priority,' Shona said.

'I'd have taken it somewhere quiet,' Jess said. 'Maybes a wee loch. Tipped it in.'

'Risky,' Kyle said. 'Someone might see you.'

'Not me,' Jess said, coolly. 'Onto a trailer, tarp over it. Use the tractor to pull it. You could drive it down the middle of the road, no one would look twice. Back into the water. Farmers dump old kit all the time.'

Jess's brothers were right to be wary of their big sister, Shona thought.

'We have tyre tracks from the night,' Erin said. 'Find the van and we match them.'

'Good point,' Ian said. 'That's a forensic link. The van is the murder weapon.'

'Okay, once we have them in custody we can search Moine Farm and Billy Fraser's cottage. Where is that?' Shona had never seen it, so it must be somewhere secluded.

'Top o' the brae, where the shelter belt is,' McCulloch said. 'It's got a canny view.'

'The key thing that's bugging me is why?' Shona went on. 'From all we know, the brothers were close. They lost their dad young, John looked up to Muir. So why steal from him? Why kill him?'

'Worth talkin' tae Maggie Maxwell again?' McCulloch said. 'Naebody kens folk better than their mothers.'

Shona looked to their FLO, Jess, who made a face. 'She's loyal to the land. I doubt we'd get anything out of her.'

'So, who?' Shona pressed.

'Anna,' Jess said. 'She's the outsider there.'

'An outsider? But she's Muir's wife,' Shona said. 'She practically runs the business. She does the accounts, and a lot of the diversification ideas came from her. When I first spoke to John about the farm shop business and how they would cope in the wake of Muir's death, he said that it was Anna, not his mother, that would see them through.'

'The business and the farm are two different things. Anna is an outsider not just because she was brought up in Edinburgh. Anna could leave the land and start again somewhere fresh but that's not something Maggie could ever do. She proved that when she stayed on after her husband's death.'

Outside, a van rolled up. Kyle went to the barn window. 'Forensics.'

'Right,' Shona began. 'Statements from the farmer. Door-to-door the neighbours in case they saw anything. Erin, start on the CCTV footage from the farm. I want anything more that can usefully identify either man. Phone records would also be good. Ian, put a stop on John Maxwell's passport and alert our counterparts at Cairnryan, in case he tries to do a flit.' She turned to McCulloch. 'Do we know where both men are now?'

'Moine Farm. I called Maggie an' said I was gettin' together more photos of suspects tae show them and what were their plans fur the day. John and Billy are oot checking fences. But they're due back at Eastcraig aroon four o'clock.'

'Okay, good. Get an arrest team together. We'll go in this afternoon at Moine. Eastcraig is too risky with the kids about. Jess and I are off to see Anna. Maybe she'll be able to tell us what this mess is all about.'

–

'Any ideas on how we're going to get Anna on her own?' Jess said as they made their way through the narrow lanes towards Eastcraig. 'I don't think she'll talk if Maggie's around. We could take her back to Newton Stewart, but that might spook her.'

'I agree,' Shona said, pulling out from behind a caravan and putting her foot down.

'Let's tell them that their statements need double-checking and that has to be done separately. Maggie told me not to bother coming back unless I'd found Muir's killer. It's ironic, but that's exactly what we're doing, though I've a feeling she knew before any of us.'

Shona took the turning for the farm. 'Looks like our luck's in.' She pointed to the field with the standing stones. Maggie had her back to them, her attention on her granddaughters, who were busy feeding the hens. 'You'll do better at keeping Maggie talking than I will. I'll find Anna.'

She parked the Audi by the house, in a spot Shona hoped was less visible from the field. She went to the back door and knocked. Surprise and wariness registered in Anna Maxwell's expression.

'Can I come in for a minute, Anna?'

'Maggie's not here. She's out with the girls.'

'It was actually you I wanted to see.'

'Oh.' Her face fell.

They went into the kitchen. Shona saw Anna was baking again. 'I'm just filling the freezer for the next time we do teas.'

'Anna, I want you to tell me truthfully how Muir and John got on.'

For a moment she just stared at Shona, then she buried her face in her hands.

Shona hurried across the kitchen. But when she reached her, Anna put up a hand and took a step backwards.

'No, don't pity me. I can stand anything except folk being nice.' She swallowed. 'The truth was they didn't get on, not really. Muir wasn't a kind person. He never hit us or anything like that, but he wasn't kind.'

'What did Muir and John argue about?'

'Petty things. I didn't really understand it. Muir felt the responsibility of the farm rested on his shoulders and it made him blinkered, thoughtless at times. He didn't always see the value in people who helped him. But sometimes John was just as bad.'

Shona thought about Jess's brothers, Drew and Ben, fighting over tasks and responsibilities around the farm. She thought about the Gallagher brothers she'd helped rescue from the sinking yacht in the Solway, brawling even though it put their own lives in danger.

'Do you know what happened?'

She shook her head.

'Where are John and Billy now?'

'Up at Uncle Pat's, Moine Farm, I mean.'

'Maggie said they were checking fences. D'you know where they'd go?'

'They're not checking fences,' Anna said with a frown. 'They're after rabbits.'

'How do you know that?'

'Because John took Muir's shotgun.'

Shona was on her phone and out the door in seconds.

'Jess,' she shouted, as she ran to the car. From behind her DC, Maggie Maxwell glared at her. Jess didn't stop to question what was wrong and dived for the passenger side door.

It felt like sprinting over corrugated iron as the Audi bumped its way up the track to Moine Farm. Then they sped into the yard, coming to a stop in a spray of loose gravel. The house looked empty; there was no sign of John's pickup. For a moment, Shona considered if John had fled, taking Muir's shotgun with him. That could lead to all sorts of bad things – hostage situations, spree killings – but she pushed the thought to the back of her mind for now. Nothing had been released to the media yet about last night's farm raid so John wouldn't know yet that they were onto him. His best bet now was to go on as normal so nobody would take any notice of him.

Shona was about to get out of the car when Jess put a hand on her arm to stop her.

'He's armed. We should wait for backup.'

Jess was right, of course, but Shona thought John's greatest danger was to himself, and she wanted him found as quickly as possible.

'I'm just going to check the house and have a wee look around the yard.'

'In that case, I'm coming with you,' Jess said. 'We're a wee bit of a sitting target here if he heard us arrive, and I'm not sure your car could stop a shotgun blast.'

'I could order you to stay here.'

'You could try.'

'House first then.'

Shona got cautiously out of the Audi, pausing to listen for any sound. But all she could hear was the burn that ran down one side of the property. There was also a low whine that seemed to come from all around them, making the hairs on the back of Shona's neck stand up until she realised it was just the wind whistling through the plastic guards on the hundreds of trees that surrounded them.

The big, blank windows of the old farmhouse stared back at them as they approached. Shona was conscious of every reflection of the surrounding trees, which seemed to shift across the glass as she scanned for any movement inside.

She and Jess knocked, then cautiously pressed their faces up against the windows but didn't see any signs of life. It looked no different to Shona's first visit here with McCulloch, but the interiors were so stark it was difficult to work out if the place was occupied even then.

'I don't think he's here,' Jess said, finally, straightening and stepping back from the window.

They walked around the building. Shona tried the back door and found it also locked. 'Maybe he's at Billy's?'

Jess nodded. 'I can't see any vehicle.'

'You check the old steading buildings. I'm going to look in the new byres.' Shona pointed to the large green metal agricultural buildings that Anna had previously told her were for overwintering cattle.

'Okay, be careful, boss.'

'You too, Jess.'

It was hard not to feel the creeping sense that you were being watched. Shona moved carefully, conscious of every tiny movement in her peripheral vision – leaves flickering in the breeze or birds darting for the undergrowth.

She found the door of the first byre unlocked. Inside, everything looked brand new. Stacked against the far wall were pallets of feed bags still in their original wrapping. She gave the place a last look over then pulled the door shut again.

The entrance to the second building was around the far side facing a cleared area of flat ground, intersected by animal pens. The gate to the pens lay slightly open and she noticed the door to the byre was also ajar.

Shona looked back towards the steading buildings that formed three sides of an open square, arranged around the flat yard where she'd parked. There was no sign of Jess.

This byre was darker and cooler. When she stepped inside, it took a moment for her eyes to adjust after the brightness. The floor was strewn with straw that muffled the sound of her footsteps.

She didn't see him at first. Shona's breath caught in her throat, but John Maxwell showed no signs that he'd even heard her arrival.

She took two steps towards him and when he didn't move she said, softly, 'John.'

At the sound of his name, he turned and Shona saw the unbroken shotgun resting across his lap.

'You've got yourself a nice spot here,' Shona said. She stayed close to the door, so he had to look backwards over his shoulder to speak to her. She hoped it would buy her some crucial fragments of time should he decide to raise the gun at her.

'You think that, do ye?' His voice was bitter. 'This place is a hole. It's cursed. Uncle Pat knew it. Ye ken both these farms were once one farm. I tried tae get Muir tae put them back thegether, but he wouldnae do it. Why should he give up what he had, he said. He ne'er cared aboot me.'

He pulled the gun upright between his knees, tucking the barrel under his chin.

'John, please put the gun down.'

He shook his head. 'It's ma father's.'

Shona felt a cold wave creep up her spine. 'Anna told me you'd done well with this place.'

She was rewarded by a sad smile.

'She doesnae know how bad things are. I tried everythin' I could think of, but I'm bankrupt. Gonnae lose this place. Muir didnae deserve her. Tell her I'm sorry. I didnae mean to dae it. But when I saw him there in front of me, I couldnae stop. I'd asked him for a loan, but he'd refused. Half of Eastcraig should've been mine.'

'And last night?'

'Thought it'd make it look like a gang. Like last year. Tell the farmer I'm sorry for the bother.'

From the tail of her eye, Shona saw Jess had come silently to the door. With a twitch of her left hand, Shona signalled her not to come any further.

'John, where's Billy?'

'Muir wanted him oot o' his cottage so he could let it to tourists. He wis born there. Billy begged him, but Muir just shoved him awa. When Billy tried again, he punched him. An old man, who gave his life tae this place. I couldnae let him go tae jail.'

'Where is he, John?'

'Up by the woods. He loved it there.'

Jess hesitated, but Shona motioned her to go. There was a slim chance Billy was still alive. In the distance, Shona heard cars approaching. John must've heard them too.

'Tell Anna I'm sorry.'

'No, John, wait…'

The blast roared through the metal byre, mingled with Shona's shouts until, at last, all was silent again, and John Maxwell was gone.

Chapter 34

It took two whole days to process the scene at Moine Farm. Jess had found the Ford Transit Connect van, still smeared with Muir Maxwell's blood, in one of the partially demolished old barns hidden behind bales of straw. It'd probably been driven along tracks between the two farms on the night of his murder, never passing a single CCTV camera. It'd been registered as scrapped three years earlier to save a cash-strapped John from taxing and insuring it. If John and Billy hadn't decided to stage a second raid, it might have been quietly disposed of as Jess had suggested, the case ultimately remaining unsolved.

They found Billy Fraser behind his cottage, in the woods where he'd played as a child. He'd been looking out at the view across Eastcraig when John had raised his father's shotgun to the back of Billy's head.

When Shona had gone to break the news to Maggie, the woman showed no grief or even shock.

'You knew what John had done, didn't you?' Shona had asked her.

'I kenned in my heart that John had kilt Muir. But I wasnae aboot tae lose another son. When your lads both have the Devil in them, what difference does it make? They're still yer children. How did you ken?'

'You said the dogs barked. But they couldn't be heard on the CCTV. They didn't bark because they knew it wasn't strangers, but John and Billy.'

'Aye well, chalk that up tae an old woman's bad memory then.' Maggie studied Shona with her piercing glare. 'Unless ye want tae arrest me?'

'I'm not sure what good that would do, Maggie.' Three generations of women would have to live with the consequences of what had happened at Eastcraig. The case was solved but never had Shona wished more that the outcome had been different.

–

Back at Coldharbour Cottage that evening, after a late supper, Shona called Simon. She hadn't meant to talk about work or tell him how low she was feeling, but somehow it all spilled out.

'I should have been more thorough at the start.'

'Everyone thinks that when a person turns a weapon on themselves,' Simon replied. 'You extracted all the data from the crime scene that you could've.'

'But I didn't get to grips with the family dynamics quickly enough.'

'People can live all their lives inside families and not understand the dynamics,' he said firmly.

Shona was silent for a moment as she thought about what that might mean.

'It's never just about the yacht,' she said. 'It's what Tommy said when we pulled those two brothers from their vessel and they turned violent. I should've listened to him.'

The Gallagher brothers had been into the lifeboat station at Kirkness to apologise for their behaviour and had left chocolates for Shona as an apology. But she doubted the loss of their father's yacht would be the last thing they'd argue about.

'And then there's Angie,' Shona went on. 'If ever there was a lesson about what people can do to their nearest and dearest it's her.'

She thought Simon might disagree with her, counsel her to give her mother another chance, but he stayed silent.

'I've been thinking about what I said to you on Sunday,' he said. 'About you moving to Glasgow.'

'Simon, I…'

'No, it's fine, listen. I think we both know you're not ready, and that's okay.' He paused. 'I don't want you to think I'm punishing you in any way, but I've been thinking about this for a while.'

Whatever was coming, it wasn't good. Shona felt it in the pit of her stomach. She clenched her fingers around her phone and tried to make her voice sound calm and light. 'What is it?'

'I've been offered a position abroad for eighteen months,' Simon said, evenly. 'Bahrain. At the Naval Support Facility. I've worked there before.'

'Oh,' was all Shona could bring herself to say.

'I'll still be back to Glasgow regularly. Gabe's there. Maybe you'll be there too?'

'I'd really like that.'

'So would I.'

She could hear the warmth in his voice. What could've escalated into a row, and even a permanent break between them, had somehow brought them closer. A minute ago, she'd been prepared for a fight. She marvelled at the unexpected turns their exchanges could take. She realised the one truth that trumped everything. Her life was better with Simon in it. The rest was details. They would work them out.

Becca was reading in the window seat when Shona came into the front room. Behind her daughter, the sun had set leaving behind a soft gloaming where the sea and sky reflected each other.

'How's Simon?' Becca said, not looking up from her book. It was a thick volume on Neolithic Galloway that she'd borrowed from Isobel Dalrymple's library.

'He's good. Sends his love.' Shona paused long enough for Becca to look up.

'What?'

Shona took a deep breath. 'I've decided I don't want to move to Glasgow, just yet.'

'Okay,' Becca said, and went back to an illustration of a pair of standing stones remarkably similar to the ones at Eastcraig Farm.

'Okay? That's it?' Shona said.

'You can do whatever you want, Mum.'

'That's youth and inexperience talking,' Shona said, though she admired the purity of the concept. 'You'll soon find out life is never that simple.'

Becca closed the book and jumped up from the window seat. 'I know it's not, but somethings can be.' She came and hugged her mother. 'I'm glad you're not leaving High Pines. I think being here with Jack has made me think about how important having a home to come back to is. I like that Kirkness is part of my life. I like seeing Tommy and Freya, and Ravi and Martin, and Murdo, and all my other friends there. So, what d'you want, Mum?'

Shona stroked Becca's long hair as she thought. 'I think I'd like to get to know Helen a bit.'

'Yes!' Becca raised her arms in a mock victory salute and began to dance around the room. 'I'll get to play with my cousins.' She stopped. 'Wow, that sounds so odd.'

Shona, caught up in her daughter's enthusiasm, laughed.

'Before you know it,' Becca grinned, 'you and Helen will be fighting over who gets to wear what and ganging up on the rest of us. God, d'you think she's as bossy as you are?'

'Worse, if Jess is anything to go by. Big sisters are always the boss in her book, and anyone who crosses them better watch out.'

'I'm not looking forward to going back to Glasgow tomorrow,' Becca said suddenly. 'Back to work.'

'Jack's coming up next week, isn't he? It'll be fine when you're all settled into the flat again, you'll see. Are you all right getting the train? I'd take you to the station but I have to see Kenny Dalrymple for a proper catch-up on cases tomorrow morning. I don't want to change the time. I think he's fitting me in around Isobel's care.'

'It's fine, Mum, honestly. Roddy can take me to the train. Can you give this book back for me and thank Isobel?'

'Sure.'

'Think I might go to bed,' Becca said. 'Get up early for a last walk around.'

'Good plan. Night, darlin'.'

'Night, Mum.'

Shona stood holding the book Becca had given her. On the back cover was a black-and-white photograph of the standing stones, known as The Sisters – two young women who'd been turned to stone after competing to see which one could summon the devil. Becca hadn't managed to visit them on this trip but had pencilled them in for next time.

The meeting with Dalrymple was to talk over current cases, but she knew the only one he'd really be interested in was Ailsa's murder. She had to decide what to say to him. Ever since her talk with Roddy, a new and troubling conclusion had been swirling in her mind. She went out to the hallway, retrieved the file from her bag, and continued on to the bench outside.

The air was soft on her cheek. A golden band sat across the horizon marking the wake of the departed sun. Now she was close to solving the mystery of who killed Ailsa Scott, the lighthouse, surrounded by its whispering, dusk-filled fields held less menace. She'd be sad to leave it behind. It had been an ally as much as an adversary during her time in Galloway, a fixed point around which the concerns of the land, as much as the sea, revolved. Shona had no doubt that the breeze through the grass stirred up the voices of the departed sailors dispatched by villagers. She hoped Ailsa had found her own place amongst them.

Shona took out the sketch of the walker that the elderly couple had seen near the lighthouse and stared at it until she was sure. Tall, slim, waterproof jacket, trousers, boots and the beanie hat. Roddy had been watching the cliffs and the coastal path and was certain no one else had come along it in either direction. If he was right, that left only one conclusion.

Chapter 35

When Shona arrived at the Dalrymple home the next morning, the nurse let her in. Kenny had just gone to pick up a prescription and would be back shortly, she said. They'd already arranged that Jess would come back to support the Maxwells if required, though Kyle had decided to train as a family liaison officer and both Shona and Jess had agreed he'd be well suited to the role.

'How is Isobel?' Shona asked.

The nurse, who was about Shona's age, folded her hands. 'It won't be long now. But you're welcome to go in and say hello. She said she'd be pleased to see you.'

As Shona came to the open door of Isobel's room, she paused. The view from the window opposite glowed like a painting itself among Ailsa's art.

Isobel must've heard her footsteps. 'Is that you, Shona?'

Shona fixed on a smile, tapped the door and went in. Isobel was lying back on the pillows. Once again, she had her make-up on, but the canvas beneath had shrunk. Her cheeks were hollow. Lifting her arm to point Shona to the chair beside her bed depleted what energy she had.

'I brought back the book you lent Becca. She says thank you.' Shona placed the book on the bedside table. 'Interesting title, *The Sisters*. Any reason you chose that one?'

A broad smile crossed Isobel's face. 'I knew as soon as we met that you'd work it out.' The smile faded fast and Shona could see Isobel was in considerable pain.

'Shall I fetch the nurse?'

Isobel shook her head. 'I'm fine. How did you know I was the one who killed my sister?'

'Roddy saw you, but he didn't make the connection. He thought you'd come directly across the fields looking for Ailsa after the alarm was raised. The walkers who gave your description had passed you earlier, close to the coastal path, and assumed you were a hiker like them. And Roddy showed me a photograph he'd taken of you and Ailsa together. Like the one in the file, but from a different angle.'

'It was the last one of us together.' Isobel smiled.

'Your jacket and beanie are in the background, hanging over the fence. The hat would've hidden your hair. Because you're almost six-foot tall, the hiker couple just assumed you were male.'

'I thought Roddy had worked it out. That's why we weren't friends.'

'He didn't know,' Shona assured her. 'He said you just drifted apart, had different interests.'

Isobel considered this for a moment, then nodded.

'I hated my sister. I can say it now. She was the star of the family, always my parents' favourite. It made me spiteful, as you can see.' Isobel tipped her head to the small, red-and-black oils showing the nightmarish, screaming faces.

'These are you?' Shona couldn't imagine what it would be like to be confronted with such ugly portraits of yourself. 'Why do you keep them?'

'To remind me, and because they are true. I killed my sister. Out of anger, out of spite. I didn't set out that day to kill her, but she'd left me to do her chores. Treated me like her servant. Her little sister. Went off painting. No point in telling my parents. Ailsa was an artist. A unique talent. She could do no wrong. I hit her with a rock when she laughed at me. Then tried to make it look like she'd just fallen.'

'When I stood at the place it happened, I wondered why her killer had gone to the trouble of posing her, as if she'd just slipped while she was painting. Why hadn't they just pushed her body into the sea?'

'I couldn't have done that to my sister.'

Isobel began to cough. Shona fetched a glass of water from the side table and held it while Isobel sipped it. Downstairs the front door slammed followed by Dalrymple's urgent voice in the hall, and the nurse's calm replies to his hurried questions.

Isobel pushed away the water and turned her eyes up to Shona's.

'I'm glad you know. I'm glad someone knows. It feels right for Ailsa. If she's waiting for me, I can ask her forgiveness.' Isobel paused and swallowed painfully. 'Will you tell him?'

For a moment, Shona didn't know the answer. Then she set down the glass and took Isobel's almost fleshless hands in her own. It was like shaking hands with death. What good could be done now by a revelation of this kind, of doubling a sorrow? There was no doubt that Isobel had examined her conscience and admitted what she'd done, if not to others, at least to herself, and served a life sentence for her crime.

Shona found she couldn't judge if that was justice for Ailsa, for a life stolen.

'Isobel, I'm not sure it's my secret to tell.'

–

Shona met Dalrymple coming up the stairs with a tray of coffee and biscuits. She could see he was already interrogating her expression for news of the cold case.

'I hope I haven't tired Isobel out. We were talking about the paintings.'

Dalrymple shook his head.

'Those awful red ones. I've tried to get rid of them,' he muttered.

'I think she feels they have as much merit as the beautiful landscapes.'

'I know. I just don't understand why you'd want to look at them all day.

Shona waited while Dalrymple took in Isobel's coffee. He was soon back out again.

'She's sleeping,' he said. 'Let's go downstairs to my study.'

They went through the Muir Maxwell murder and its aftermath and Shona congratulated him on the diligence of his team. They briefly touched on whether John Maxwell's and Billy Fraser's lives could've been saved, with Dalrymple assuring her she couldn't have predicted the outcome. The arrest of Midge Elliot, and the break-up of a substantial drugs operation, was a feather in Galloway CID's cap. Eventually, they returned to the bread and butter – dog attacks on livestock, damage to ancient monuments, minor fire-raising, puppy farms, road rage against tractors and horse riders.

Finally, Shona couldn't put it off any longer. She steeled herself, looking around at the family pictures and paintings. There in plain view of Dalrymple's desk was the final picture of Ailsa and Isobel with their arms around each other. It was possible, she realised, to destroy a life, even after it had been lived, and she had no desire to bring any more pain into a house that was already filled with it.

'Ailsa's murder,' she said, taking the file from her bag and placing it carefully on his desk. 'You did all you could. The original conclusion was probably the right one. The walker. An opportunistic attack, perhaps even accidental, and they panicked. I can't claim to understand what their motive was. One good thing is that there's no evidence they've ever done anything like this again. It would've flagged somewhere in the system. So, you shouldn't burden yourself with the idea that there's a potential threat still at large.' She gave him a reassuring smile and saw a weight lift from his shoulders. She considered whether to mention Ian Smith's history with the case, but the idea that a member of his staff had kept something that important from him would only raise more questions than it solved.

'I'm not sure if my conclusion will change your feelings about Graham McLean and Bruce Campbell. They may be the cross you'll have to bear.'

'You can say that again,' he acknowledged with a small smile. 'Thank you, Shona. I really mean that, for everything you've done.'

'What will you do now?'

'After Isobel's gone? I think I'll probably sell the house. It was always too big for us, but Isobel loved the view of the lighthouse. I think it's served its purpose now.'

-

Shona spent the rest of the day in the CID office. When she'd arrived, George McCulloch had got to his feet and offered her his hand, congratulating her on both the drugs case and the murder enquiry. They acknowledged the outcomes weren't all they could have wished but each assured the other that they were jobs well done. She'd realised McCulloch had felt hurt by Dalrymple appointing Shona to review the cold case, instead of his trusted lieutenant, so she'd told him he was right. Dalrymple had done a thorough job. That it was the unidentified walker was likely the correct conclusion. She'd found nothing new. He'd accepted the news with good grace. If they'd got off on the wrong foot, at least they were finishing on the right one.

Later, she'd taken Ian Smith aside and delivered her verdict on Ailsa's murder to him too. He'd looked uncertain, loathe to give up a conviction of a lifetime that Graham McLean or Bruce Campbell had been responsible. But eventually his features relaxed; she saw he was relieved that the original investigation, and his own part in it, hadn't been as flawed as he'd come to believe.

Though there'd been no formal acknowledgement, it felt like her time there was drawing to a natural end. The Super had indicated that a DI from Kilmarnock would be sent, to ease Dalrymple through the rest of his leave. At lunchtime Shona went out for a walk, conscious that she'd seen nothing of Newton Stewart itself since she'd been there. Her time in Galloway had put her through the mill, but with its untamed nature and rugged beauty, this *land of the saints* as Isobel had called it, had found a place in her heart.

When her phone rang, she assumed it was Becca, but when she saw the name her heart sank.

'DI Oliver, it's Dave Hennessey from the NCA. How are you?' The tone was relaxed, friendly even. She remembered him from their single previous meeting, more than a year ago, when he'd turned up at her office. Thirties, angularly slim, his casual clothes bordering on shabby. If she met him in the street she'd expect to be asked for *any spare change*.

'I'm very well. What can I do for you?'

'I'd like you to come in for a chat. Shall we say our London offices at two p.m. tomorrow?'

'Okay.' She'd need to get the early train from Carlisle. The NCA was south of the river, but it wouldn't take her long after she arrived at St Pancras. 'Is there anything I can help you with now?'

'We'll chat tomorrow.'

The cheek of him, Shona thought, knowing all the while that his cheek might be the least of her problems.

Chapter 36

As the train pulled into the concrete box of London Euston, just after midday, Shona took a deep breath. Around her, passengers were already in the aisles, hauling down bags and gathering up their possessions, but she was in no hurry. London often felt like a homecoming. She enjoyed spending time visiting her old haunts, though the city changed so quickly there was never any guarantee they'd still be waiting when she got there. This time she would just be glad to get the visit over with.

Isobel had died early that morning. From the tone of Dalrymple's message, it seemed she'd decided not to confess to him that she'd been responsible for her sister Ailsa's death. It was probably a kindness. Shona would be back in Galloway for the funeral in the next few weeks. Then, she'd know for sure. If Dalrymple had any doubts he'd be sure to ask her then.

There was also a backlog of work to do at High Pines. She picked up her phone to check on the bookings. The seasonal shift into autumn was approaching and their position on the estuary meant repairs and maintenance were best done before winter arrived. And Becca would soon be back at university, hopefully with Jack, and there were always last-minute arrangements, which frequently fell into Shona's lap.

'DI Oliver?'

Shona looked up. The carriage had emptied. In place of her fellow passengers stood two men, broad shouldered and dressed alike in dark suits, hair shaved to a stubble. She knew at once who they were. One of them smiled and leaned forward. Too late she realised what was happening. He gripped her wrist and slipped on a handcuff.

'Wait.' Instinctively, she pulled back her other hand, shrinking against the wall of the carriage. 'What d'you think you're doing?'

'If you please, ma'am,' he said smoothly, as if he was guiding her to her seat in a fancy restaurant. He held out his hand for her other wrist. Stunned, she let him cuff her.

'Shona Oliver, I'm arresting you for Misconduct in Public Office. You do not have to say anything…'

Shona didn't hear the rest. There was a roaring in her head. She just wanted to get out of the train and run. If the NCA were going to arrest her, she'd thought they'd do it at High Pines. That sleekit little shit Dave Hennessey had tricked her.

The two men helped her from her seat. They gathered up her suit jacket, bag and phone, which the taller one slipped into his pocket, and nodded to the nervous, red-headed train steward who'd been preventing the cleaners from entering the carriage. As they marched her down the busy platform, sticking close, one of them looped her jacket over her handcuffs, she presumed to save her from the embarrassment. She didn't care. All she could think about was Becca and High Pines and the lifeboat crew and her team back in Dumfries CID. It wasn't self-importance, but she knew this would rock all their lives. She trusted them and they trusted her. Now, that trust would be broken and thrown back in all their faces, and there was nothing she could do about it.

They put her in the back of a black saloon car, the taller one climbing in with her while the other officer took the wheel. Streets flashed past. They were going south, through Soho, past Westminster and over Vauxhall Bridge, to the office in Spring Gardens.

They turned off the Albert Embankment and passed under the railway bridge, but as they approached the offices, instead of turning into the carpark, they sped up.

'Stop the car! Where are you taking me?' It only struck her then that she couldn't remember seeing their warrant cards on the train. 'Who are you? Show me your ID.'

When neither replied she began to struggle in her seat belt. 'Stop the car now!'

'Please remain calm, ma'am,' the officer next to her said, his hand closing over hers, pinning the cuffs painfully into her wrists.

Her mind was racing and a dreadful possibility hit her. Had Delfont's corrupt contacts got her? Had he reached from beyond the grave to have his revenge?

The car took a hard right and she was forced against the door. She tried to reach the handle, but whoever this guy was had a tight grip on them. The car turned again, this time into a narrow road flanked on one side by a line of railway arches. She'd traced the route and knew exactly where she was. There were shops, galleries, pubs nearby where she could ask for help. If she could get free, escape... but they'd be watching her like hawks. Her best hope would be to talk her way out. If she could just find out what it was they wanted.

'This way, please.' They helped her from the car and pushed her towards a red roller shutter, next to a wine merchant's unit.

‘Let go of me,’ she said as calmly as she could, pulling her elbow away, determined they wouldn’t feel how much her legs were shaking.

Inside, the concrete floor was bare beneath strip-lighting in the arch above, the space echoing with emptiness. The temperature had dropped twenty degrees, and this near the river the place smelled of damp. Light spilled from the corner office at the back. When they were almost there, one of the men took hold of her cuffs and unlocked them. Shona stood for a moment stunned, then walked towards the open door. A figure was seated in the corner.

‘DI Oliver,’ Dave Hennessey said, pressing his palms together. ‘Please excuse the manner of your journey.’ He wore a suit like the others. Gone were the street clothes and the earrings. She had no doubt he was NCA, so what the actual fuck was going on?

‘Am I under arrest?’ She rubbed her wrists where the cuffs had raised fine red weals. ‘Because if I’m not, I’m walking straight out of here.’

‘You are under arrest,’ he replied, his tone regretful. ‘But I need a little chat before we formally charge you. We know the part you played in DCI Delfont’s murder by helping Thalia Brookes escape from the scene.’

Only Thalia, Cumbrian DC Dan Ridley and herself knew what had happened. Thalia wouldn’t have told them, and Dan she trusted with her life.

‘You’re bluffing,’ Shona said.

‘I assure you I’m not. We had a chat recently with DC Ridley.’

‘What?’ Shona couldn’t believe it. He’d said he would always protect her, as she would him. But deep in her heart she’d known his moral core meant he’d never lie on the stand.

'He's quite the rising star in counterterrorism and organised crime,' Hennessey went on. 'He knew we'd join the dots eventually. Loyalty is everything, isn't it? And he was loyal to you. Until we spoke to him, we thought you and Thalia Brookes had planned it together. And I really do think he was trying to protect you. What he didn't realise is quite how valuable you've become recently.'

'What d'you mean?'

Hennessey gave her a cool smile. 'You and your husband, Rob, are getting divorced, is that right?'

'I don't see how that's relevant,' Shona bristled.

'Just makes things simpler. Tell me again what happened with DCI Delfont?'

'Why? Do you enjoy hearing about men who assault women?'

'I just want to check I've got the facts right.'

Shona gritted her teeth. 'It was a leaving-do in a pub. I had one tonic water. No alcohol. I woke up in my car on the hard shoulder of the Limehouse link expressway with a traffic cop tapping on my window. I was driven back to the police station. It was then I discovered my underwear was on back to front. DCI Delfont was there. Since my breath test was negative he persuaded them I was "overtired". It was swept neatly away. Later I discovered he'd filmed himself assaulting me.'

'Anything else?'

'He also had evidence against Rob. It came between us. We were looking over our shoulder every day. I don't think any marriage can survive that.'

'Two years after you moved to Scotland, your husband was convicted of money laundering. It didn't strike you as odd that your husband was able to start up a high-end boutique B&B?'

'He told me it was profit from the sale of our Camden house. From investments.'

'And the amount he was spending on gambling?'

'I didn't know about the gambling.'

'And yet your boss, Detective Superintendent Munroe, didn't instigate a professional standards case against you.'

'I had no case to answer.'

'Did you know your husband was a criminal while you were a serving police officer?'

'No, I did not. Why are you questioning me on this? I wasn't the only woman Delfont assaulted. The CPS sank the case because when there was delay after delay, one of his victims killed herself and another withdrew her accusation. There was only Thalia and I left, though I'm sure there were others.'

'And your husband's crimes?'

'You honestly think I knew? That I was covering for him?'

'Were you?'

'No!'

'What about anyone else? Is there anyone else you're covering for?'

'How fucking dare you!'

The air between them was heavy. It stretched on until the silence was broken by the rumbling thunder of a train passing overhead.

'You see, Shona, big, organised serious crime cannot survive without corruption. It's as simple as that. And not just corrupt police, it's the legal profession, it's in banking because of money laundering. It's a fact of life. The bigger the crime the more they need corrupt individuals to facilitate their work. But what makes corrupt cops? How does it happen? What makes someone go bad?'

Shona glared at him.

'Most corrupt cops are really good cops. They're smart, grafters, brilliant with informants. So why does it happen? A small favour becomes a big one years later. You cannot be half-corrupt, Shona. Once you step over that line, you're corrupt forever.'

'So, are you corrupt?' Shona said. His definition was simplistic. Yes, she'd perverted the course of justice, but only when justice was dead in the water. It was a salvage operation. She was entitled to her reward, even if that was the satisfaction of knowing that Delfont had paid with his life for all the lives he'd ruined.

'Am I corrupt?' Hennessey mused. 'I don't find that's a productive question to ask myself. I just like locking up bad guys. I suspect you do too.' He reached down to a rucksack at his feet and pulled out a laptop, then opened it and turned it to face Shona.

For a moment she held back from looking at the screen. She hated Hennessey. She hated being manipulated. It was like Delfont all over again and she wanted to grab Hennessey by the throat, feel the spasming of his windpipe beneath her fingers while she slammed his head repeatedly against the brick wall of the arches. His cronies were outside, but they'd be too late. When the next train came over there'd be so much noise they wouldn't hear his skull split.

While she waited for the train, she pulled the laptop towards her.

It was a social work file. Bradley Woolf, a Canadian citizen, in and out of jail for drug offences in his youth. Now a big-name hood in Ontario, looking to expand overseas.

'Word is,' Hennessey said, 'he's fixed on Glasgow as his stepping stone into Europe. He's coming home to Scotland from Canada after more than forty years away.'

'Why are you telling me this?'

'Look at the next page.'

When she saw the name, her breath caught in her throat. Bradley Woolf hadn't always gone by that name. Before his adoption he'd been Michael MacDonald. Her brother.

The next paragraph told her he'd been split from their sister Helen by social workers due to his 'malign influence'. At four years old, he'd tried to drown his baby sister in a toilet. At five, he'd pushed a neighbour's child in front of a car. Investigations showed he'd been smoking cannabis stolen from his mother. In care, the tally of troubling behaviour escalated until he'd battered another child with a shoe, knocking out their teeth. When he'd been adopted by a couple moving to Canada, the social workers had thought it for the best and likely breathed a sigh of relief. No wonder they'd told her sister Helen that he wasn't coming back. Only now, it looked like he was.

Her mind was racing through likely scenarios, connections sparking and dying as she tried to make sense of what she was hearing.

'What d'you want?'

'Just to know if he gets in touch.'

'You want me to help catch him, don't you?' When he didn't answer, she said, 'What do I get in return?'

Hennessey held his arms out. 'The world. Your slate wiped clean.'

-

It was dark when she arrived back at High Pines. The familiar outlines of the house above the estuary should have felt welcoming, but they seemed as strange to her as they did when she'd first arrived there nearly five years before. Everything had changed. It was not the turning of a new page but the destruction of the whole volume.

Tomorrow, she'd feel different, more sanguine. The chances of her brother getting in touch, even if he came back to Scotland, were slim. He'd never shown any interest in his birth family. She didn't know about him, so he probably didn't know she even existed. It was fine. She'd got the better end of the deal and she could close the book on Delfont. A move to Glasgow might be something she'd come to welcome in time.

In the morning she'd have coffee with Freya and Tommy and talk about the lifeboat and High Pines. She'd soon be back at her desk in Dumfries, her team hard at work, Murdo moving among them, oiling the gears.

She dropped her bag in the kitchen and turned on all the lights. There was a stack of mail on the countertop but she'd leave it until the morning. She texted Becca to say she was back at High Pines and everything was fine. She'd call her tomorrow to explain. She was about to put her phone down when she saw an email. It had been forwarded from Scottish Connection, a message board for those seeking family abroad, who she'd contacted after that first email from Helen.

It was there, in the subject line.

'Hello Sis.'

Acknowledgements

I've learned something very important in the writing of this book: if you ever need inspiration, you can do worse than talk to a bookseller. In this case it was a query from Joyce Cochrane – who, with her husband Ian, runs The Old Bank Bookshop in Wigtown – that set the cogs turning. Will DI Shona Oliver ever solve a crime in Galloway? Might she be seconded? It was such a delicious prospect to bring Shona to this wild and ruggedly beautiful place that I began to think of ways to make that happen. And indeed, two books later, Shona found herself at the westernmost part of her beloved Solway, where it meets the Irish Sea. I hope you enjoyed the result.

As a writer, I am very lucky to be represented by Anne Williams of the Kate Hordern Literary Agency, who has an unerring eye for story and for what makes characters tick. Thank you for all your support and wisdom.

I am immensely grateful to my editor at Canelo, Executive Publisher Louise Cullen, whose input makes the books better every time, and to the stellar team of editor Alicia Pountney, assistant editor Aidan Kavanagh, development editor Bonnie Macleod and copy editor Laurel Sills and proofreader Vicki Vrint.

A special thank-you to sales, marketing and publicity teams, in particular publicist Kate Shepherd, whose hard work ensures that readers can find their way to books they seek. That goes too for all the bloggers, reviewers and readers around the world who spread the word on social media about the novels they love.

Once again, I am indebted to all the RNLI volunteers who have taken time to chat about their work and correct my misconceptions. Also, the Scottish Partnership Against Rural Crime, National Farmers Union Scotland, NFU Mutual for their insights into the crime risks faced by farmers and Education Scotland for their resources on the Scots language as spoken in Galloway.

Thanks to my family – Mickey, Chloe, Leo and Sam, Eric, Netta and John. Also, to my fellow authors, the alumni of UEA's MA Crime Fiction – Sharon Bale, Katherine Black, Libby Brookes, Hannah Brown, Mandy Byatt, Alan Jackson, Denise Kuehl, Simon Margrave, Helen Marsden, Pat Page, Sue Thomas, Gigi Vernon – who are a constant source of support, fun and creativity. And thank you to Charles Simpson for being just the ideas guy.

Finally, a word of thanks to you for picking up this book – I hope you enjoyed it. Publication of *A Cold Harbour* marks five years since DI Shona Oliver first appeared in print. I'm loving the journey so far and it's great to have you with me. I can't wait to see where it takes us next.